Also by James W. Morrison

Bedford Goes to War: The Heroic Story of a Small Virginia Community in World War II

Bedford Goes to War (A Historical Drama)

"Bedford County and D-Day" in *Bedford Images, Vol. 2, Celebrating 250 Years of History*

Poems, Essays, and Drama in *Voices from Smith Mountain Lake*, an anthology

"Europe" (with Jeffrey Simon and Charles Barry) in *Strategic Assessment 1995*, INSS/National Defense University

Vladimir Zhirinovskiy: An Assessment of a Russian Ultra-nationalist

NATO Expansion and Alternative Future Security Alignments

CLASS OF 1940

Coming of Age in World War II

To Bart and Pat Storky,
with appreciation
and best wishes,

James W. Morrison

A Novel

James W. Morrison

Class of 1940: Coming of Age in World War II is a work of fiction. All dialogue and all characters, with the exception of some well-known historical and public figures and one unnamed minor-role character, are products of the author's imagination and are not to be considered real. Some incidents reflect events that actually happened during World War II, but these incidents, as presented, are fictional in terms of characters, situations, and/or dialogue. In all other respects, any resemblance to persons living or dead is purely coincidental.

Copies of *Class of 1940* and the author's history *Bedford Goes to War: The Heroic Story of a Small Virginia Community in World War II* are available from Amazon.com and other retail outlets and on Kindle and other devices.

ISBN 978-14949-27882

Book Cover Photographs Identification and Credits

Front cover: At top, a photo taken by the author in Bedford County, Virginia, showing rolling hills and mountains of southwest Virginia. At bottom, a photo by a U.S. Coast Guard photographer and now in the collection of the National Archives, of soldiers leaving a landing craft during the June 6, 1944, D-Day Invasion of Normandy, France.

Back cover: Photos illustrate what life might have been like in the 1940s. Three photos at the top are from 1940 yearbook of Bedford High School, Bedford, Virginia, used with permission of the Bedford County School System. In upper center is the Class of 1940; in upper-left corner is the football team; and in upper-right corner are female students forming the letters HI-Y club. In left margin, in descending order, are: (1) 116th Infantry's Company A, a former National Guard company based in Bedford, marching in Ivybridge, England, 1943 or 1944 (photographer unknown, courtesy of Allen M. Huddleston); (2) GIs aboard landing craft on D-Day, June 6, 1944 (photo by Coast Guard, National Archives, photo # 26-G-2340); (3) GIs in Belgium, January 1945 (National Archives, WWII photo #113); (4) GI guarding German POWS (National Archives, WWII photo #208); (5) prisoners of a Nazi concentration camp liberated by Allied forces (National Archives, WWII photo #178). In right margin, in descending order, are: (1) U.S. Army nurses in training at Aberdeen, Maryland (photo by U.S. Army Signal Corps, National Archives, 111-SC-121195); (2) U.S. Army nurses boarding a transport (National Archives, 111-SC-136562); (3) U.S. Army nurses of an evacuation hospital in Italy (National Archives, 111-SC 182769); (4) surgery performed with the assistance of U.S. Army nurses,132nd General Hospital (National Institute of Health, Record 101443149); (5) damage done by enemy fire to U.S. Army 56th Evacuation Hospital in Italy, September 1944 (National Institute of Health, Record 101442610).

For Edie

Chapter 1

July 2009, Halesford, Virginia

In the kitchen of the old, Virginia farmhouse, Jeb Fletcher, his wife, and their twelve-year-old great-grandson sat quietly around the table, amid the lingering aroma of a breakfast of bacon, eggs, and biscuits. Jeb lowered his newspaper, took a sip of coffee, and looked at the boy. Billy, on the first full day of his visit, was hunched over playing the electronic game he had brought with him.

Jeb glanced at his wife, who sat at the end of the table sewing. Their eyes met, and they shook their heads. They had talked earlier about wanting meaningful time with the boy. At their age, there wouldn't be many more visits. Chicago was a long way away.

Jeb flipped the page to the obituaries and then peered over the top of the paper. "Dick Drumheller died yesterday."

The old woman looked up from the shirt she was mending. "Oh, that's too bad. I just saw his wife the other day. They've had a hard life."

"Is that his third or fourth wife?"

"You really didn't like Dick, did you?"

"Nope. He was a mean S.O.B."

"Jeb!" his wife said sharply, nodding toward the boy.

"Well, I guess we'll have to go to the funeral. He did save my life in France." Jeb put down the paper and stared out the window. "This makes me the last survivor around here from Company O."

Billy looked up from his game. "You're talking about World War II, aren't you, Grandpa?"

Jeb took a sip of coffee. "Yes, Billy."

"Dad's told me you were in the Army, but he says he doesn't know much about what you did or where you served. Did someone really save your life? Did you ever have to shoot anybody?"

"Oh, it's a long story. Maybe I'll tell you someday." Jeb resumed reading the paper.

Billy went back to playing his game.

The woman frowned and shook her head at the lost opportunity for Jeb to share details of his wartime experience with his great-grandson. "Men," she muttered. The room fell quiet again.

A minute later a sharp COCK-A-DOODLE-DOO shattered the silence as a rooster announced his presence just outside the screened door to the back porch.

Billy, sitting with his back to the porch, bolted upright. He jerked his head up from his game and swiveled around in his chair toward the source of the noise. It wasn't the rooster, however, that caught his eye. What he saw was a gun, hanging above the door lintel.

"Oh, wow! That's a really old shotgun." Setting his game on the table, Billy jumped up from his chair and hurried over for a closer look. Then he turned to Jeb. "Can I shoot it, Grandpa?"

Jeb, who had watched the boy bolt from his chair, looked down at his newspaper. *Damn,* he thought. *I should have put that gun away before Billy arrived, like I did last time. Does he even know how to shoot?* He took a sip of coffee. *Why have I even kept that damned gun, with its horrible memories?*

The woman cleared her throat, as though preparing to speak, but then said nothing. She put her mending down on the table and went to the sink to wash some vegetables she'd picked earlier in the morning.

Jeb looked up at Billy. "You mean 'May I shoot the gun,' don't you, Billy?"

The boy didn't know his great-grandfather well, but he knew he was a stickler, for proper English and just about everything. He smiled. "May I shoot your shotgun, Grandpa?"

The woman shut off the water and turned to face her husband as she dried her hands on her apron.

Jeb glanced at his wife, who shook her head "Well, I don't know," he said.

Billy looked again at the gun and then back at Jeb. "Who made this gun?"

"It's an Iver Johnson. A Champion model."

"I've heard of Iver Johnson."

"Really?"

"I've seen their guns on the internet." Billy raised his arms and took a shooter's stance. "But I've never had a chance to shoot one."

Jeb rubbed his chin.

"Dad's taught me how to handle guns, safety rules and all. He says you taught Grandpa Franklin and Grandpa Franklin then taught Dad. I've heard you're really strict about safety."

"How old are you, Billy? Twelve?"

"Twelve and a half."

Jeb looked again at his wife.

She pursed her lips and shook her head again. "It'll be noontime before long—time for dinner."

Jeb arched his eyebrows.

"Don't you mean lunch, Grandma?"

"Around here in southwest Virginia, Billy, we have dinner in the middle of the day and supper in the evening."

Jeb scooted his chair back. "Well, I think we have time." He started to stand, but he'd been sitting too long, and the muscles in his 87-year-old legs were stiff. He struggled for a moment, put his hands on the table, and pushed up, lifting his lean, nearly six-foot frame.

His wife saw his difficulty in getting up, something she had noticed more and more in the past few weeks. She stepped forward to help.

Jeb waved her off with one hand. Finally standing, he steadied himself for a moment. From a cabinet drawer behind his chair, he took out a box of ammunition, picked out four red and brass shells, and dropped them into one of his pants pockets. He walked over to his wife, bent his head down, and kissed her on the forehead. She was almost a foot shorter than he. He lingered, drawing in the scent of her freshly shampooed hair, a smell that had pleased him for the more than sixty years they had been married.

She looked up at him, a frown on her face. "Be careful, Jeb," she said quietly.

He gazed into her eyes, winked, and kissed her lightly on the lips. "Yes, dear."

Heading for the door, he reached up and took down the shotgun. He checked to make sure it was unloaded and then handed it to Billy. "O.K. Let's go to the woods out back. On the way, you can tell me everything you know about gun safety." He pushed open the screened door and held it for Billy.

"Now don't you be long out there, Jebidiah Fletcher," ordered his wife. "I'm going to start some chicken."

As Jeb followed Billy through the doorway, he turned at the last second and caught the screened door before it slammed. Having narrowly avoided one of his wife's pet peeves, he smiled at her through the screen. "We won't be long, especially as we're having fried chicken."

He picked up two empty, plastic milk jugs from the porch and joined Billy in the back yard. They headed down a lane that cut across the fields to the woods.

From the kitchen window, the woman watched the old man and the boy walking side-by side. *They have the same walk—must be in the genes. I hope Billy also got the genes that'll help him grow up to be as good a man as his great-grandfather.* Then she saw Billy pause, switch the shotgun from the crook of his right arm to that of his left, and hurry to catch up with Jeb. *Why in heaven's name did Jeb agree to let Billy shoot that gun?*

Chapter 2

"So, what do you know about gun safety, Billy?" asked Jeb as they walked down the lane.

"The first rule is never point a gun at something you don't intend to shoot."

"Good. What else?"

"Never assume a gun is unloaded."

"That's very important."

Billy continued talking about gun safety, but Jeb's mind moved elsewhere, back to a day seventy-five years earlier, a day still burned into his memory, despite his efforts to erase it.

Once again, he was twelve. He was hunting in these same fields with his father and his Uncle Jonah. A bright October sun lit the morning sky, and the smell of harvest filled the air. The three of them walked along, spread out in a row, Uncle Jonah in the middle. No one spoke, as they advanced quietly, looking for quail. A sudden flutter of wings beating upward broke the stillness, followed by the loud BOOM of a gunshot and immediately the BOOM of a second shot. Then came the deep scream—the scream that seemed for Jeb to have no end.

Billy's voice intruded. "How old is this gun, Grandpa?"

"What?" Jeb shook his head and released a long, deep sigh as his mind struggled back to the present.

"This gun is pretty old, isn't it? It's only a single shot."

"Yes, pretty old. Almost as old as I am. I got it when I was your age."

"Didn't you ever buy a new one?"

"No."

"Why not?"

"I don't know. I thought about getting rid of the gun— thought about it many times. I suppose I kept it because it was a present from my father."

"Dad's got a new Mossberg 500 pump action. It's really cool. You can fire six shells, one right after another, and you can switch barrels from 12 gauge to 20 gauge."

"That sounds pretty nifty." Jeb came to a stop as they reached a clearing at the edge of the woods. "This looks as good a place as any. I'll set up a couple of targets." He walked ahead about thirty feet and set one of the milk jugs in front of a tree and the other on a three-foot-high stump. He returned to where Billy stood. "Do you know how to load this gun?"

"I think so."

Jeb handed the boy a shell and watched as he loaded it. "Aim for the jug in front of the tree. Watch out for the kick. The gun's got a real bite."

Billy put his left foot forward and turned sideways to the target. He raised the gun's stock and pressed it into his right shoulder. With his left hand curved under the barrel handle, he raised the end of the barrel toward the target. He pulled the gun tighter into his shoulder, lowered his head and aimed down the barrel. Then he curled his right index finger around the trigger.

Pretty good, thought Jeb.

Billy pulled the trigger. BOOM!

The same sound as seventy-five years ago, thought Jeb. He shook his head to clear away the noise and memories.

Billy winced. "Wow, that gun does have a kick!" He lowered the gun and set it against a tree. He rubbed his right shoulder with this left hand.

The shot had missed the jug.

"Want to try another shot?" asked Jeb.

Billy glanced at the gun and rubbed his shoulder. "O.K. I think my shot was too high and to the right."

Jeb handed him a second shell. Billy picked up the gun and loaded it. He raised the gun to his shoulder, aimed, and fired again. BOOM!

This second shot was too low, but one or two pieces of shot hit the jug.

He's rushing his shot, thought Jeb.

Billy lowered the gun, held it in the crook of his right arm, and again rubbed his right shoulder. He then held the gun out to Jeb. "Would you like to try, Grandpa?"

"I haven't shot this thing in a long while."

"I'll bet you're a pretty good shot."

Jeb took the gun. "Well, we'll see if I'm still any good." Jeb loaded a shell and raised the gun to his shoulder. He hesitated and then lowered it. He removed his glasses and stuffed them into his shirt pocket. His sight at a distance was better without glasses.

He raised the gun and aimed at the second milk jug, the one atop the tree stump. As he sighted down the barrel, he thought, for an instant, that he saw a man squatting. The gray bark of the stump matched the color of a German soldier's uniform.

Jeb blinked a couple of times and brought the milk jug back into focus. Now, however, he had trouble holding his aim. The end of the barrel swung slightly from side to side. He took a deep breath and exhaled. Then he took another breath, partially exhaled, held it, aimed, and squeezed the trigger. BOOM! The jug flew off the stump, shredded into pieces. He exhaled and relaxed. *All right! Not bad.*

"Great shot, Grandpa! You really blasted that jug."

"Well, I guess I haven't forgotten everything."

"Can I try one more time?"

"You mean 'May I?'"

"Yes. May I try once more?"

"Your shoulder isn't too sore?"

"No, I'm fine."

"Well, O.K. We have one shell left, and that jug in front of the tree is still almost intact." Jeb handed the gun and last shell to Billy. "Now relax, and don't rush your shot. Take a breath, exhale part of it, hold the rest, aim, and squeeze the trigger gently."

"O.K." Billy loaded the gun. To relax, he pulled his shoulders back, took a deep breath, and exhaled. He raised the gun, took a breath, let part of it out, aimed, and gently squeezed the trigger. BOOM! Billy's third shot hit the jug dead center and shredded it.

"Nice shot, Billy! Third time's a charm."

Billy beamed.

"That's good shooting, especially with this old gun."

"Thanks, Grandpa."

"You handle the gun well, and you do it safely. Your dad must be a good teacher."

"He's pretty good, but I'm glad for the advice on breathing and squeezing the trigger."

"How's your shoulder?"

Billy looked down at the ground. "It's O.K."

"Really?"

Billy looked up. "Well, it does hurt a little."

"A little?"

"Actually, a lot."

Jeb smiled and then laughed softly. "My shoulder will probably hurt tomorrow, too. Well, the important thing is you kept trying—and you kept getting better. Now run and pick up what's left of those jugs. We'd better get back to the house, or Grandma will skin our hides, and that would hurt a lot more than the kick of that gun."

As they walked across the field toward the house, Billy said, "When you were in World War II, did you ever have to shoot anyone?"

Jeb walked along for some time without answering. Scenes from his training in the United States and then in England flashed through his mind, followed by scenes of combat in France and Germany. He had tried to forget those times but hadn't fully succeeded. As they neared the house, Jeb finally spoke. "So, you're twelve and a half, right?"

"Yep. I'll be a teenager soon."

"Well, after we have our dinner, I'd like to take you some place."

"Where?"

"That's my surprise."

Chapter 3

Jeb pushed his chair back from the table and, again with some difficulty, stood up. "Thanks for the tasty dinner, dear. The chicken was delicious." He picked up his dishes and carried them to the sink.

Billy stood up and patted his stomach. "The blueberry pie was out of this world, Grandma." Following his great-grandfather's lead, he, too, carried his dishes to the sink.

"Why, thank you, boys. You two are a pleasure to cook for, especially with nice compliments like that. Now, why don't you both run along? Grandpa told me where he's taking you, Billy, and I'm sure you're going to enjoy it." She stood and began clearing the rest of the table. "I'm going to clean up here and then take a nice, long nap."

Jeb walked over to his wife and gave her a quick kiss. In the past year, whenever one of them was leaving the house, they had taken care to give each other a kiss, as though this might be their last opportunity. "We'll be back in time for supper," Jeb said, as he walked toward the back door, followed by Billy.

"Bye, Grandma."

"Bye, boys."

Jeb led Billy to the barn and opened the two large doors. Inside, back in a dark corner, sat a vehicle, covered with a tarp. Jeb pulled off the tarp, revealing an antique pickup truck. The truck—painted a shiny dark green with varnished, natural wood railings on the sides and back of the bed—glistened.

"Wow! That's a beauty!" Billy ran his finger over a front fender. "It's spotless, and it looks like it's in perfect shape."

Jeb smiled. "This is the second most beautiful thing in my life—after Grandma. Hop in, boy." Jeb climbed in behind the steering wheel.

Billy jumped in on the passenger side and began surveying the inside of the truck. "That's a pretty simple dashboard."

"Yeah, compared to all the gadgets on today's dashes." Jeb put a key in the ignition and started the truck. It ran roughly at first but then smoothed out. As the engine warmed up, the smell of oil inside the cab grew more distinct. Jeb clicked on a hip-level seatbelt. "Put on your seatbelt. I don't have shoulder belts, but these should work pretty well." As Billy put on his seatbelt, Jeb put the truck into first gear and drove slowly out of the barn.

"How old is this truck?"

"It's a 1934 model—a Ford. It was my father's. He bought it new."

"Wow! That makes this truck 75 years old."

"That sounds about right. You must be pretty good with math."

"I like math."

Jeb eased the truck into second gear and continued down the gravel lane leading from the farm house to the road, driving slowly to avoid stirring up too much dust.

Billy surveyed the inside of the cab. "Did your father give you this truck? I hope my father will give me a car or truck someday."

"My father died the year he bought this truck. My mother then drove it, and eventually it became mine."

"You must have been young when your dad died."

Jeb looked straight ahead down the lane. "I was twelve."

"Gee, my age. How'd your dad die?"

"It's a long story." Jeb slowed the truck as they neared the end of the lane and then pulled out onto the paved road.

"What was your dad's name?"

"Jeremiah. Jeremiah Jacob Fletcher."

"'Jeremiah,' huh? I've heard that name in Sunday school. And you're 'Jebidiah.' Those are unusual names. They sound like they came from the Bible. How'd you happen to name my grandfather 'Franklin'?" That's not from the Bible, is it?"

Jeb looked straight ahead. "That's a long story, too. Maybe I'll tell you later."

Billy looked ahead down the road. "Where are we going?"

"We're going over into the next county—Bedford County."

"What's in Bedford County?"

"That's a surprise. You'll just have to keep your britches on and wait until we get there." Jeb came to a stop sign and turned onto a state highway.

Billy looked out the window for several minutes but then picked up the electronic game he had brought with him and began playing.

Jeb glanced at the boy and his game and shook his head. *Why doesn't he put that damn thing away and look at this beautiful countryside?* Jeb stared straight ahead and soon was lost in thought, thinking of the place where they were headed.

After about thirty miles, Jeb slowed the truck as it reached the city limits. A sign by the side of the road read "Bedford, Virginia. World's Best Little Town."

Billy looked up from his game and saw the sign. Neither he nor his great-grandfather had spoken for more than half an hour.

"Is this really the world's best little town?"

Jeb straightened up. *I'm glad he finally looked up from that confounded gadget that he carries everywhere.* He looked toward Billy and smiled. "Lots of people around here think so. I'm partial to it myself."

"How little is it? How many people live here?"

"About 6,000 in the town of Bedford. There're probably over 65,000 people in all of Bedford County."

"That's pretty small. We've got about three million in Chicago, I think, almost ten million counting the suburbs. That's what Dad says."

"Is that so," Jeb said, smiling slightly.

They resumed their silence. Billy turned back to his game. Jeb continued to drive. Soon he pulled onto Main Street.

Billy again looked up from his game when he saw the red brick storefronts and the old-fashioned, black lampposts, all decorated with small American flags. "This sure isn't Chicago, Grandpa."

"You've got that right," Jeb said with a chuckle. He made a turn off Main Street and soon turned onto a side road. Approaching a large, formal gate area, he slowed the truck. "We're here."

Chapter 4

Bedford, Virginia

Ahead were two enormous, black-enameled, iron-picket gates hanging on hinges attached to concrete pillars. The gates were open. Large black letters mounted on a concrete wall read "National D-Day Memorial."

"What's D-Day?" asked Billy.

"I'm going to tell you all about that, once we get to the top of that big hill ahead."

Jeb drove up a long incline toward the highest point in the town, an elevation of some 500 feet. As they neared the top, a large American flag and a nearly 50-feet-high, dark-green, granite arch, topped with black and white concrete stripes, came into focus. Upon reaching the top, Jeb pulled the truck up to a gatehouse.

"Good morning, Mr. Fletcher," said the attendant, smiling broadly.

"Morning, Mack. How're you doing today?" Jeb stretched out his arm, and the two men shook hands. Jeb held up his pass to the memorial, and Mack waved his acknowledgement.

"Couldn't be better, on a beautiful day like this." He leaned down to look inside the truck. "Who's this with you?"

"This is my great-grandson, Billy. He's visiting from Chicago. He hasn't been to Bedford before. Now that he's twelve and a half, I thought I'd show him around. Billy, this is my friend Mack Conklin."

Billy gave a slight wave. "Hello, Mr. Conklin."

"Welcome to the National D-Day Memorial, Billy. You're a lucky young man. You've probably got the most knowledgeable man there is to show you around here. Your great-grandpa comes up here at least a couple of times a week to walk around and study all the plaques. He gives special tours, too. He's one of the few actual D-Day veterans we have. So, you're in good hands." Conklin stepped back from the car. "Well, you two have a nice visit. Billy, it was nice to meet you. Next time you come, bring some people from Chicago with you. They ought to see this memorial."

"O.K., Mr. Conklin. Nice to meet you, too."

"Thanks, Mack," said Jeb, as he put the truck in gear and pulled into the drive circling the memorial. About three quarters of the way around the circle, he parked the truck and got out. Billy got out on his side. Jeb paused on the sidewalk in front of the truck and swept his right arm out in front of him, gesturing toward the structures ahead. "This is a memorial to some of the bravest Americans and Allies of America who fought in World War II. It honors those who, on June 6, 1944, helped with the Allied invasion of Normandy, France."

"I know a little bit about World War II, but not much," said Billy.

"Well, the war in Europe started in 1939, when Germany invaded western Poland, and Britain and France then declared war on Germany. The Soviet Union invaded eastern Poland a few weeks later. Then in 1940, the Germans invaded and conquered France and other countries in Western Europe. The Germans also occupied much of Eastern Europe, and, in 1941, they attacked the Soviet Union, most of which you may now know as Russia, and several other countries. With the Soviets fighting to defeat the Germans in the east, we Western Allies launched an invasion from Great Britain to help liberate Western Europe and advance troops into Germany to defeat the Nazis. The invasion, which took place in the coastal area of France known as Normandy, began on June 6, 1944. That's the day generally known as "D-Day.""

"What's the 'D' stand for?"

"The 'D' really doesn't stand for anything. 'D-Day' means the first day of an invasion or attack. It's been used to indicate the first day of other battles, too. For most people now, it means the invasion that began on June 6, 1944.

'D+1' means the second day of the invasion, 'D+2' the third day, and so forth."

"Were you part of D-Day?"

"Yes, I was."

"What did you do that day?"

"Well, maybe I'll tell you about that later. Right now I just want to show you some things."

At that moment, one of the volunteer tour guides, leading a group of five tourists, approached. "Good afternoon, Mr. Fletcher," the guide said.

Jeb tipped the National-D-Day-Memorial-souvenir cap he had put on before getting out of the truck. "Good afternoon, Bob."

"May I introduce you to these folks visiting from Indiana?"

"Certainly. I'm always glad to see Hoosiers here."

"Folks, let me introduce Mr. Jeb Fletcher. He's a D-Day veteran, one of the few who lives around here now."

"Good afternoon, folks. What Bob means is one of the few still living." Jeb chuckled, as did the tourists and guide. "It's nice of you to come to visit the memorial. This is my great-grandson, Billy. He's a Mid-Westerner, too, from Chicago."

"Good afternoon, Mr. Fletcher," said one of the tourists, who wore a cap reading "Korea & Vietnam Vet." "We don't want to interrupt your time with your great-grandson, but we'd like to thank you for your service."

The other tourists also expressed their thanks.

Jeb held out his hand to the first tourist who had spoken, the one with the veteran's cap, and the two men shook hands. "And thanks for your service," said Jeb.

Billy looked quizzically at the visitors and then at his great-grandfather. *What's that all about?*

Jeb put his hand on Billy's shoulder. "I hope you folks enjoy your tour. Thanks for visiting the memorial and honoring those who served." Jeb guided Billy down the sidewalk.

Once they were alone, Billy said, "Grandpa, I don't understand why those people thanked you."

"Well, most Americans appreciate the men and women who serve in our armed forces and who put themselves at risk to defend this country. Most Americans nowadays— now that we have a volunteer force—have never served in the military. People seem to want to express their thanks to those who have served and are now serving."

"But why did that man with the hat thank you? He had served in the military, too, hadn't he? And why did you thank him?"

"Yes, I'm sure he'd served. I've had many veterans of later wars, such as that veteran, thank me. Many of those who served in Korea and Vietnam were not thanked when they came back from those wars, and it's important that they be appreciated, too. As for us D-Day veterans, people know how important D-Day and World War II were to our freedom. They also know that many of us old veterans won't be around much longer."

"What do you mean, exactly?" asked Billy.

"Some 1,000 of us World War II veterans die each day."

"Really? That's too bad."

"Well, that's part of life. You know, Billy, when people thank me for my service, it's a little embarrassing, for me and them. But it's a nice gesture. Whenever anyone thanks me, I accept the thanks on behalf of all veterans."

"I think I understand."

Jeb pointed ahead. "O.K. Now let's walk over to the area that resembles a garden. Most of the planning and preparation for the Normandy Invasion was done in England, so this section resembles an English garden."

Billy pointed to a feature made of stones. "Those stones look like they're in the shape of a sword."

"They are shaped like a sword. The uniform shoulder patch for our top Allied command headquarters had a crusader's sword on it, and that stone structure and other features resemble the shoulder patch."

Billy pointed to some sculptures. "Who are all these statues of?"

"Well, that larger-than-life statue under the dome is General Dwight D. Eisenhower. He was the supreme commander of the Allies—the top leader—of our forces attacking the Germans. We affectionately called him 'Ike,' but not to his face."

"He was one of our presidents, wasn't he?"

"That's good, Billy. General Eisenhower was elected president seven years after the war."

"Did you know him?"

"Yes. I met him once, in an unusual situation, and then later I served on his staff as a junior officer."

"That must have been cool."

"It was." Jeb pointed to six pedestals capped with the busts of military officers. "These statues—called busts—are of some of the top-ranked American and British commanders. They were subordinate to General Eisenhower—they worked for him. The plaques under the busts tell about the men. Maybe sometime you can come back and read them. Now, however, I want to show you some areas of the memorial that mean a lot to me."

Chapter 5

Jeb led Billy to a series of bronze plaques honoring units that fought in the D-Day operation. He pointed to a large one. "This was my division—the 29th Infantry Division. There were about 15,000 men in our division."

"That's a lot of men," said Billy.

"We were a National Guard division before the war. We were citizen soldiers. We worked at our regular civilian jobs and drilled one evening a week with our local unit, Company O. We also went to camp for a couple of weeks in the summer."

"You went to summer camp just like I do. Was your camp fun, too?"

"Well, like your camp, Billy, it was an adventure, and I shared it with friends. It was a chance to get away, and we got to shoot rifles. The training, however, was tough, and I doubt if I got to have as much fun as you."

"What are these other plaques?"

Jeb pointed to a smaller plaque. "This is my regiment, the 116th Infantry, one of three infantry regiments in our division. Each regiment had nearly 5,000 men in it, and below the regiments were battalions."

"What are these plaques—the ones that read 'Company'?"

"Companies were smaller units, below battalions." He pointed to a plaque. "This is my company—Company O. Before the war, almost everyone in my company was from Halesford County, where our farm is. As the war continued, however, some of our men were reassigned, and our company grew in size. Many of the new men who were added to our company came from the North, so we had a mix of Southerners and Northerners. Our division was called the 'Blue-Gray Division', symbolic of the colors of the Union and Confederate uniforms during the Civil War."

"How many men in a company?"

"Ours had over 200 men by D-Day. Now I want to show you the heart of this memorial."

Jeb led Billy to the middle plaza. "This depicts the invasion across the English Channel. Our forces landed on five beaches on the Normandy coast in northern France. My company landed on what we called Omaha Beach, the second from the west. The Germans were up on the cliffs on high ground, many in concrete bunkers, shooting down at us. Our bombers and ships were supposed to have bombarded the Germans before we landed, but they seemed to have bombed too far inland, perhaps to avoid hitting us. When we landed at low tide, we had to cross some 400 yards of beach before finding protection behind a seawall."

"You had to run across 400 yards of beach? That's like running the length of four football fields! And the Germans were shooting at you, too?"

"Yes, and we carried 60-pound packs plus our weapons."

"Wow, that's amazing."

"Those statues in the water over there represent men wading ashore, crossing the beach, and falling wounded or killed in the surf and on the beach. The statue of the four soldiers scaling the cliff represents Rangers climbing a place called Pointe du Hoc, at the western edge of Omaha Beach. The Rangers had to scale a 100-foot-high cliff, with the Germans shooting down at them."

"Are the popping noises and splashes in the water supposed to be bullets hitting the water? They sound like it."

"Yes, that represents German gunfire aimed at our troops as they approached and landed on the beach."

"They seem almost real."

"Yes, they do, but with all the firing that day, especially from heavy guns, the noise was overwhelming."

"Did you wear ear plugs?"

"Not back in those days. Now, let's step over to this wall. I want to show you something special. See those plaques?"

"You mean the ones with names on them."

"That's right. There are about 4,413 names on this wall—about 2,500 Americans and the rest from our Allied countries. Those men were killed on D-Day, all on just one day, June 6, 1944."

"That's awful—so many men killed on one day. Were any of them from your company?"

Jeb led Billy to one of the plaques and touched one of the raised names on it. "Yes. This man was one of the best friends I ever had." Jeb's voice quavered, and he paused to clear his throat. "The names of several other men from my company are here on this wall, too." Jeb's voice broke, and he turned away. He dabbed at his eyes with his handkerchief, cleared his throat again, and took a deep breath. "Well, we'd better get home." Jeb put his arm around the boy's shoulder and led him to the truck. Before getting in, Jeb turned back toward the memorial. "See that arch up on the top level? That's the Victory Arch. It symbolizes the success of the invasion, which helped lead to our victory in the war."

"What's the meaning of that word on the arch—'Overlord'? And whose flags are those around the arch?"

"'Overlord' was the codename for the D-Day operation, and those are the flags of the twelve Allies that participated in the operation."

"This is a cool memorial, Grandpa."

"Yes, I think so. Now we'd better get back home. We don't want to be late for supper. Grandma would be mad at us, and your dad should have arrived by the time we get there."

Chapter 6

As the truck pulled up the lane to the farmhouse, Jeb and Billy saw Billy's dad, William Jebediah Fletcher, Sr., and Grandma sitting in rockers on the front porch.

Bill Fletcher got up and walked out to greet them.

When the truck stopped, Billy jumped out and ran toward his father. "Hey, Dad," he yelled.

Bill called in return, "Hey, Billy." Father and son shared a hug. "Gee, I'm sure glad to see you. We missed you while you were away at camp."

"I missed you and Mom, too."

Bill then turned toward Jeb, who was coming around the side of the truck. He smiled. "Hi, Grandpa."

"Hey, Bill," said Jeb, returning the smile and extending a hand. Jeb was old school, not much of a hugger. The two men shook hands and patted each other on the shoulder. Jeb motioned Bill toward the porch. "How was the drive from Chicago?"

"It was fine. Thanks for driving down to North Carolina to pick up Billy from camp. We had a major flap at work, and I just couldn't get away in time."

"Oh, we were glad to fetch him. It was a nice drive."

"Susie sends her best. She's sorry she couldn't come. She'd planned to drive out with me, but she's on a big project, and her firm needed her all this week."

"That's quite all right. We're just glad to have at least you and Billy here for a few days."

They climbed the steps to the porch and joined Billy and his grandmother.

"Grandma and I have been talking," said Bill, "but she wouldn't tell me where you two went. She said that was your story to tell. I hope Billy was good for you." He winked at Billy.

Jeb glanced at Billy and nodded. "He's was a perfect young gentleman. We went to Bedford this afternoon to see some of the sites."

"Dad, we went to the D-Day Memorial."

"The National D-Day Memorial," Jeb said, correcting the boy.

"Really? That must have been nice," said Bill.

"It was cool," said Billy.

"All right, you men," interjected Grandma, as she stood. "It's time to come in and wash up. Supper's about ready to come out of the oven. You can talk while you eat."

"You mean between bites, don't you, Grandma?" said Billy, with a smile. "Not while we have food in our mouths."

"Exactly, Billy," she replied, returning the smile as she headed toward the dining room.

During supper, they discussed the afternoon visit to the memorial.

Later in the evening, after they had finished supper and Billy had gone to bed, Jeb and Bill sat on the front porch in the warm summer air, drinking coffee. The night critters had begun their chirping and croaking. Grandma was in the kitchen baking an apple pie for the next day.

"Why did you take Billy to the memorial today?" asked Bill. "You've always been reluctant to take me when we've been here for visits. Why Billy, and why today?"

"Oh, I don't know. I didn't plan to take him there. One thing just seemed to lead to another. I guess it started with the shotgun."

"The shotgun?"

"Yes, Billy wanted to shoot the shotgun, and we went out back and shot at some milk jugs."

"You mean the old shotgun that hangs above the kitchen door?"

"Yep."

"When I came on visits when I was younger, I asked many times to shoot that gun, but you never let me."

"I remember. So, would you like to shoot the gun while you're here?"

"Yes, I would, but tell me, why was it that now, today, you let Billy shoot that gun and then you took him to the memorial? Did you tell him about your wartime experiences, too?"

"No, I didn't talk about my involvement in the war, not really, not in any detail."

"You know I'd like to hear about what you did in the war. I'm sure Billy would, too. I've wanted to know for a long time."

"You know, Bill, when I got back from Europe, I wanted to put much of what happened out of my mind, to put it behind me. I did some things over there that I'm proud of, but I also did some things I'm not so proud of. I also saw some horrible things, and I've had some nightmares."

"Dad told me you used to have nightmares."

Jeb sighed. "It seemed that when I thought of those things during the day, I had nightmares about them at night. So I just tried to put it all out of my head. I also wanted to get on with my life here, with getting married, raising a family, and working in this community. I wanted to look forward, not backward."

"I can understand that."

"When Tom Brokaw's book, *The Greatest Generation*, came out in 1998, I read it and started to think that maybe we veterans needed to share our stories, to honor our wartime buddies, and let the younger generations know what we went through."

Bill took a sip of coffee. "I've heard that a lot of veterans began opening up after reading Brokaw's book."

"I think that's true, but I guess I just wasn't ready." Jeb, with some difficulty, stood up, pushing down on the chair's arms to help him rise. He stretched his legs and back and then eased himself back down into the chair. "Then after I retired and the National D-Day Memorial opened in Bedford, I began visiting there. I read several books about D-Day. I learned a lot about what happened that day, things I never knew when I was there, seeing only my small piece of the action. What one individual can see is so little, and war is so confusing. I began participating in special events at the memorial, and later I even began giving tours. I let people know I was a D-Day veteran, but I didn't really go into much detail about my personal experiences."

"What triggered today's events?"

"Well, more recently, I've come to realize that I'm not getting any younger and if I'm ever going to share some of my experiences, it'll need to be soon. Billy's interest in the shotgun today just seemed to trigger something in me. I wanted to connect with him. I could see that I needed to offer something interesting that we could do together if I was ever going to get him away from that confounded gadget he carries everywhere."

Bill shook his head. "Oh, yes, all the kids have those games. Susie and I limit the time Billy can play with it, but perhaps not enough. Well, for tomorrow, how about taking Billy and me back to the memorial?"

Jeb took a sip of coffee. "You really want to go?"

"Yes, and I'd like to hear all about your wartime service. I heard hints from Dad, but he never told me much before he died."

At the mention of the death of his son, Franklin, Jeb took a deep breath, gazed up at the stars shining in the nighttime sky, and let out an audible sigh. Tears welled up, and he was silent. He took out his handkerchief and wiped his eyes.

Bill followed his grandfather's gaze up into the sky. It seemed there were thousands, maybe even millions or more, of bright, shining stars. He imagined for a moment that his father was out there somewhere.

Jeb broke the silence. "I miss your dad."

"So do I. He was a wonderful man."

"Yes, he was. I was devastated when he was killed. What's it been—seventeen years?"

"Eighteen years this past January."

"I never encouraged him to join the Army, but I didn't discourage him either. After he was killed, I did a lot of second guessing about trying to influence him. Maybe if I had told him more about what I went through in World War II, then maybe he wouldn't have made the military a career. He was just so strongly attracted to the Army, and he did so well—one promotion right after another, a bird colonel by the time he turned 42. Your grandmother and I were more concerned during his two tours as a lieutenant in Vietnam than we were when he went to the Gulf as a colonel."

"I remember seeing him off. I was home for the summer, after my first year of college. We had a good talk before he left."

Jeb sighed. "You and Billy remind me of your dad. I wish you could have seen him as a child. He was such an active, inquisitive boy. We had some great times together." Jeb inhaled deeply and sighed. "It's hard losing a child, at whatever age you are. We're not meant to outlive our children."

"It's hard losing a father, too," said Bill.

"I know that only too well, too. As I told Billy today, I was twelve when I lost my father. You were somewhat older when you lost your dad." Jeb paused and took a deep breath. "Well, it's wonderful having you and Billy here."

"I'm glad we could come. You know, it's never been clear to me how much Dad knew about your time in the Army. He said you have wounds on your shoulder and several other places, but he never told me much."

"I never told him much."

"I wish I had asked Dad about a lot of things. Now it's too late, but it's not too late for us, and this visit is a perfect time. Would you tell Billy and me as much as you can about what you did in the war? Then tell us everything you remember about my dad."

Jeb stared back up at the stars for several seconds. Then he took a deep breath and looked at Bill. "All right. Tomorrow we'll go back to the memorial. Afterwards, we'll stop at a couple of cemeteries. Then I'll tell you all about what I did during the war. Maybe we can even get your Grandma to talk about her experiences."

"Grandma?"

"Oh, yes. She has quite a story, too. I'm sure we can get her to share it with you. Then after we've shared our stories, we'll try to tell you everything we remember about your dad."

Chapter 7

The next morning, Jeb, Bill, and Billy piled into the pickup truck and headed for Bedford. Jeb drove, with Billy squeezed into the middle of the bench seat. Bill and Jeb talked of Chicago and Bill's job.

Billy pulled out his electronic game and began playing. The two men glanced at Billy and then shot each other a look, as they continued to talk.

Jeb drove back up to the National D-Day Memorial and stopped at the gatehouse.

Mack Conklin emerged from the gatehouse and walked over to the truck. "Good morning, Mr. Fletcher." He paused to think. "And 'Billy,' isn't it?"

Jeb nodded. "Good morning, Mack. You've got a good memory."

"Mr. Conklin," said Billy, "you told me yesterday that the next time I came here I should bring someone from Chicago with me. Well, we've brought my dad with us today."

"I didn't expect to see you back so soon, but it's super that you brought your dad, Billy."

Jeb introduced the two men to each other, and they shook hands, reaching in front of Jeb and Billy. Conklin wished them a good visit, and Jeb drove ahead on the circular drive around the memorial and parked the truck.

Jeb led Bill and Billy on a tour, adding even more detail this time. They read the detailed information on the plaques honoring Jeb's Company O and Company O's parent battalion and regiment. They also read the plaques under the statue of General Eisenhower and the plaques under the busts of Eisenhower's two American deputies, Generals Omar N. Bradley and Walter Bedell Smith, as well as plaques for four British deputies to Eisenhower.

"Grandpa," said Billy, "yesterday you said you had met General Eisenhower. Did you meet General Bradley and General Smith?"

"You met Ike?" asked Bill.

"Yes, both General Eisenhower and General Bradley, and toward the end of the war I served on a special staff that worked for General Smith."

"The plaque says that General Smith's nickname was 'Beetle,'" said Billy. "That's funny. Did you call him 'Beetle'?"

"Heaven's no! General Smith got his nickname, 'Beetle,' from his middle name, 'Bedell.' We always called him 'General Smith,' when speaking to him or referring to him when he wasn't around. He'd have bitten our heads off if he'd ever heard us call him 'Beetle.' He was a tough, no-nonsense, taskmaster."

Jeb lead Bill and Billy to other parts of the memorial. Ending the tour at the majestic Victory Arch, Jeb said: "The Victory Arch stands forty-four feet six inches high. It's symbolic of the sixth day of the sixth month of 1944—June 6, 1944, D-Day. When the construction crew started to build the memorial on this hill, the highest spot in the town of Bedford, they had to chop off the top of the hill in order to have a flat place to build. One of the guides likes to joke that after the builders cut off the top of the hill and erected the Victory Arch, they then put in the mountains in the background." Jeb pointed to the Blue Ridge Mountains some three miles northwest of the memorial, as Bill and Billy laughed. "Those two high mountains are part of the Peaks of Otter—Sharp Top on the left, and Flat Top on the right. The Blue Ridge Parkway runs along near the top of the mountains."

"This is an absolutely beautiful place for a memorial, especially with the mountains in the background," said Bill.

"I agree. When I give tours, I also mention that a B-25 bomber on a training mission from South Carolina crashed into Sharp Top in February 1943."

"What happened to the people on board?" asked Billy.

"The crash occurred on a cold, wintry night. A local search team was formed. When they got to the site, they found no survivors. All five members of the crew were killed. Several years ago the Boy Scouts placed a memorial at the site of the crash."

"That was a nice thing to do," said Billy. "I'm a Boy Scout."

"Good for you, Billy," said Jeb. "Well, that completes the tour. Let's go over to the memorial's gift shop. I want to buy something."

While walking to the gift shop, Jeb continued talking. "Besides the National D-Day Memorial and the memorial at the B-25 crash site, you can find memorials all around Bedford and Halesford Counties honoring those who served and those who died in World War II. There are memorials at the courthouses, at the museums, in some of the schools, and in many of the churches."

"How much of an impact did World War II have on this area?" asked Bill.

"I get that question sometimes when I give tours. From what I've read, I believe that some 13 percent of the people in this area served in the military during the war. So just about everyone in the county had a loved one in the service or personally knew someone in the military."

"That's sure different from today," said Bill. "Of course, we have a smaller military and an all-volunteer service."

"Yes, the draft reached into every community. About 16 million men and women served in uniform during World War II. On the home front, just about everyone contributed in some manner. Some made equipment or food for the military. Almost everyone bought war bonds and contributed to the Red Cross and charities like the USO that serve those in the military. Many salvaged scarce materials like tin and rubber, and, with rationing, everyone had to restrict their consumption of food and other items."

"That's far different from today, too," said Bill. "We civilians haven't had to sacrifice much during our wars since World War II."

"That's true."

"How many men from this area were killed in the war?" asked Bill.

"Too many. I've read that Bedford County lost over 140 men throughout the war, and I think Halesford County lost almost as many. Bedford County's special tragedy was losing 20 men on D-Day alone, including nineteen in Company A. That's probably the highest loss per capita on D-Day of any community in America. It was because of this loss that the people of Bedford helped get the National D-Day Memorial established here.

"That's tragic, for those who died and for all their families," said Bill.

"Yes, and, of course, many more were wounded. There were such tragedies all across America. More than one million American service men and women were casualties in World War II—they were either killed or wounded—and over 405,000 of those died."

"Memorials like this are important. The new generations need to know of this sacrifice, so all of us never forget," said Bill.

They arrived at the gift shop and went in. Jeb greeted the volunteers running the shop, all of whom seemed to know him, and he bought a book on D-Day.

When they got back in the truck, Jeb gave Billy the book. "I thought maybe you'd like to learn more about D-Day, Billy."

"Gee, thanks, Grandpa." The boy, who had pulled out his game, put it away and began looking through the book.

"O.K.," said Jeb, as he backed out of the parking slot. "Now I want to take you to see a couple of other hallowed places, one here in Bedford and one in Halesford."

Chapter 8

Jeb drove the truck down the long hill leading out of the memorial and headed for the center of Bedford. He drove past the stores and then northeast on Longwood Avenue. At the end of a stretch of residences, they came to a large cemetery, actually three cemeteries. Jeb took the last entrance and drove slowly to a section marked by several large trees. Pulling the left two wheels off the asphalt and onto the grass, he stopped the truck under an old oak.

As Jeb eased himself out of the truck, the creaking of his knees broke the silence. "Come on, fellows. I want to show you the graves of some real heroes."

Bill climbed out of the truck, but Billy hesitated, looking at the surrounding tombstones. It was his first visit to a cemetery. He slid cautiously out the passenger door and stepped onto the grass.

Jeb walked a short distance among the tombstones, with Bill and Billy following closely. He stopped in front of one family tombstone that read "Fellers." "Right around here are buried some of the famed 'Bedford Boys.' The 'Bedford Boys' were in Company A of the 116th Infantry Regiment, 29th Infantry Division. Company A had been a Virginia National Guard company based here in Bedford before it was activated for federal service. It was made up mostly of men from Bedford County, including the town of Bedford. Their company was very much like the company that I served in over in Halesford County."

"Did you know any of the men from Bedford in Company A?" asked Bill.

"Yes, we were at the same bases and trained together. I've also read several stories about them. They've become pretty famous."

"How'd they become famous?" asked Billy.

"Company A was one of the first units to land on Omaha Beach on D-Day, and they suffered many casualties. I mentioned back at the memorial that the Bedford community lost nineteen men on D-Day from Company A, plus one man assigned to another company."

"Twenty men in one day. That's a real tragedy," said Bill.

"Yes, it is. Right around us here are buried some of those men." He pointed at one of the graves. "Here is the grave of Captain Taylor Fellers, Company A's commanding officer. Over there is the grave of Master Sergeant John Wilkes, Company A's top sergeant. His sister Rubye is buried next to him."

"Did she serve in Company A?" asked Billy.

"Oh, no. The infantry units were all male. I've read that she joined the Army Nurse Corps shortly after her brother and the rest of Company A were called up to active duty in early 1941. She went on to serve 26 years in the Army and ended up as a lieutenant colonel."

"Wow!" said Billy.

"Other men from Company A are buried nearby. John Reynolds is buried over there, and across the road under that oak tree is the grave of Frank Draper. Here's the grave of Ray Stevens, one of a set of twin brothers in Company A. His twin brother Roy's landing craft sank in the channel, and Roy and the other men in the boat were taken back to England, re-outfitted, and then returned to Normandy, where Roy found Ray's temporary grave. Roy, himself, was seriously wounded three weeks after D-Day, but he survived the war and returned to Bedford. Toward the end of his life, Roy used to come up to the National D-Day Memorial almost every day."

"Are all 20 of the Bedford men killed on D-Day buried here?" asked Bill.

"No, I've been asked that question when I give tours. Nine are buried in the American military cemetery in Normandy, France, and the names of two are listed on the tablets of the missing at that cemetery. Nine families accepted the government's offer in 1947-48 and had the remains of their loved ones returned for burial here in this cemetery or elsewhere in the county."

"What happened to the two men who were missing?" asked Billy.

"Well, they probably were shot and died in the surf or on the beach, and their bodies probably washed back out into the English Channel."

"That's sad," said Billy.

"Yes, it is. Well, we'd better go now. I want to stop in a cemetery over in our county and show you some of the graves of men that were in my company."

They walked back to the truck, and Jeb drove them to a cemetery closer to home. There, Jeb led a tour to several graves of his World War II comrades. As they made their last stop, Jeb stared silently at the grave for nearly half a minute. "This is the grave of one of my best friends. We grew up together. We were in the same class in school, and we were almost inseparable. He was killed on D-Day."

"I'm sorry you lost your friend," said Bill.

"Me, too," said Billy.

"Thanks. One of the hardest things I ever had to do was to go visit his parents when I came home from the war. I know they appreciated the visit, and I know they were glad I had survived, but I could tell—I could just sense it—that they were asking themselves the unanswerable question—*how come Jeb survived the war but our son didn't?*" Jeb paused and wiped a tear running down his cheek.

"That's a tough question," said Bill.

"I've thought a lot about why I survived while others didn't. Some people might say, 'There but for the grace of God, go I.' I don't buy that—that God would help or save me but not others, that somehow I'm worthy of God's grace but others aren't. That's not the God I know. I also don't buy into fatalism—the idea that a bullet had someone's name on it."

"Don't training and conditioning help explain why some survive and some don't?" asked Bill.

"In a very general sense, yes, but when you get down to specifics, all the men in my unit had similar training and conditioning. The only answer I'm left with is luck. I was lucky—it's as simple as that. But luck isn't a very satisfying answer, is it?"

Bill felt the need to move the conversation elsewhere. "What year did you graduate, Grandpa?"

"1940. We were the Halesford High School Class of 1940."

"1940? That's sure a long time ago," said Billy.

Jeb laughed. "You're right there, Billy. Well, we'd better get back home. Grandma will have supper waiting for us."

They walked to the truck.

"Bill, would you mind driving? I'm feeling a little tired, and I wouldn't want to fall asleep at the wheel."

"Mind? Are you kidding? I'd love to drive your truck."

They climbed in, Bill in the driver's seat and Billy again squeezed in the middle.

"Just turn right out of the cemetery, and about a half mile down the road you'll see the highway," said Jeb.

"O.K.," said Bill. "Once we get on the main highway, I know the rest of the way to the farm."

After they had driven about five minutes, Bill asked, "Will you tell us more about your wartime experiences?"

"Yes, please, Grandpa," said Billy, looking up from his book on D-Day.

"We'll do that tomorrow. You know, if we're going to talk about those days, you ought to ask your grandmother to tell her story."

"You mean her life story?" asked Bill.

"Yes, including World War II."

"What did she do in World War II?" asked Billy.

"That's her story to tell," said Jeb. "If you ask, I think she'll tell you."

"We'll do that for sure," said Bill.

"You do know that she's not really your grandmother, don't you?"

"Oh, sure, Grandpa," said Billy. "She's really my great-grandmother, but it's just easier to call her 'Grandma.'"

"Right. She's my grandmother," said Bill.

"Not really," said Jeb.

"What do you mean 'not really'?" asked Bill, momentarily taking his eyes off the road to look at his grandfather.

"Well, she's really your step-grandmother, Bill, and, Billy, she's your step-great-grandmother."

"What? How can that be?" said Bill, looking over again at his grandfather. "I never heard anything about that."

Jeb looked at Bill. "Your father never told you?"

"No. You mean you were married once before, to a woman who was my real grandmother?"

"No, not exactly," said Jeb.

"I don't understand this, Grandpa," said Billy, scratching his head.

"I don't understand it either," said Bill, whose face was flushed. "What's this all about?"

"No more questions now, boys. I'm tired, and I need to close my eyes for a few minutes. I see we've got lots to talk about tomorrow."

Chapter 9

September 1939, Halesford

"Hey, Mother. I'm off to school," Jeb yelled up the stairway. "I've got football practice this afternoon. I won't be home until six."

"O.K., dear," his mother called down. "I'm headed to work shortly. I'll have dinner ready by the time you get home."

"Thanks. See you then." Jeb picked up his books and walked out the door of the small rental house where his mother and he lived.

Upstairs, Helen Fletcher, as she finished dressing, thought of the day ahead of her. *I'm going to be really busy today at the mill. Learning that new loom is a challenge, and I have to stand most of the day. It'll be great after supper to sit down, get my feet up, listen to the radio, and read the newspaper. Maybe if Jeb doesn't have too much homework, he'll have time to sit with me and listen to George Burns and Gracie Allen.*

Helen and Jeb had tried to make a go of it on the farm after her husband's death six years earlier, but they had soon found the farm to be more than the two of them could handle. Helen found a job at the woolen mill in Halesford. She sold the farm, and she and Jeb moved into town. To help pay the rent and other expenses, Jeb worked at a gas station on Saturdays throughout the school year and also on some weekdays during the summers.

From their house, Jeb had to walk only six blocks to Halesford High School. In the second block, he saw a classmate leave her house on the opposite side of the street and head toward school. He felt his heart beat faster and a feeling of unease rise in his stomach. He thought Virginia Jackson was the prettiest girl in his senior class, indeed in the whole school.

Ginny, as everyone called her, had long, strawberry-blond hair and a light complexion. Her eyes were blue, and she had an almost perpetual smile. She had a cute figure, too. She was smart and would surely be the class valedictorian. Best of all, she was nice, nice to everyone.

Jeb knew that Ginny was going steady with Dick Drumheller, the star fullback on the football team. For the life of him, Jeb couldn't see what attracted Ginny to Drumheller. In Jeb's view, Drumheller was a bully and a jerk.

Jeb cleared his throat and called across the street, "Hey, Ginny."

Ginny paused and turned toward him. "Oh, hello, Jeb."

"Wait up, and I'll walk with you."

Ginny glanced around. *I hope no one's watching.*

Jeb jogged across the street. *What should I say to her, what can we talk about?* When he reached her, he smiled. "How're you doing?"

"I'm fine," she said, with a slight smile. She thought Jeb was a nice boy—smart, friendly, and polite—but he was young looking, more like a sophomore than a senior, and he always seemed nervous around her.

They began walking. Ginny was closest to the curb. After a few steps, Jeb awkwardly cut behind her and then came forward between her and the curb, forcing her to the inside of the sidewalk. Jeb's father, when he was alive, had taught Jeb on family trips into town on Saturday evenings that men, who were to protect ladies, were to position themselves next to the curb to absorb any splashing and dangers from the street.

Ginny had to suppress a smile at Jeb's awkward maneuver. Dick wouldn't have bothered. "So, how are you doing, Jeb?"

"Oh, I'm fine. Are you ready for the English exam?"

"As ready as I can be."

They walked along in silence. In the next block, another classmate, Charlotte Biggs, came out of her house.

The moment Ginny saw her, she called, almost too eagerly, "Hey, Charlotte, come walk with us."

Charlotte joined them, but there wasn't enough room for three to walk abreast, so Jeb fell in behind the two girls. The girls chatted easily, while Jeb walked along quietly.

Once they reached the school, the girls stopped to talk to some friends, and Jeb headed for the senior lockers. There he found his best friend, Cal Barton. "Hey, Cal."

"Hey, Jeb. I saw you as you came onto the school grounds. Pretty nice company you're keeping. How do you manage having two girlfriends, while I don't have any?"

"Don't make too much of it, wise guy. Ginny and Charlotte live just down the street from me."

"Right. Maybe I should hang out at your house more often. I could swing by and walk to school with you."

"Sure. The more the merrier," said Jeb, chuckling, as they headed together toward their history class.

"I'd walk with Charlotte, leaving you to walk with Ginny. Of course, you'd have to deal with Dick Drumheller." Cal grinned broadly.

"I was just being friendly with Ginny. Don't let your imagination run away with you."

"I hear you, pal."

Chapter 10

In the afternoon, after classes, Jeb and Cal walked the ten blocks from school to the football field. In the locker room under the stands, they changed into their practice uniforms and jogged out onto the field with the rest of the team.

After warm-ups, Coach Reese Ruffner split the team into two lines, with the first player at the head of one line facing the first player at the head of the other line about five yards away. "Boys, we're going to have a little one-on-one drill. I want to toughen you up."

"I could do without one-on-ones," Cal muttered to Jeb.

"Me, too," Jeb replied quietly. Jeb especially disliked one-on-one drills when he came up against a bigger boy. Jeb was five feet, ten inches, tall, but he weighed only 140 pounds. He was still growing, but many of the other boys were taller and outweighed him.

Boys in one line were to be the ball carrier, and boys in the other line were to be the tackler. The ball carrier was to try to run over the tackler, while the tackler was to try to tackle and stop the ball carrier. It was head-to-head, one-on-one.

Coach Ruffner threw the ball to the first ball carrier and called, "Go!" The ball carrier and the tackler ran at each other and collided. CRACK! Both boys ended up on the ground flat on their backs. "All right, get up and go to the back of your line," shouted Ruffner. "Next time, Laughner, hold on to that tackle."

The second boys in each line then moved up. Ruffner threw the ball to the second ball carrier, and the carrier and tackler flew at each other. CRACK! This time the tackler hit the ball carrier right above the knees, picked him up off the ground, and threw him onto his back while falling on top of him. "That's the way to hit, Abbott," yelled Ruffner.

Jeb was third in line. He was to be the tackler. He looked up at the boy in the other line facing him. It was Tommy

Price, the smallest kid on the team. *Good*, thought Jeb. Before Ruffner could throw the ball to Price, the player behind Price pulled Tommy back and moved up into his place at the head of the line. Jeb gulped. *Oh, man. Dick Drumheller.*

Drumheller was over six feet tall and weighed at least 180 pounds. Ruffner tossed the ball to Drumheller and yelled, "Go!" Drumheller charged full speed ahead, as Jeb moved forward in a crouch. The big fullback lowered his shoulder just before the collision. CRACK! He hit Jeb squarely in the chest, knocking the breath out of him and bowling him over backwards to the ground.

Lying there, Jeb tried to inhale but couldn't. He gasped for air, imagining a drowning man cut off from oxygen. Finally, he was able to suck in some air. He looked over and saw Drumheller lying on the ground next to him. Somehow he had been able to hold on and bring the big fullback down.

Drumheller put a hand on Jeb's chest and, with all his weight, began pushing himself up from the ground. In a voice low enough that the coaches couldn't hear, Drumheller said, "Someone saw you with my girl this morning. Stay away from my girl."

Jeb lay on the ground, as air began filling his lungs. He rolled over, spat dirt from his mouth, and wiped his lips. He watched Drumheller walk away with a slight limp.

Ruffner barked, "Good job, Fletcher. Now get up and get back in line."

Jeb got back in line. Cal, after making a tackle, got in line behind Jeb.

"Wow!" said Cal. "Drumheller looked like a freight train bearing down on you, but you held on. Pretty amazing."

Ten minutes later, Ruffner switched the assignments for the lines, so that when Jeb advanced to the front of his line he was the ball carrier. Cal was still behind him.

Opposite Jeb was Tommy Price. Drumheller was behind Price but made no move to replace him.

"Oh, shit," muttered Cal. "I've got Drumheller.

Ruffner threw the ball to Jeb.

Jeb caught the ball but then turned, handed the ball to Cal behind him, and stepped back into second place in line so that he would go up next against Drumheller.

"What are you doing, Jeb? Are you doing this for me?" muttered Cal under his breath.

"No, I'm doing this for me. I'm not backing down."

"You're one crazy guy," said Cal, as Ruffner yelled, "Go!" and Cal ran over Tommy Price.

Ruffner again threw the ball to Jeb. Drumheller, at the front of the opposing line, sneered. Jeb squatted into a running back stance. *Here goes nothing.*

Ruffner yelled, "Go!"

Jeb sprinted forward at full speed, lowering his right shoulder in an attempt to run over his opponent. Drumheller burst ahead and lowered his helmet toward Jeb, trying to spear him. Drumheller's helmet hit Jeb's shoulder pad and then his helmet. CRACK! The boys and their helmets bounced off one another, and both fell backwards to the ground. Lying prostrate, Jeb saw darkness and flashing lights. His ears rang. He looked over and saw Drumheller lying beside him.

Coach Ruffner stood above them. "Now, that's the way to hit, boys! Good job!" He turned to the rest of the team. "Did you see that? These boys have spirit! They're going all out, and it's only practice. They want to make this team, and they want this team to win. Now let's see some of the rest of you hit like that!"

As the two boys slowly got up, Drumheller looked at Jeb and muttered, "You haven't seen the last of me."

Chapter 11

Ginny Jackson sat in the dining room having breakfast on Saturday morning with her parents, Randolph and Ruth Jackson, and her 13-year-old brother, Tim.

"Ginny," said Ruth, "when you left the house yesterday morning, I saw Jeb Fletcher join you on the walk to school. How are the Fletchers?"

"They're fine, as far as I know. Why do you ask, Mother?"

"Oh, I was just wondering. I saw Helen in church last Sunday, and she looked tired. These past few years can't have been easy for her—losing her husband, having to sell the farm, and now working at the woolen mill."

"Well, Jeb seems to be fine, at least."

"What did you talk about?"

"Oh, I did most of the talking. He seems really shy when he's around me."

"Is that right?" asked Randolph.

"He's active and popular in school," said Ginny. "I don't know why he's so quiet around me."

"Jeb's neat," interjected Tim. "Even though he's on the football team, he sometimes plays ball with us younger kids down at the park. Maybe he's so quiet around you, Ginny, because it's hard to get a word in edgewise. I know the feeling."

"Very funny, little brother," said Ginny, showing her teeth in a mock smile.

"Jeb appears to be a nice boy," said Randolph. "As the captain of the football team, he spoke at the sports banquet last week. He seemed mature beyond his looks and his age."

"Losing a father and having to take on responsibilities might do that to a boy," said Ruth.

"How'd Jeb loose his dad?" asked Tim.

"In a hunting accident," replied Randolph.

"What happened?" asked Tim.

"I don't really know. There were rumors, but no details were ever released. I don't pass along rumors."

"So, Ginny, how's Dick?" asked Ruth, changing the subject abruptly.

"He's fine."

"He didn't come into the house last night when he came to pick you up," said Randolph.

Ginny looked down and began buttering a piece of toast. "He called and asked me to meet him out front. He was running a bit late."

"Did you two have a good time?" asked Ruth.

"We did."

"What did you do?" asked Randolph, taking a sip of coffee.

"We went to the sock hop at school."

"That must have been fun," said Ruth.

"What did you do after the dance?" asked Randolph, looking down at his plate, cutting off a piece of melon, and stealing a glance at his wife.

Ginny took a bite of toast and chewed for several seconds. "Oh, we got something to eat and then went for a drive."

Randolph looked directly at his daughter. "I got up at half past midnight to get a drink of water and the light was still on in the living room."

Ginny said nothing.

"Ginny," said Ruth, "you probably need to get home earlier. You're still in school, and you study so hard and are in so many activities. You need plenty of sleep."

"O.K., Mother," said Ginny. She glanced at her watch. "Excuse me, please. I've got to get going. We have cheerleader practice this morning." She stood up and rushed out the door.

Tommy stood up, too. "I'm going to shoot some baskets with the gang."

"Have fun, but be back by noon," said Ruth.

"O.K.," said Tommy, heading out the door.

Ruth and Randolph sat quietly for a few minutes, finishing their breakfast. Ruth poured more coffee for each of them.

"Randolph, you pressed Ginny pretty hard about last night."

Randolph took a sip of coffee. "I haven't had a chance to tell you, but Walt Littlefield dropped by the office late yesterday afternoon."

"Walt? What did he want?"

"Walt and I've known each other a long time. We went to school together, and he's a client of mine." Randolph took another sip of coffee. "He said he was reluctant to come see me, but he and Martha are concerned about Ginny."

"Concerned about Ginny? What do you mean?"

"He said he and Martha think very highly of Ginny. What they're concerned about are Ginny and Dick Drumheller. Their daughter Becky used to date Dick. Walt said he didn't want to go into details, but Becky told Martha some things, and it appears that Dick, as Walt put it, was 'too amorously aggressive.' He was even mean when Becky resisted his advances. Walt and Martha forbade Becky from having any more dates with Dick. They're aware that Ginny is dating Dick, and they're concerned Ginny might get hurt in some way. I thanked Walt and told him I would tell you but no one else of the conversation."

"Oh, dear." Ruth picked up her coffee cup but then set it down without drinking. "I must say that I've had reservations about Dick."

"Me, too. I don't like that boy."

"What should we do?"

"Well, we need to keep a close eye on Ginny—make sure she gets home at a reasonable hour. We ought to sit down and talk to her, too."

"I agree. I hope she'll outgrow Dick."

"I hope so, too, and soon," said Randolph, downing the rest of his coffee and standing up to leave the table. "Let's talk to Ginny after supper tonight. She'll probably be going out with Dick later in the evening."

Chapter 12

After supper, Ginny and her mother worked together cleaning up the dishes. Tim had gone to a friend's house.

"Ginny, your father and I would like to talk to you."

"What about?"

"Let's go sit down in the living room."

They joined Randolph, who was in his favorite chair reading the newspaper. Ruth sat on the sofa, and Ginny sat in a straight chair opposite them.

Randolph put down his paper and took his feet off the hassock. "Ginny, I'm going to be rather blunt. Your mother and I are concerned about your dating Dick Drumheller."

"Why?" asked Ginny, sitting up straight.

"We have some concerns, dear," said Ruth.

"What concerns?"

"Well, we just have a feeling about him," said Ruth.

Ginny sat back and crossed her arms. "Could you be more specific?"

Randolph began filling his pipe with tobacco. "I'll be blunt again. We've heard that Dick doesn't have the best reputation."

"Where did you hear that, Dad?"

"I'm not going to tell you, because it was said in confidence, but I consider the source very reliable. We're concerned that you're going out with someone who may not be good for you, and you're staying out late with him."

"Yes, dear," said Ruth. "We're concerned that you might get hurt in some way."

"Well, I appreciate your concern, but I'm eighteen. I think by now I know how to take care of myself."

"We know," said Ruth, "but if you ever find yourself in a situation that makes you uncomfortable, you can always come and talk to us at any time."

Randolph lit his pipe, and the smell of cherry tobacco wafted through the air. "Yes, and be sure to get home no later than midnight."

"We have your best interests at heart, dear."

"I know you do. I'll be home by midnight."

"I have to catch up on some work I brought home from the office, so I'll probably still be up when you get home." Randolph picked up the newspaper and turned the page.

"While we're talking, could I raise another subject?" asked Ginny, leaning forward.

Randolph slowly lowered the paper. "What's that?"

"I've been thinking about going to nursing school next year."

"Nursing school? I thought you wanted to go to Roanoke College," said Ruth.

Her father dropped the paper on his hassock. "Where did you ever get the idea of becoming a nurse?"

"Some of us girls were talking. We want to help people, to really make a difference, instead of just getting married and raising a family or finding a job just to make money. Also, a diploma in nursing would give me lots of opportunities throughout my life."

Randolph took a deep draw on his pipe. "What do you know about nursing?"

"I've been doing some reading, and a couple of us have taken a tour of the Halesford Hospital."

Randolph paused, exhaling some smoke. "Look. I tip my hat to nurses. They were nice to me when I had my appendix removed last year. But they have to do a lot of unpleasant, even demeaning, physical work—keeping people clean, helping with bedpans and emptying them, messing around with needles and blood, and such—a lot of pretty disgusting things."

"That's true," said Ruth, "and I would think nursing would require a lot of—what shall I say—rather intimate contact, with a whole range of people. Some people, including potential suitors, might think being a nurse is inappropriate for a proper young lady. You could also be exposed to lots of diseases, and I understand nurses' hours are quite long and they're not paid well."

"What you say may be true, at least in part," said Ginny, "but don't you agree that nursing is a noble profession, that nurses are dedicated to helping others. Every Sunday in church we hear about loving our neighbors and taking care of others."

"Like your father, I have lots of respect for nurses," said Ruth. "I'm not sure I could do all the things they have to do. I'm glad there are women willing to do those things."

"Dad, I've checked out the costs of attending Roanoke College and nursing school, and nursing school is much less expensive."

"Is that right?" Randolph took another draw on his pipe. "Well, I might want to look into that. Business is finally picking up a bit, but it won't be long before Tim graduates and starts looking at colleges. What's the deadline for applying to schools for next year?" he asked.

"I have about three months left."

"Good. We'll have plenty of time to discuss this." He picked up his paper and resumed reading.

Chapter 13

May 1940

Halesford High School held its graduation ceremony in late May. Ginny, the Class of 1940 valedictorian, was recognized as the outstanding senior girl for her academic achievements, her service as yearbook editor and head cheerleader, and her membership in several school clubs. Speaking to the graduating seniors and their families and friends, Ginny emphasized the duty of graduates to repay the community by being good, hard-working citizens and helping others.

Jeb was selected as the outstanding senior boy. He had the highest academic achievement of the boys in his class, but his class rank was sixth, behind five girls. At the awards ceremony, he received third-year chevrons for football and baseball. The chevrons would be sewn onto the sleeves of his leather letter jacket.

Cal, who ranked in the middle of the class and received only a chevron for football, ribbed Jeb when the scholastic rankings were announced. "Maybe with your academic abilities you should go to college and join a sorority with the five girls that ranked ahead of you."

Jeb merely chuckled. Going to college was not something he could laugh about. Cal wasn't even considering college, but Jeb still had hopes.

A reporter for the *Halesford Bulletin* newspaper came to the school to interview some of the graduating seniors. He asked Ginny about her plans for the next year and for the future.

"I want to be a nurse," said Ginny. "I plan to start nursing school in the fall."

"Why do you want to become a nurse?"

"I'd like to help others, and nursing seems to offer lots of opportunities."

"What kind of nursing do you want to do?"

"I don't really care, except that I don't think I'd want to serve in an emergency room or an operating room. Those jobs are probably very stressful, and I'd probably be a little squeamish about helping with surgery. I might like to work with children, maybe in the children's ward at a hospital."

In a separate interview, the reporter asked Jeb about his plans.

"I'd like to go to college, but I'm not sure that I'll be able to go this year," said Jeb. "I may get a job for awhile and save my money toward college. Eventually, I'd like to become a businessman."

Earlier in the year, Jeb had talked to his mother about his future. "Mom, is there any chance I could go to college next year?"

"I really wish it was possible, Jeb, but I'm afraid we just can't afford it. You'd need money for tuition, books, and room and board, and there would be other expenses."

"Do you think I could work part-time and go to college?"

"That would be difficult. If you worked around here, you'd have to commute a good distance to a college, and I need our truck to get to work."

"Well, maybe if I worked for a year, I could save up enough money to go to college."

"Well, maybe, but you'd need to go to college for four years to graduate."

"Maybe I should find a job now and save enough money for at least a year or two of college. Once I'm in college, I could work part-time during the school year, full-time during the summers, and perhaps get a scholarship so that I could continue and finish in four years."

"That sounds like a good plan, Jeb. You're a hard worker. If you manage your money well, you might just be able to start and finish college. I'll try to put some of my earnings aside and help to the extent I can."

"Thanks, Mother. I know I can always count on you."

Chapter 14

On the morning after graduation, Jeb walked to Gibbs Lumber Yard, where two days earlier he had seen a help wanted sign. The Gibbs establishment, located five blocks from the center of Halesford, along the railroad tracks on the western edge of town, was the only lumber yard in the county. As such, it was a popular place for both homeowners and contractors.

As he approached the front door of the office, Jeb hesitated and then walked on past the door. *I really need a full-time job. I need this job. Just relax and be yourself.* He turned around and walked back. Pausing and clearing his throat, he took a deep breath and entered.

The combination office and display room bustled with activity. All the clerks were helping customers write up orders or choose from the tools and other materials on display. Jeb surveyed the store as he walked over to a tool display and waited patiently for a clerk. The store was neat and clean. A scent of floor wax and furniture polish wafted through the room. The clerks were friendly, and the customers seemed to be treated well.

Looks like a nice place to work. Jeb picked up an electric saw. It gave off a clean, new-metal smell. He felt the blade. It was sharp. He put the saw down and picked up a hand-cranked drill, turned the crank a couple of times, and set the drill back on the shelf.

A clerk approached. "May I help you?"

"I'd like to speak to the owner, please."

"That would be Mr. Gibbs. Are you, by any chance, here about the job that's posted in the window?"

"Yes, sir."

"Mr. Gibbs is interviewing someone else right now, but they should be through soon. Why don't you just look around some more, and I'll come get you when Mr. Gibbs is free."

Jeb thanked the clerk and picked up a hand saw. He ran his fingers down the sharp teeth. As he set the saw down, he looked up just as someone emerged from the hallway that appeared to lead to the back offices.

Dick Drumheller looked as surprised as Jeb felt. Drumheller paused, sneered at Jeb, and said, "You're too late, boy."

Jeb didn't reply. *He beat me to the job.*

Drumheller swaggered ahead and out the front door.

The clerk came over to Jeb. "Come along with me, and we'll see if Mr. Gibbs can talk to you now."

I guess I should go ahead, even if Dick has beaten me to the job. Jeb followed the clerk down the hallway.

At the end of the corridor was an office, with its door open. A gray-haired man sat at a desk, scribbling on a yellow tablet.

The clerk rapped on the door frame. "Mr. Gibbs, there's a young man here to see you about the job."

Gibbs looked up from his desk. "Thanks, Charlie."

The clerk turned and headed back toward the display room, leaving Jeb standing in the doorway.

"Come in, young man." Gibbs stood, came around from behind the desk, and extended a hand. "I'm Gerald Gibbs."

"Good morning, sir," said Jeb, shaking Gibbs's hand. "I'm Jeb Fletcher."

Gibbs pointed to a chair. "Sit down, please." He returned to his place behind the desk, picked up the tablet, turned to a new page, and wrote something along the top margin. "Jeb Fletcher, huh?"

"Yes, sir."

"So you're interested in the job we've posted?"

"Yes, sir, if it's still open."

"We're looking for someone to help take care of customers—to write up what they want, figure out their bills, take the money and give them change, and then help load their purchases into their vehicles. I've interviewed several applicants. Matter of fact, one just left."

"Yes, sir. I know him."

"You know Dick ...," Gibbs paused, as he flipped backward through the pages of his interview notes.

"Dick Drumheller. Yes, sir." *That may be a good sign that he didn't remember Dick's last name.*

"Right, that's the name, Drumheller. How do you know each other?"

"We just graduated together from Halesford High School."

"Congratulations."

"Thank you."

"Tell me a little about yourself. What qualifications do you have for working in a lumber yard?"

Jeb sat up straight. "Well, I'm a hard worker, and I'm in good physical shape. I like to talk to people. I had good grades in high school."

Gibbs wrote on his tablet. "So you're part of the Class of 1940, huh?"

"Yes, sir."

"I was in the Class of 1905. My, but that sounds like a long time ago, doesn't it?" Gibbs laughed. "So you had good grades. Just how good?"

"Almost all A's."

"That's great. Where'd you rank in your class? I'm not going to tell you where I ranked." Gibbs again laughed. "My daughter, however, was first in her class, several years ago."

"I was sixth."

Gibbs wrote again on his tablet. "Do you know who was ahead of you?"

"Yes, sir. Five girls."

"Five girls?" Gibbs chuckled. "You let five girls beat you?"

Jeb squirmed in his seat. *Getting beat by those five girls still rankles me.* "Well, they were pretty smart, and they probably had more time to study than I did."

"Is that an excuse?"

"No, sir. They were probably just smarter than me."

"Why didn't you have more time to study?"

"I played sports and had a lot of chores. I also had a part-time job."

"What sports did you play?"

"Football and baseball."

"What position did you play in football? I played halfback back in '05."

"I played halfback, too."

"Oh, sure, now I recognize your name. You spoke at the sports banquet this year, didn't you?"

"Yes, sir, I did."

"I remember hearing you speak. You were pretty good, for a young man your age."

"Thank you, sir."

"Who's your dad?"

"My dad was Jeremiah Fletcher."

Gibbs wrote on his tablet and then looked up at Jeb. "Jeremiah Fletcher...from Wild Cat Creek?"

"Yes, sir. We used to live on Wild Cat Creek."

"Your father..." Gibbs hesitated, searching for the right words. "He's no longer alive, right?"

"Yes. He died about six years ago."

"I knew him. I was sorry when he, uh, passed away."

"Thank you, sir."

"I know your Uncle Jonah. Good biblical names in your family—Jeremiah and Jonah. Is 'Jeb' really your first name?"

"No, sir. It's a nickname. My real name is Jebidiah. Dad told me it's a cross between the Bible and the War Between the States. He was a big fan of Jeb Stuart, so he took the biblical 'Jedidiah' and changed it to 'Jebidiah' and nicknamed me 'Jeb.'"

Gibbs laughed. "That's good, that's good. Sounds like something your father would do. How's your mother? Helen, isn't it?"

"Yes, sir. She's doing pretty well. She's been working at the woolen mill since we moved into town."

"She's a nice lady. I see her sometimes in the grocery store and around. You be sure and tell her I said 'hello.'"

"Yes, sir."

"What kind of grades did you get in math, Jeb?"

"Straight A's. Math was one of my favorite subjects."

Gibbs wrote again on his tablet. "Who was your math teacher?"

"In my senior year, it was Delamaude Saunders."

"Oh, my gosh, I had Delamaude Saunders when I was in school."

"I guess she's been around a while," Jeb said with a smile.

"You can certainly say that. I wonder how old she is now. She was a tough taskmaster. Does she still pile on the homework?"

"Yes, sir. She used to give us about an hour each night, but I learned a lot from her."

"I did, too. I guess you always remember the teachers who really made you work."

"I think so, and I'll always remember Miss Saunders."

"What can you tell me about Dick Drumheller?" asked Gibbs, twirling his pencil between his fingers. "Did he do well in math?"

Jeb hesitated, shifting in his chair. *Mother always said not to speak ill of other people.* "I don't really know Dick all that well, and I don't know how he did in math. I do know that he worked hard at football."

Gibbs leaned forward. "Anything else you want to share about him? I've heard some rumors."

Jeb shifted in his chair. "No, sir. As I said, I really don't know him all that well."

"You said you worked part time. Where?"

"At Newton's Gas Station. I've been working at Newton's every Saturday, from seven in the morning until five in the afternoon during the school year. During the summers, I've worked the same hours on Saturdays plus Thursdays and Fridays."

"How long have you been working at Newton's?"

"Two years."

Gibbs made a note on his tablet. "During the school year, that made for a pretty long week, didn't it?"

"I have Sundays free—in my family we've always kept Sunday as a day for church and for rest."

Gibbs put the tablet and pencil down. "Well, I know Joe Newton, and I know he wouldn't have kept you on if you weren't a good worker. I'll give Joe a call just to confirm that you don't think two plus two is five. You don't do you?" Gibbs grinned.

Jeb smiled. "No, sir."

"Sit here a minute, while I go and call Joe."

While Gibbs was out of the office, Jeb sat quietly, looking around the room. On the wall hung a diploma from Roanoke College, and on a shelf behind Gibbs's desk sat pictures of his family. The center of the desk was clear, but papers were stacked all around the edges.

In a couple of minutes, Gibbs returned and took his seat. "Joe said that if I steal you away from him, he's going to give me a bad tank of gas the next time I stop by."

Jeb chuckled. "I don't like leaving and causing any problems for Mr. Newton. He's been very good to me. But I need a full-time job."

"In all seriousness, Joe said he thinks the world of you and that he just wished he had a full-time job for you."

"That's nice of Mr. Newton to say that. I think he could easily find someone to take my hours. Several of my friends are looking for part-time work."

"Well, Jeb, now that Joe has vouched for you, I want to tell you that you're far above the others I've interviewed."

Jeb slid up to the edge of his chair as his pulse quickened.

"You seem to be a personable young man, and if your math skills are what you say they are, you should be able to handle the job well. The job is yours."

Jeb let out a barely-audible sigh of relief. "Thank you, Mr. Gibbs."

"The job is full-time, from 7 a.m. to 5 p.m. Mondays through Fridays plus Saturday mornings from 7 a.m. to noon. We close at noon on Saturdays. We give an hour for lunch, so that comes to fifty hours a week. You'll get two weeks of vacation a year, paid. When can you start?"

"I could start today. I wore my Sunday shirt and pants, so I'd probably have to go home and change first."

Gibbs laughed. "Why don't you plan to report to work here tomorrow morning at 7 a.m.?"

Jeb smiled. "That would be super."

"We didn't talk about wages. We can start you at thirty cents an hour. You'll get time-and-a-half for over forty hours." Gibbs paused, calculating in his head. "That would come to $16.50 a week. Does that sound fair?"

"Yes, sir." *A full time job and $16.50 a week. What could be better?*

Gibbs stood and came around from behind his desk, extending his hand.

Jeb stood, and they shook hands.

"That seals the deal. Now come along and let me show you around and introduce you to some of our other employees."

As they walked down the hall, Gibbs stopped momentarily. "Oh, by the way, I'll call the other applicants and let them know the job has been filled." Gibbs looked at Jeb with raised eyebrows and a smile. "That is, unless you want to tell Dick Drumheller."

Without smiling, Jeb responded, "No, sir, I think it would be best if you did that." He scratched his elbow, a nervous habit he had. *What will Dick do when he hears?*

Chapter 15

The first Saturday after graduation, Dick invited Ginny to go
out for dinner. Ginny was surprised, because sharing a meal
with Dick usually meant grabbing a hamburger somewhere.

The evening of their date, Dick drove to her house,
parked, and walked up to the front door. He rang the bell.

Ruth answered, opening the door less than half way. She
peered out and said, "Good evening, Dick."

"Hi. I'm here for Ginny."

Realizing that she had opened the door less than half way
and had held it so, even after she recognized Dick, Ruth
opened the door fully. "Oh, come in, won't you. Ginny will
be ready shortly."

Dick entered the living room. Randolph was sitting in his
easy chair reading the newspaper. Tim sat reading a
magazine.

"Good evening, Dick," said Randolph, putting his paper
down.

"Hi, Dick," said Tim.

"Hello," said Dick, standing and jingling the keys in his
pants pocket.

"Won't you have a seat?" asked Randolph.

Dick sat down on the arm of the sofa, near where he was
standing.

Ruth looked at Dick and then glanced at Randolph. The
Jacksons had always been strict with their children about not
sitting on the arms of the furniture. She sat down in a
straight-backed chair. "Are you glad graduation is over,
Dick."

"Yeah, but I'll miss football next year."

"What are your plans?" asked Randolph.

"My plans? You mean for next year?"

Randolph nodded. "Yes."

"Well, I'm looking for a job."

"Jobs are still fairly scarce, I'm afraid," said Randolph.

"That's true," said Ruth, "but I heard that Jeb Fletcher just got a job at the lumber yard. I saw his mother at the grocery store, and she told me."

Dick scowled. *So it was Fletcher that Gibbs chose for the job. Bastards, both of them.* He started to say something but stopped when he heard steps on the stairs.

Ginny appeared, dressed in a skirt and sweater. "Hi, Dick," she said with a smile.

Dick stood. "Hi. Are you ready to go?"

"Yes. Are we late?"

"No, but we probably need to get going."

"O.K." Ginny turned to her parents. "I'll see you later. We won't be real late."

"That would be good," Randolph said.

"I hope you have a nice evening," said Ruth.

"Thanks, Mother."

Dick and Ginny walked out to Dick's car. He walked around to the driver's side and got in. Ginny had to let herself in on the passenger side.

They drove to a restaurant in the center of town and had dinner. Afterwards, Dick drove out along a road by the golf course and parked.

He leaned over and put his arm around Ginny. She slid closer to him on the seat.

"Ginny, I'm glad school is finally over. I've been thinking about the future. I want to get a good job here in town. I've already applied at a couple of places. And I've been thinking about us."

Ginny's eyes locked on Dick. "About us?"

"Yeah, about us. Will you marry me?"

Ginny turned her head and looked down at the floor of the car. "Oh, Dick." Her voice reflected her surprise. She scooted back several inches toward her side of the car and then looked at Dick.

He stared at her intensely. "We could find a house to rent. Maybe you could find a job. We could start a family—not right away, of course. Ronnie and Catherine are getting married later this month, and Ronnie has already found a rental house."

"Dick, I'm sorry." She spoke softly. "I really can't accept your proposal now."

Dick wrinkled his brow. "You can't? Why not?" Then his eyes narrowed. "Is there some other guy? Has this got anything to do with Jeb Fletcher?"

"Jeb Fletcher? What in the world does Jeb Fletcher have to do with this?"

"I've always suspected that he had a crush on you, and when I came to pick you up your mother mentioned him, saying he'd landed a job."

"Really now, Dick. Jeb's just a classmate and neighbor. He lives down the street from me. I've never been out with him—we're just casual friends, maybe not even that."

"Well, if you're not interested in Fletcher, is there someone else?"

"There's no one else."

"Then why won't you marry me?"

"I'm not ready to get married and settle down. I've been accepted to nursing school in Richmond. I'm really looking forward to that and becoming a nurse." Ginny slid further away across the seat.

"You really want to go back to school?"

"Yes. I like school. I like to learn new things, and I want to learn things that will help me help other people."

"How're you going to pay for nursing school?"

"My parents are very supportive of my decision, and they're going to pay."

"How long does it take to complete nursing school?"

"Three years."

Dick sat quietly, thinking.

"It's getting late, Dick. I think I'd better be getting home."

Dick started the car and drove Ginny home in silence.

Chapter 16

On a Saturday afternoon in mid-June, Jeb and Cal drove out into the country to their favorite swimming hole in Wild Cat Creek.

Jeb had started his job at Gibbs Lumber Yard. Cal worked with his father on the family farm.

The two young men dived into the creek and swam for almost an hour. When they tired, they stretched out on the bank, soaking up the sun.

"Hey, why don't we join the National Guard?" said Cal.

"Do what?"

"Join the National Guard."

"Why would we want to do that?"

"Well, Ralph Thomson joined, and he says the National Guard pays him a buck for every training session."

"How often do they train?"

"Once a week, for a couple of hours. That's a buck a week."

Jeb sat up. "That's pretty good money. When do they train?"

"Monday evenings, from seven to nine."

"That's a big commitment—every Monday night."

Cal sat up, drying his hair with a towel. "Yeah, but it's a pretty good deal, if you ask me. The Guard goes to summer camp for two weeks in the summer, and that's additional pay."

"Where do they go?"

"Ralph tells me they go to an Army base either here in Virginia or down somewhere in the Carolinas. I'm probably going to live on a farm in Halesford the rest of my life, and this would be a chance to see at least a little country outside of Halesford."

"And what do they do at summer camp?"

"Ralph says they camp out in tents. Best of all, they get to shoot high-powered Army rifles and other weapons."

I haven't picked up a gun in six years, since the accident, thought Jeb.

"Ralph says the food is good, and there's plenty of it."

"But the summer's a two-week commitment. I'd have to miss work, and I'm not sure Mr. Gibbs would let me off. The summer is probably the busiest time at the yard."

"You could ask your boss."

"Did Ralph mention any other drawbacks?"

"Oh, he says there's some chickenshit stuff, you know, polishing your boots and cleaning your rifle, but overall it's a pretty good time."

"Cal, you know, don't you, that there's a lot of threatening stuff going on in Europe. The Germans have taken over much of Central Europe and now they've moved against Western Europe. My uncle Jonah fought in France in 1918. He was gassed by the Germans. He hasn't been right since."

"Oh, I think that's just that weird little guy, Hitler, acting tough. All that won't amount to nothing in the end."

"You think so?"

"Sure. Say, your dad served in France, too, didn't he?"

"He did. He wouldn't talk about it much, except to say it was pretty bad. He was proud of his service, though."

"Look, Jeb, if we joined the Guard, we'd make some pretty-good extra money. We'd have some good times, even go camping, and see a little of Virginia and the Carolinas. And we'd be serving our country, and you'd be continuing a family tradition. How can you beat that? What do you say?"

"I don't know. I guess we could go talk to the Guard people, but I'm still not sure how Mr. Gibbs would feel, whether he'd be willing to let me off for summer camp."

"Let's go Monday evening and talk to the Guard."

"I guess it wouldn't hurt just to talk. No commitment, O.K.?"

"O.K. No commitment."

Chapter 17

On Monday evening, Jeb and Cal drove to downtown Halesford. Cal parked along the street, and the two young men walked to the courthouse. The National Guard Armory was in the basement of the courthouse. They descended the dimly-lit, concrete steps leading down from the sidewalk. When they opened the door, they were greeted by a pungent odor of mildewed equipment.

Inside, sixty uniformed men were milling around. Jeb didn't immediately recognize anyone. They all looked older than Jeb had expected, most appearing to be in their mid-twenties. *They're a tough looking bunch. I thought they'd be closer to my age.*

One of the soldiers noticed the boys. He turned and spoke to another man who had several stripes on his sleeves and was writing something on a clipboard. The man with the stripes looked over at the visitors and headed toward them.

Too late to back out now, thought Jeb.

"Hi, boys, I'm Master Sergeant Buck. What can I do for you?"

Cal spoke first. "I'm Cal Barton, and this is my friend Jeb Fletcher. We're thinking about joining the Guard."

"Well, we'd like some information, at least," said Jeb.

"Cal Barton and Jeb Fletcher," said Buck, as he scribbled their names on his clipboard. "Nice to meet you. You've come to the right place at the right time. We're looking for more young men to fill out our company. How'd you happen to come here?"

"My friend Ralph Thomson joined," said Cal, "and he told me some things about the Guard."

"Good for Ralph," said Buck. "We like our men to help recruit others. Now, Jeb, what kind of information do you want?"

Jeb could see several of the other soldiers looking at them. "Well, sir..."

Buck cut in. "You don't have to call me 'sir.' We reserve that for officers. You can call me 'Master Sergeant.'"

He's friendly enough, but a simple 'sir' would be a lot easier than 'master sergeant'.

"I was wondering," said Jeb, "if you can confirm that your unit meets every Monday evening for two hours and that a soldier earns a dollar for each drill session, plus more when the unit goes to camp for two weeks in the summer."

"That's right. One dollar for each Monday evening drill, and then much more when we deploy for two weeks in the summer."

"What kind of commitment would we have?"

"Assuming you pass the physical exam, you'd have a one-year commitment."

Cal, turning to Jeb, said, "That sounds good to me, Jeb. Let's sign up."

"I have another question, Master Sergeant," said Jeb. "What happens if our country somehow gets into the war in Europe?"

"Do you really think that's going to happen?" asked Buck, scowling.

"No, but what if it happens?"

"The regular Army is trained and ready. The Army could be expanded and deployed. It's possible our company could get called up to active duty—there are no guarantees—but it's unlikely. Should we happen to get activated, at least you'd be serving in a unit with a bunch of guys you know, rather than some unit where you didn't know anyone."

"I'm not sure I see anyone here that I know," said Jeb.

"You may not know anyone here right now, although at least one of you seems to know Ralph Thomson. He's not here tonight, and some others are absent, too. My point is that you'd get to know the men in this unit well before there was any chance of our unit getting called up. Do you have any other questions?"

"I don't have any more questions," said Cal.

Jeb looked down at the floor. *I just don't know how Mr. Gibbs would feel about me having to take two weeks off during the busy summer period. Then, of course, there's my mother. She could have a conniption fit with me joining the Guard. But I'm old enough now to make my own decisions, and it's only a one-year commitment.* He looked up. "No more questions."

"Good," said Buck. "If you don't have any more questions, how about signing some papers?"

Cal looked at Jeb and nodded his head encouragingly.

Jeb took a deep breath and exhaled. "O.K."

Buck led them over to a table to fill out the paperwork, the first step in a long journey.

Chapter 18

When Jeb returned home that evening, his mother was sitting in her easy chair in the living room reading a magazine.

"What have you and Cal been up to tonight?"

Jeb sat down on the sofa. "I know I should have talked to you first." He looked down at the floor.

Helen lowered the magazine. "About what?"

Jeb looked at his mother. "Cal and I just signed up to join the National Guard."

Helen dropped the magazine in her lap. "What?"

"We signed up for the Guard."

Helen shook her head. "Why in heaven's sake did you do that?"

"Cal and I have talked for several days about joining the Guard. Ralph Thomson joined earlier this year, and he likes it. I'll earn a dollar a week for training on Monday evenings and more for summer camp. Dad and Uncle Jonah served in the Army, so I'll be carrying on a family tradition."

"Why didn't you ask me first?"

"I should have. We were going to the Guard meeting tonight just to get some information. I really didn't plan to sign up. I'm sorry I didn't talk to you first."

"Did you think this through? With all that's going on in Europe—why, I was just reading about some of the things Hitler's done recently. We could get involved in the war before too much longer. You know what happened to your dad and Uncle Jonah when they went into the Army and were sent to Europe, don't you? Both your dad and Jonah said it was terrible."

"It's not clear that America will get involved, Mother. Besides, I'd rather serve with a group of guys I know than be drafted and placed with guys I've never met."

"Have you made a firm commitment?"

"Yes, I signed the papers. I still have to pass the physical, but that shouldn't be a problem. I know you're upset, rightfully so, but it's not like I've done something bad."

"No, Jeb, what you've done is not bad, although I do wish you had talked to me first. It's just that if something happened to you, I don't know what I'd do."

"I'll be O.K. You needn't worry."

"Have you talked to Mr. Gibbs about this?"

"No. I'm going to tell him tomorrow. Well, it's late, so I'd better get to bed. Goodnight, Mother."

"Goodnight, Jeb." Helen sat alone for almost an hour worrying about the future of her son.

Jeb tossed and turned in bed for an hour before finally drifting off.

At breakfast the next morning, Helen was the first to speak. "I had trouble sleeping last night. I thought about you and Cal joining the National Guard, and how your serving could be dangerous. Then I thought about all the bad things I've read about that Hitler's doing in Europe and the Japanese are doing in China, and I realized that our country has to be ready to defend itself. While I may worry myself silly, I'm very proud of you."

Jeb stood up, stepped around the table, and hugged his mother. "Thanks, Mother."

Chapter 19

At work that day, soon after the lumber yard opened, Jeb
went to Gerald Gibbs's office. The door was open as usual,
and Gibbs sat at his desk, using a hand-cranked adding
machine. Jeb knocked on the door frame. "Mr. Gibbs?"

Gibbs looked up, smiled, and waved his hand toward a
chair. "Come in, Jeb."

Jeb sat down and edged forward in his seat. "Mr. Gibbs, I
need to tell you something."

Gibbs leaned back in his chair. "O.K."

"I signed up for the National Guard last night."

"Well, that's news," said Gibbs, picking up a pencil and
spinning it with the fingers of both hands.

"I meant to tell you I was thinking about joining the
Guard, but things moved faster than I thought. I still have to
pass the physical, but passing should not be a problem. I'll
probably have to ask for a few hours off work to take the
physical later this week or early next week. We drill on
Monday nights. That won't interfere with work here, but I'll
need to go to summer camp with the Guard for two weeks in
the summer. Maybe I could use my vacation for that."

Gibbs set the pencil down and put his hands together in
front of him, fingertip to fingertip, almost as in prayer. He
said nothing for several seconds. "Well, Jeb, I admire you for
joining the Guard. I served in the Army in 1917 and 1918,
even went to France. Then in 1924, when a National Guard
company was formed here in Halesford, I joined the unit."

"I didn't know you served."

"Yes, I think I served a total of six years. When we
opened this lumber yard and I got busy with my family, I had
to drop out of the Guard. But I always thought I benefited
from my time in the military, and I was proud of my
service."

"That's nice to hear."

"I'll tell you what. You're the first man from this lumber yard to join the Guard since I served. When I was in the Guard, I went to summer camp for two weeks, and then in September I took two weeks of vacation. We'll do the same for you. You can go to summer camp for two weeks. We won't pay you for those two weeks, but the Guard will. Then we'll give you two weeks of vacation with pay in September after the summer rush is over. Is that a deal?" Gibbs stood up and put his hand forward.

Jeb stood up and shook Gibbs's hand. "Yes, sir, that's a very good deal. Thanks, Mr. Gibbs."

"You're welcome. In some ways I miss the Guard. Maybe every once in a while you can tell me how things are going in the unit."

"Sure thing, Mr. Gibbs."

As Jeb walked out of the office, Gibbs watched him and grimaced. *I was once that young and naïve.*

Chapter 20

Later in the week Jeb and Cal reported to the armory in nearby Roanoke, the closest large city where military physicals were given.

"All right, you men, line up in a row facing me," shouted a sergeant. After the men had formed up, the sergeant barked out a question. "What do you think are the two main reasons a man will fail his physical?"

"Syphilis and gonorrhea," wisecracked one of the men.

"In your case, knucklehead, that's probably right. But for most men, at least those who can keep their peckers in their pants, the two main reasons are bad teeth and bad eyes. So, form two lines, facing toward those tables to your left. We need to check your teeth and have you read an eye chart."

The men lined up. Those who failed the cursory dental and eye tests were pulled to the side.

A young man, pulled out of line after the vision test, complained. "Oh, come on, Doc. My old man's a veteran of the Great War. He and my girlfriend won't understand if I go home rejected."

The doctor replied, "Son, almost half the young men across the nation fail the eye and dental exams. Now you report to that check-out table over to your right and then go home. You did your bit—you tried, and you reported for the physical. Some day you may actually appreciate what happened today."

The men who passed the preliminary tests, including Jeb and Cal, were kept in the main room.

"All right," shouted the sergeant. "Now we're going to look at more than your teeth and your eyes. So, start stripping."

"You mean take off our clothes?" asked one of the men.

"That's exactly what I mean," barked the sergeant. "Drop your clothes right where you are."

"Even our undershorts?" asked one of the recruits.

"Yeah, even your undershorts. What's the matter? Are you shy? I'll make a special case for you. You can take your undershorts off and stick them over your head. That way, we won't be able to tell who you are."

The men burst out laughing.

"Strip—now," bellowed the sergeant.

The men began to undress. Jeb moved slowly and left his underpants on until last. He felt self-conscious, even though he was used to walking around naked in his school's football and baseball locker rooms. He was proud of his body. He was muscular and had no fat, unlike many of these men, but he didn't know anyone in the room except Cal.

Other men, especially those who had not been on sports teams and experienced locker rooms, seemed shier and undressed more slowly.

As soon as all the men were naked, the sergeant shouted, "All right, form a file here in front of the doctor. Once you've been through this line, been checked, and answered all the questions, then get dressed."

The doctor gave each man a quick exam, checking first for signs of venereal disease and then, after he told the man to turn his head and cough, probing the groin for hernias. The doctor checked for hearing loss and flat feet and asked several questions.

When the testing was done and the men had dressed, the sergeant bellowed, "All right, line up again. We need you to sign some papers. Once you've signed those papers, all I have to say is 'Congratulations! You're in the National Guard.'"

"Hot dog, we made it," said Cal, a broad smile on his face.

"Yeah, we made it," replied Jeb, quietly. *What are we getting ourselves into?*

Chapter 21

The next Monday evening Jeb and Cal drove together to the
drill meeting of Company O in the basement of the
courthouse.

"Are you nervous?" asked Jeb, as Cal parked the car.

"Nervous? Nah. What's there to be nervous about?"

"Oh, I guess nothing," replied Jeb, belying his thoughts.
*Actually, there's plenty to be worried about. We don't know
these guys and almost all of them are several years older
than us. They've been in the company for a while and are
experienced. As new recruits, we might get hassled.*

They walked to the front of the courthouse and descended
the stairs into the armory. The room was again bustling with
the activity of some sixty men, all in uniform. Some were
talking and laughing. Others seemed busy with tasks.

Jeb surveyed the men. "Oh, my God," he said, in a voice
intended only for Cal.

"What is it?" asked Cal.

"Over in the far right corner—Dick Drumheller."

"Oh, no," said Cal, spotting Drumheller.

As they stood looking, Drumheller, who had been talking
with several other men, turned and saw them. His eyes met
Jeb's. Drumheller was in uniform and had two chevrons on
his sleeve, indicating the rank of corporal. While Drumheller
had been in the Class of 1940 with Jeb and Cal, he was older
and had been in the National Guard for more than a year,
unbeknownst to the two new recruits.

Drumheller started toward them. "Hey, guys," he called to
the men around him, in a voice loud enough for Jeb and Cal
to hear, "look what we have here—a couple of real
greenhorns."

Jeb braced. *Here we go.*

Drumheller stopped in front of Jeb, licked the index finger
of his right hand, and swiped it behind Jeb's left ear. "Look,

this one's still wet behind the ears." Drumheller laughed, as did other soldiers nearby.

Jeb thought about pushing Drumheller away but stood still.

A voice rang out. "All right, Drumheller. Leave those two alone," barked Master Sergeant Buck.

Drumheller glowered at Jeb but then walked away, muttering something in a low voice that made his buddies laugh again.

Buck walked over to Jeb and Cal. "How'd the physicals go?"

"We passed without any problems," said Cal. "We brought our medical exam records." Cal and Jeb passed their papers to Buck.

"Good," said Buck. "Now I need you to sign some other papers to make you officially part of Company O. Come on over to the table."

The three went to the table and sat down. Buck handed each a set of papers. Jeb and Cal glanced through the papers and signed.

"Hey, Sarge, will we get paid for tonight's drill?" asked Cal. "And when will we get our uniforms?"

"You two are now officially part of Company O. You'll call me Master Sergeant or Master Sergeant Buck. Is that clear? And stop asking so many damn questions. Just keep your eyes open and our mouths shut and follow orders, and we'll get along just fine." Buck abruptly stood up and walked away.

Jeb and Cal glanced at each other and raised their eyebrows.

"All of a sudden, Buck doesn't seem so friendly," said Cal quietly.

"Yeah, as fast as the stroke of a pen."

Buck walked over to an area of the room where there were two flags, the American flag and the flag of the Commonwealth of Virginia. He shouted, "Fall in." Except for Jeb and Cal, the men fell into squad and platoon formations, standing at attention with heels together and arms straight down at their sides. Buck ordered, "At ease," and each man spread his legs and feet apart and locked his arms behind him.

Jeb and Cal didn't know where to go and so stood in place, off to the side.

Addressing the platoons, Buck continued. "We have two new recruits joining us—Private Jebidiah Fletcher and Private Cal Barton. I'm assigning both of them to Third Platoon, Third Squad." Addressing the platoon sergeant in charge of the Third Platoon, Buck ordered, "Staff Sergeant Tucker, get those two new men in uniforms."

"Yes, Master Sergeant," said Tucker.

While Buck read announcements to the rest of the company, Tucker walked over to Jeb and Cal and pointed to a rack of uniforms in a back corner of the room. "Go to that rack and find uniforms that'll fit you. We'll get you something more permanent later."

"Yes, Sergeant," Jeb and Cal said in unison. They hurried over to the rack and searched for uniform pants and shirts that would at least come close to fitting them.

Buck finished with his announcements. He ordered the three platoon sergeants forward to talk with him, leaving the rest of the company standing at ease.

Jeb and Cal found suitable uniform parts and began stripping out of their civilian clothes down to their underwear.

Drumheller stood in formation only ten feet away. He let out a loud wolf whistle, one which he usually reserved for buxom young women. His buddies and most of the men in formation laughed.

Cal, standing in his shorts and undershirt, called to Drumheller. "What's the matter, Dick? Do my shorts turn you on?"

Jeb muttered, "Cal, control yourself."

Drumheller's face turned red, and one of the other men muttered, "Oh, no, here we go."

Buck, whose back had been to the men as he talked to the platoon sergeants but who seemed to have eyes in the back of his head, whirled around and glowered. "Sergeant Tucker, why are two of your men not yet in uniform and in ranks?"

"No excuse, Master Sergeant," answered Tucker.

"Well, at the end of tonight's drill, your platoon will run 5 laps around the block, with Barton, Fletcher, and Drumheller setting the pace."

"Yes, Master Sergeant," replied Tucker.

The men of Third Platoon glowered at the three culprits.

Jeb and Cal quickly finished donning their uniforms, and Tucker directed them to their places in the Third Platoon formation.

Buck continued. "All right, platoon sergeants, I want you to have your men draw rifles and then for an hour I want you to drill your platoons outdoors in rifle position drill and close order marching. Sergeant Tucker, get your two new men some personal instruction. Reassemble at 2015 hours."

The platoon sergeants took over the direction of their platoons. Two of the platoons drew rifles from the racks and marched out the door and up the stairs to the street level in front of the courthouse, where they started their drills.

Tucker kept Third Platoon in place. "Corporal Drumheller, front and center," he ordered.

Drumheller walked quickly to the front of the platoon and stood in front of Tucker. "Yes, Sergeant."

"Drumheller, I've got an important mission for you tonight."

"Yes, Sergeant."

"As a junior non-commissioned officer, your mission tonight is to teach Privates Fletcher and Barton the basic drill positions. You've got forty-five minutes. I'll be back to test them."

"But…"

"That's an order, Drumheller."

"Yes, Sergeant."

Tucker ordered the other men in the platoon to draw rifles from the racks and then marched them toward the door, leaving Drumheller with Jeb and Cal.

Drumheller faced the two recruits. "All right you two peckerheads, I'm going to demonstrate the basic drill positions. You'd better damn well pay attention. If you don't pass Sergeant Tucker's test, I'll have your asses. Now get a rifle." Drumheller walked to the gun rack and picked up a rifle.

Jeb and Cal each picked up an M-1 rifle from the rack.

Jeb examined the rifle from the tip of the barrel to the butt of the stock. He noticed that his hands shook slightly. *This is the first time I've handled a gun since the accident.*

Drumheller began instructing the two recruits in the drill positions for a soldier armed with a rifle.

After about ten minutes, a man in his forties, graying at the temples, walked up behind Drumheller. "Corporal Drumheller," he said.

Drumheller, reacting to the disruption, muttered "yeah" and wheeled about. His face reddened. "Oh, Captain Harrison. Excuse me, sir. Good evening."

"Good evening, Corporal Drumheller," said the captain. "Are these our two new recruits?"

"Yes, sir. I'm instructing them in drill positions."

"Good." Turning to Jeb and Cal, the captain said, "Men, I'm your company commander, Captain Charles Harrison. Welcome to Company O." He held out his hand.

"Good evening, sir," said Jeb and Cal, almost in unison, as they shook his hand, Jeb first, followed by Cal.

"I've looked at your paperwork," said Harrison. "You should both be fine assets to this company. I know some of your family. You can tell them I'll take good care of you."

"Yes, sir," the two recruits responded, again almost in unison.

The captain seems nice, thought Jeb.

Drumheller, standing to the side, rolled his eyes.

"All right, Corporal Drumheller, carry on, and take good care of these men." Harrison turned and walked away.

"Yes, sir," replied Drumheller, in a voice lacking in sincerity. *Yes, sireee! I'm going to help you take care of these two, Captain.*

Drumheller turned to the two recruits. "Captain's pets, huh? Well, we're going to have to make sure he isn't disappointed in you. Let's see how well you remember everything I just taught you." Drumheller barked out a series of orders, "Right shoulder arms! Damn it, Fletcher, get that right forearm horizontal! Left shoulder arms! Barton, get your right arm down to the side. Port arms! Damn, you two greenhorns have a lot of work to do."

What a jerk! thought Jeb. *What have we gotten ourselves into?*

If I'd known Drumheller was in this unit and had rank on us, I probably wouldn't have suggested Jeb and I join thought Cal.

By the end of the forty-five minutes, both recruits were tired from drilling with their ten-pound rifles. Sergeant Tucker returned and quickly gave several drill commands to test Jeb and Cal. "All right, that's good," said Tucker to Jeb and Cal. "You men must be faster learners."

Drumheller stood to the side, frowning. *They learned because I'm a good teacher. Thanks a lot for the compliment, Sarge.*

The platoons began filing back into the armory. Buck ordered the units back into assembly formation. "All right, men, you did well tonight. We ought to score high in the unit competitions this summer. We'll drill the same time next week. Sergeant Tucker's Third Platoon owes me five laps around the block. Get them moving, Sergeant."

"Yes, Master Sergeant," replied Tucker. "Third Platoon, file out onto the street and form up." The Third Platoon filed out the door, with Drumheller, Fletcher, and Barton bringing up the rear.

"As for the rest of you men," ordered Buck, "DISMISSED!"

Outside, Tucker ordered, "Drumheller, you know the route, so you take the point. Fletcher and Barton, you follow Drumheller, then the rest of the platoon. Five laps. Now move!"

The men began their run. The grumbling and resentment against the two new recruits grew with each lap.

Chapter 22

August 1940, A.P. Hill Military Reservation, Virginia

In late August, Company O, along with other units of the 29th Infantry Division, deployed by truck to A.P. Hill Military Reservation, north of Richmond, for two weeks of intense training.

At the reservation, named for the famous Confederate general, the division's leaders organized competitions among the sub-units, especially the companies, as a way of motivating the men and building esprit de corps. The companies competed in formation marching, orderliness and cleanliness of their bivouac areas, and even the skills of their cooks. The most intense competition, however, was rifle marksmanship.

To prepare for the shooting competition scheduled for the next to last day of camp, Captain Harrison ordered that Company O's riflemen practice firing on the rifle range for two hours each day. There were to be no exceptions, since the target scores of all the riflemen in the company counted.

Harrison ordered special training on the rifle for Jeb and Cal, who had no experience with the M-1 Garand rifle. Poor shooting on their part would drag down the combined score of the company. Harrison gave the order to the company executive officer, who relayed it to the lieutenant who led the Third Platoon, who passed it to the platoon sergeant of the Third Platoon, Staff Sergeant Tucker. Tucker would select a junior non-commissioned officer to give the special training to Jeb and Cal.

On the afternoon of the first day of camp, Master Sergeant Buck ordered the company into formation, with rifles, preparatory to being trucked to the rifle range. As the platoons stood at ease, Sergeant Tucker addressed the men in his Third Platoon. "This afternoon we're going to begin our practice on the firing range. If you put in maximum effort, our company stands a good chance of winning the competition at the end of the two weeks. Last year, this platoon lead the rest of Company O, and our company won the division competition. This year, however, we have some new men—Privates Fletcher and Barton. They're not experienced with the M-1. We need to give them some special attention in learning how to disassemble, clean, and reassemble their rifles. After that, we'll show them how to shoot. Now, while most of us go to the firing range, I need one well-trained non-com to stay behind to teach Fletcher and Barton how to strip, clean, and reassemble their pieces. Are there any volunteers?"

All the non-coms in the platoon looked down at their boots to avoid eye contact with Tucker. None wanted to be stuck training the new men and missing a chance to shoot on the firing range.

"No volunteers, huh?" said Tucker. "O.K. then, Corporal Drumheller, you're the man."

"What?" cried Drumheller, raising his arm in exasperation and breaking out of his "at ease" stance. "Why the hell me, Sarge?"

"You did a fine job teaching them the drill positions," said Tucker. "You're a good teacher."

"Yeah, I am, but how about having one of the other guys now instruct these two greenhorns. I had my turn."

"You're the best man for the job, Drumheller," said Tucker. "You should be proud."

One of the men in the front row snickered. Drumheller glowered at him.

"O.K.," said Tucker. "Drumheller, Fletcher, and Barton, fall out." He turned to the others. "The rest of you, load onto the trucks." Then he turned back to the three who were to stay behind. "When we get back from the range, Drumheller, I'll test these two to see how well you taught them." He turned and hopped aboard a truck.

Drumheller glared at Jeb and Cal. "Damn it! Now look what you've done." He kicked the ground. "I wanted that range time. I need it. The other guys will get a leg up on me now."

"It's not our fault," said Cal.

"Shut the hell up. It is your damn fault." Drumheller watched the trucks pull out. He took a deep breath and spit on the ground in front of Jeb and Cal. "All right. We've got work to do. Get your sorry asses in gear and follow me."

Drumheller led Jeb and Cal to one of the buildings used for instruction. Inside, he had the two privates lay their rifles on a training table. He took one of the rifles and showed them how to disassemble, clean, and reassemble it. Then he had Jeb and Cal disassemble and clean the parts of their rifles.

Jeb began cleaning his rifle. *This is the first time I've cleaned a gun since before the accident.* He started to recall walking out in the field that October day with his father and uncle. Distracted, he dropped one of the parts he was cleaning. It fell on the table with a sharp crack.

"Damn it, Fletcher. Watch what you're doing. You're going to damage those parts, and then there'll be hell to pay."

Jeb refocused his attention on cleaning the rifle.

Drumheller repeatedly had Jeb and Cal take their rifles apart and put them back together. After several iterations, he began clocking them. They became more proficient with each attempt.

At the end of nearly three hours, the rest of the company returned to the bivouac area. Tucker came looking for the three left behind. "How'd they do, Drumheller?"

"I explained everything in simple terms, showed them how to do it, and then drilled them over and over. As dimwitted as they are, I think they got it."

"All right," said Tucker, "let me time them. Fletcher and Barton, when I count to three I want you to disassemble your pieces and then reassemble them."

When Tucker reached three, Jeb and Cal went to work. They quickly disassembled their rifles and began

reassembling them. Jeb finished a couple of seconds before
Cal.

"Well done, men. Drumheller, you did such a good job
today that tomorrow I want you to teach these two how to
fire their pieces."

"For Lord's sake, Sarge, give me a break."

Tucker turned and left the building.

"You two are a real pain in the ass," Drumheller said to
Jeb and Cal.

The next afternoon Company O again rode out to the rifle
range. Tucker ordered Drumheller to take Jeb and Cal to the
far right end of the firing line and instruct them in firing
from the prone, sitting, and standing positions.

Drumheller led the way to the end of the firing line, away
from most of the others. "O.K., damn it. Now watch me as I
get into the prone position." He faced toward the targets. He
explained his movements as he held his rifle chest high
across his body, dropped forward onto his knees and then,
using the butt of the rifle as leverage, eased himself forward
until he lay on the ground. He extended his left arm forward,
put his left elbow on the ground, bent his forearm upward,
and cradled the front hand guard of the rifle in his left hand.
He jammed the butt of the rifle into his right shoulder,
planted his right elbow on the ground, bent his forearm
upward until his right hand grasped the rifle at the narrow
point of the stock, with his right index finger on the trigger.
In position, he sighted down the barrel of the rifle. He looked
up at Jeb and Cal. "Did you see everything I did?"

Jeb was about to answer when the loud CRACK of a
gunshot erupted behind him. One of the other men on the
firing line had fired a first round. At the sharp sound, Jeb
instinctively ducked. It was the first time he had heard
gunfire since that October day six years before. Within
seconds a series of CRACKS erupted as the other men on the
firing line fired their first rounds. Jeb stood frozen. Then all
became quiet as the men evaluated their shots.

"What the hell's the matter with you, Fletcher?" shouted Drumheller. "Don't tell me you're gun shy."

"Are you O.K., Jeb?" asked Cal, quietly.

Jeb took a deep breath. "I'm O.K."

"I asked you two a question," barked Drumheller. "Did you see everything I did?"

"Yes, we did," said Cal.

"All right, then, assume the prone position," ordered Drumheller.

Jeb and Cal dropped to their knees and eased forward into position. Drumheller critiqued them, criticizing their wrong movements but not complimenting their good ones.

The other men began firing again.

"I'm missing a lot of practice because of you two," complained Drumheller, as he looked at the other men firing away. He then demonstrated the sitting and standing positions and critiqued the efforts of the two privates to implement what he had shown them. Next, he instructed them in aiming and squeezing the trigger.

Finally, Drumheller loaded a clip of ammunition into his rifle, dropped to the prone position on the extreme right of the firing line, aimed at the far right target, and fired a round. He stood, took his binoculars out of their case, and surveyed the target. His shot hit Ring 4 at 3 o'clock, several inches to the right of the bull's eye.

"All right," said Drumheller, as he handed an ammunition clip to Jeb and Cal each. "Assume the prone position and engage the target. You each get one shot only."

Sergeant Tucker approached from down the firing line and stood behind the three men.

Cal dropped into position to the left of the one used by Drumheller and fired at the target second from the right—CRACK.

Drumheller raised the binoculars. "Ring 4 at 6 o'clock." Several inches straight below the bull's-eye.

"That's pretty good, for a first shot," said Tucker.

Jeb stepped up to the firing slot on the far right of the line, the same slot Drumheller had used, with the same paper target. His stomach churned and his body shook as though he were cold. *I haven't shot a gun for six years.*

"Get a move on," ordered Drumheller.

Jeb dropped into position. He sighted down the barrel at the target. One second he saw the target; in the next second it seemed to have become a quail. He was short of breath, and his arms shook. The tip of the barrel wobbled. He shook his head and again saw the target. He took a breath, held it, aimed, and squeezed the trigger. CRACK. The rifle recoiled into his shoulder. The pain of the recoil felt similar to the kick from his old shotgun. This pain, however, came with a sense of relief—despite the hunting accident, he could again fire a gun. He felt good.

Drumheller lifted the binoculars. Jeb's shot had hit the bull's eye. *That damned Fletcher, a bull's eye.* Drumheller, however, called out loudly, "Ring 4 at 3 o'clock," a spot several inches to the right of the bull's-eye, the spot on the target Drumheller had hit when he had fired minutes earlier.

"Also pretty good for a first shot," said Tucker.

Chapter 23

Late August 1940, Halesford

"Be careful with my new suitcase, Tim," Ginny shouted from the Jackson's front porch, as her brother struggled down the walk to the car. "I don't want it all scratched up even before I get to Richmond."

"What do you have in this thing, anyway?" Tim yelled back, setting the bag near the trunk of the car.

"Nothing that a good, strong boy shouldn't be able to handle." Ginny went inside the house for a last armful of hanging clothes.

When she came back out, her parents followed. Her father carried two boxes, and her mother carried one box and a picnic basket for the road trip. The three of them paused on the front porch.

"Is that everything?" asked Randolph.

"I think so, Dad."

Randolph set his boxes down on a chair and pulled out his keys.

Ginny watched as her father secured the front door. When he moved away, she continued to stare at the locked door for several seconds.

Randolph put his arm around Ginny's shoulder. "Well, this is the day our little girl flies the nest—off to the big city and the Medical College of Virginia. How do you feel?"

"I'm excited. I'm also a little bit scared."

Her mother kissed her on the cheek. "We probably don't tell you this often enough, dear, but we're very proud of you. You've been a wonderful girl, and now you're becoming a wonderful young woman."

Both women dabbed with their fingers at the tears forming in their eyes.

Randolph cleared his throat. "We're very proud of you, Ginny. You did so well in high school, and now you've been accepted at a top-notch college. You have the world before you."

Tears rolled down Ginny's cheeks, and she was barely able to speak. "You've been wonderful parents."

Randolph handed her his handkerchief. Ginny dried her eyes and handed it back.

"Hey," called Tim from curbside, "are you ready? It's hot out here, and I'm getting hungry."

"We'd better be going," said Randolph, leading the two women toward the car.

Tim watched them approach. "My gosh, with all those things, plus the things we've already loaded, the four of us will have to squeeze into the front seat."

Ginny pinched Tim's cheek. "No, there'll be plenty of room. I'll sit in the front seat with Mom and Dad, and we'll tie you on top of the car."

Tim swatted her hand away. "Very funny. Hey, have you been crying?"

"None of your business, small fry."

Randolph finished packing the car. "O.K., everyone. Climb in." He held the door for Ruth as she got into the front passenger seat. He then walked around and got into the driver's seat. Ginny and Tim squeezed into the back seat, with a pile of Ginny's things wedged in between them and boxes covering part of the floor.

As the car pulled away, Ginny looked back one more time at the house she had grown up in. *I'll miss home, but my folks and Dick might come see me in Richmond, and I'll get to come home for Thanksgiving.*

The car was hot inside, and everyone rolled down their windows.

Tim scooted forward in his seat. "Mom, since Ginny's moving out, can I have her room? Hers is much bigger."

Ginny grabbed hold of his belt and pants and pulled him back in the seat. "Nice try, squirt, but my closets are still full with my winter and spring clothes. I'll be coming home for

Thanksgiving to check on you and make sure you're not moving into my room."

Randolph laughed. "Gee, we're going to miss all this fussing between the two of you."

"It's going to be so quiet around the house," said Tim. "Maybe now I'll be able to get a word in at the dining room table."

"Yes, Tim," said his mother, "now we'll have only you to quiz at supper."

"Oh, I hadn't thought about that," said Tim, settling back in his seat.

Ginny reached over and patted her brother on the head and laughed. "Now it's your turn."

Tim scowled and looked out the window.

As they drove away from Halesford, Ginny took a deep breath of the clean, sweet smelling country air. She looked out at the Blue Ridge Mountains. The sky and the air were clear, and only a little blue haze blurred the mountains. *The mountains are so beautiful, so fresh and inviting. I'll miss them. But they're not going anywhere. They'll be here for me when I return.*

As the car moved along, leaving the mountains behind and proceeding over the relatively flat land toward Richmond, Ginny looked out at the ever-changing scenery and thought about what lay ahead. *Nursing school and Richmond—both should be exciting. I love to learn new things, and there's so much to learn about medicine and caring for patients. Being in a large city and being on my own should be fun. This is going to be an adventure.*

After they had driven nearly an hour, Tim, who had fallen asleep in the hot car, woke up. "Are we going to stop and have lunch? I'm hungry."

Randolph and Ruth spoke for a few seconds, and Randolph pulled the car off to the side of the road under some large pine trees. Everyone got out.

"Tim, would you get the picnic basket from the trunk of the car," Ruth said as she spread a blanket atop a bed of pine needles."

"Why doesn't Ginny get it?"

"Tim, your mother asked you to get it," said Randolph, standing with his hands on his hips. "You're going to have to learn to help out more, now that Ginny's leaving."

Tim bowed his head. "Yes, sir." He retrieved the basket, and they all sat down on the blanket for lunch.

Twenty minutes later, Randolph stood. "We have more than an hour's drive left. Does anyone need to visit a tree?"

No one did, and they all climbed back into the car.

An hour later, Randolph announced, "There it is. There's Richmond."

Ginny moved up on the edge of her seat and peered out the window. "It's a big city, isn't it? Look at those tall buildings."

"Look at the size of the river," said Ruth.

"What river is that," asked Tim.

"It's the James," said Randolph, as he pressed down slightly more on the accelerator. "Look, you can see the capital building off in the distance."

As they neared the center of the city, Tim asked, "What stinks?"

"That smell? That's tobacco, from the tobacco factories," said Randolph, as he stopped at an intersection.

"My but it's hot," said Ruth. "It seems several degrees hotter here in the city than back in the country. We almost bake when we come to a stop."

"Yes, I hope the car doesn't overheat," said Randolph.

The car behind them started honking when the light turned green. Randolph hurried and turned onto Broad Street, the busiest road downtown. A large, noisy truck passed them going the opposite way, spewing black exhaust fumes toward them.

"I'd almost forgotten how noisy and dirty the city can be," said Ruth.

Ginny slid forward on her seat. "Look at all the people."

"They're all sizes, shapes, and colors," said Tim.

"Too many people for me," said Ruth, fanning herself. "I'd get lost among them all."

"It may be noisy and dirty, but I think I'm going to like Richmond," said Ginny.

"Now if we can just find the nursing school in this big city," said Randolph.

Chapter 24

Richmond, Virginia

Randolph drove on until he found the university, its medical school, and the dormitory for student nurses. This was where his daughter would live with thirty other young women in her first-year class. He parked the car in a lot near the dormitory's front door.

Ginny was the first out of the car. "Let's go find my room. We can come back for my clothes and things later."

Inside the entrance to the three-story dormitory was a table. Behind it sat a woman of about 50 years of age, dressed in a starched, white uniform, white stockings and shoes, and a white cap. She looked up but did not smile. "Are you here to report in for school?"

Ginny stepped forward. "Yes, my name is Virginia Jackson."

"Jackson. I don't recall seeing a Jackson on the list."

Ginny glanced at her parents and then looked back at the woman. "I have a letter from the college."

The woman looked down at a list of names on the table. "Oh, yes, here you are."

Ginny's sigh of relief was audible.

The woman made a checkmark on the list. "I'm Miss Rathman. I'm the matron of this dormitory."

"How do you do, Miss Rathman. These are my parents, the Jacksons, and my brother Tim."

Miss Rathman stood, still not smiling, and Ginny's parents stepped forward to greet and shake hands with her. Tim held back.

Miss Rathman sat back down and looked again at the list and then at Ginny. "Your room is 312. That's on the third floor. Your father and brother may help take your things upstairs. This is the only day men are allowed in the dormitory. The dormitory rules are posted on the inside of the door in each room. You should read them right away. The stairs are over there."

"Thank you, Miss Rathman." Ginny walked over to her parents and said quietly, "Maybe we should go out to the car and get my things now." Ginny walked out the door, and her parents and Tim followed.

"What a grouch," said Tim, as they walked to the car.

"Hush, Tim," Ginny said, putting an arm around his shoulder. "Someone might hear you."

At the car, Ginny picked up most of her hanging clothes, her mother grabbed a box and the remaining clothes, her dad took two boxes, and Tim grabbed the suitcase.

As they walked back into the dormitory and headed for the stairs, they quietly passed the table where Miss Rathman was greeting another student and her family. Ginny paused and shifted the clothes to the other arm, while trying to listen.

"McCall. I don't remember seeing a McCall on the list."

"But I was notified that I was accepted."

"Let me see. Oh, yes, here it is. McCall, Martha."

Ginny hurried to catch up with her family. *Miss Rathman either has a very short memory or she's playing games with us.*

The Jacksons climbed the three flights of stairs and paused at the front of the third floor hall to catch their breath. It was hot, and they could feel no breeze.

"I guess the new class always gets the third floor, where you have to climb the steps and suffer the rising heat," said Randolph, between pants.

As they walked ahead, they saw a few girls and a couple of other families down the hall.

They soon came to Room 312. The door was open. Inside, a young woman sat on a bed looking through a brochure. A pile of clothes lay on the bed, and unpacked boxes were on the floor.

Spotting the Jacksons in the hallway, the young woman stood, smiled, and walked to the door to meet them, holding out her hand. "Hi, I'm Liz. Officially, Elizabeth Hawkins, but I prefer 'Liz'." She was a pretty brunette, slightly taller and more buxom than Ginny.

Ginny smiled and shook her hand. "I'm Ginny Jackson."

"Hi, Ginny. It looks like we're going to be roommates."

"Yes, it does. Oh, these are my parents and my brother, Tim."

Liz and Ginny's parents greeted one another and shook hands. Tim stood off to the side.

"Hi, Tim," Liz said with a big smile.

Tim blushed, lowered his head, and muttered, "Hi."

Liz smoothed out the bedspread on which she had been sitting. "My folks dropped me off about an hour ago. I've just been sitting here reading. I didn't want to claim a bed or any furniture until you arrived."

The Jacksons surveyed the room—two beds, two desks, two dressers, and a closet to share for hanging clothes. The ceiling and the bare walls were painted white. The floor covering was gray asbestos tile.

"Do you have other things I can help you bring up?"

"Thanks, but we got everything," said Ginny.

"Well, we'd better be leaving," said Randolph. "You don't need to walk us out to the car, Ginny."

Ginny walked over and gave him a hug. "Thanks, for bring me over here, Dad."

"Bye, sis," said Tim, giving a small wave.

"Bye, Tim. Thanks for lugging that big suitcase up the stairs. Remember now, no room poaching back home."

Tim glanced at Liz and then at the floor. "Nice to meet you, Liz."

Liz smiled at Tim as he raised his head. "Nice to meet you, too, Tim."

Ginny turned last to her mother. They gave each other a big hug.

"My little girl," whispered Ruth, before releasing her daughter. Both Jackson women wiped away tears.

"Write us when you can," said Randolph. "We'll try to come see you some Saturday or Sunday this fall. If you need to, call us on the phone. Call collect."

"Thanks, Dad."

"I'll write and let you know what's going on in Halesford," said Ruth. "We'll come get you for Thanksgiving."

"I'll look forward to your letters, Mother."

"Liz," said Ruth, "it's nice to meet you."

"It's very nice to meet all of you Jacksons, too."

"We know you and Ginny will have a wonderful year together," said Ruth.

Liz smiled. "I'm sure we will. I'll take very good care of your daughter."

Chapter 25

After the Jacksons left, Ginny and Liz selected their respective beds and desks, unpacked some of their things, and then sat and shared their general life histories.

"I'm from Halesford," said Ginny.

"Where's that?"

"You haven't heard of Halesford?"

"Afraid not."

"It's sort of between central and southwest Virginia, not far from Lynchburg and Roanoke. Where are you from?"

"Big Stone Gap."

"That doesn't ring any bells."

"I'm not surprised. Few have heard of it, and even fewer have visited. It's near the far southwestern tip of Virginia. You have to drive so far that by the time you get there you're almost as far west as Detroit."

"Detroit? You mean Detroit, Michigan?"

"Yes."

"You must be joking."

"Ah!" said Liz. "A doubting Thomas, or a doubting Ginny."

"Are you serious?"

"Ah, ye of little faith." Liz reached over to her desk and picked up a map. "I brought this with me. I wanted to see where all my classmates are from." Liz opened up the map. "See, Big Stone Gap is almost as far west as Detroit. There's only 15 miles difference in longitude. I measured it."

"I never would have guessed. I'll never doubt you again, Liz," Ginny said with a smile.

"Now, don't get carried away. You hardly know me, and I've been known to exaggerate sometimes. Show me where Halesford is."

Ginny took the map and pointed out her home town.

For the next couple of hours the two young women unpacked their things while they talked about their families, home towns, high schools, and the boys in their lives.

Ginny said her father was an insurance agent and her mother had been a secretary before she got married and began raising Ginny and Tim.

Liz said her father owned a large timber company and her mother had always been a housewife and mother.

Ginny told Liz about Dick and how he had proposed marriage.

"That's pretty serious," said Liz. "I had a steady boyfriend, but I broke up with him two months ago. I wanted to come to Richmond unencumbered. How's that for a word?"

"That's a mighty big word. Are you a nursing student or an English major?"

"I'm looking for all the skills I can master, including how to wrap men around my little finger. Speaking of men, my folks and I stopped on campus for lunch. I saw a flyer on a bulletin board inviting girls to a dance at the College of Richmond Saturday night. What do you say we check out some of these Richmond boys? Maybe we'll find Rhett Butler."

Ginny laughed. "You know, Liz, I thought I detected a resemblance between you and Scarlet O'Hara."

Liz stood up straight, lifted her chin, and, with her best Southern accent, said, "Tomorrow is another day."

They both burst out laughing.

"When we're not studying our textbooks, we can talk about *Gone with the Wind*," said Ginny. "I read the book when it first came out and loved it."

"I did, too, but with all the eligible young men in Richmond, surely we're not going to lock ourselves in our dorm room with books."

"No, of course not. I wouldn't want to be locked in this room. It's a little Spartan, don't you think?"

"Spartan? That's being kind. The Big Stone Gap jail is decorated better than this."

"Don't tell me you've been in jail."

"No, I wasn't in jail. I was visiting someone who had been incarcerated."

"Oh, first 'unencumbered' and now 'incarcerated.' You do have a big vocabulary."

"If you've got it, flaunt it. If you don't have it, fake it."

Ginny laughed. "Speaking about being incarcerated, did you meet Miss Rathman? I have a suspicion she could be more than a matron—perhaps a warden."

"I had a similar impression."

"She put me on the defensive right at the start by saying she didn't remember my name being on the list of new students. I overheard her do that with another student, too. Then she found both our names on the list."

"I'll be darned. She did that with me, too. My father was about to hit the roof before she finally found my name on the list."

"Well," we're not going to let her spoil our year, are we?"

"Absolutely, not."

Ginny walked to the door and looked at a paper attached to the back of the door. "These look like the dormitory rules Miss Rathman told us to read. Have you read them?"

"No."

"She said to read them first thing."

"Oh, all right, let's read them."

After they had read a quarter of the rules, Ginny said, "Look. We have a 10 o'clock curfew on weekday nights and a midnight curfew on Friday and Saturday nights. This sounds like a convent."

When they got to the half-way point on the list of rules, Liz said, "No, it's more like a monastery or nunnery."

"What's the difference?"

"A young woman can leave a convent. She can go off and get married. With a nunnery, you're in for life. We're not going to let these rules keep us from having a good time, are we?"

"No, we're going to have a wonderful year."

Chapter 26

During Ginny's first month of school, Dick visited her on two weekends, and they spoke a few times on the phone, but it was difficult for Ginny to find a phone and nearly impossible for Dick to reach her by phoning. She wrote him once a week. He sent her only one short note.

The second month, Dick came to see her only one weekend, and phone calls and correspondence were less frequent. Ginny thought Dick had begun to see someone else.

Ginny and Liz relished their new lives in Richmond. Nursing school was stimulating. Ginny enjoyed the book-learning, while Liz particularly liked the practical aspects of nursing. Ginny thrived on learning something new every day. Liz liked school, but she loved the weekends.

The course work was demanding, and most of the evenings the women spent studying. There was so much to learn in so many areas—chemistry, mathematics, anatomy, physiology, hygiene, and all the practical skills of nursing.

Friday nights and all day Saturday were times to relax. By late Sunday afternoon, it was time to study for the next week.

The two women grew to be the best of friends. Ginny felt good helping Liz with some of their tougher nursing courses. The more socially-active Liz kept Ginny supplied with dates. They often double-dated on weekends. They dated around. Neither had a serious beau.

Chapter 27

Late 1940, Halesford

As the year 1940 came toward an end, Jeb and Cal continued to work, Jeb at the lumber yard and Cal at the farm, while they trained weekly with the National Guard.

Dick had found it difficult to find a job in Depression-era Halesford. He dropped out of Company O and left the area. Few people knew where he had gone. Rumors circulated that he had joined the regular Army.

With Hitler's aggression in Europe, Mussolini's adventures in Africa, and Japan's aggrandizement in China, the United States tried to walk a tightrope, balancing between staying out of foreign wars, on the one hand, and helping friends in opposing aggression and becoming more militarily prepared itself, on the other. In September, the United States instituted the first peacetime military draft in its history. Later in the fall, word began to spread that National Guard units might be called to active duty for extended training.

One Friday evening in November, Jeb and Cal stopped at a diner for something to eat. They talked about work and their lack of success with girls. Then the discussion turned to the war.

"What do you think about the war in Europe?" asked Jeb. "It seems to be heating up."

"It's not good."

"What do you think will happen to the Guard and to us?"

"I don't know, Jeb. We could get called up to active duty with the Army. That's the rumor."

"I guess we're in for the ride."

"Yeah. I don't think they'd let us out now," said Cal.

"Besides, we've gotten to know the other men in Company O pretty well now. We couldn't just walk away—abandon them, I mean. I couldn't live with myself."

"Me neither."

* * * * * * * *

In December, word spread within Company O that its parent unit, the 29th Infantry Division, would probably be called to active duty in early 1941.

On Christmas, during an early afternoon turkey dinner his mother had prepared, Jeb was unusually quiet. Finally, over their dessert of pumpkin pie, Jeb paused and put down his fork. "Mother, I want to share something with you."

"What's that, son?"

"It looks like Company O may get called up to active duty for training. All of the 29th Infantry Division will probably be called."

Helen wiped her lips with her napkin. "I've heard rumors to that effect, too."

"You have?"

"Oh, yes, it's hard to keep a secret in this small town."

"We hear we could be called up as early as February."

"That's what I've heard, too."

"Why didn't you say something?"

"I was waiting for you to tell me, Jeb. I knew you would eventually."

"I guess I'll have to give up my job at the lumber yard. I hope I'll make enough to send you some of my military pay, to help with the expenses here."

"I don't think you'll have to do that. There'll be only one mouth to feed here, and I don't eat nearly as much as you." She smiled and took a bite of pie.

Jeb laughed. "Well, that's true. We'll see how things go, O.K.? People in Company O are saying we'll be on active duty for just one year of training, probably here in Virginia or the Carolinas. Then we'll be deactivated and return home."

"I certainly hope so. If America gets involved in the war and you go off somewhere to fight, I don't know what I would do."

"I don't think it'll come to that. President Roosevelt seems intent on keeping us out of the war."

"Well, I could not be more proud of you than I am, Jeb. You're working hard at the lumber yard. I bumped into Mr. Gibbs the other day at the market. He said he wanted me to know that you are one of his best employees. I'm also proud that you're serving in the National Guard. If you're called up to active duty, I hope it won't be for long. I'll miss you dearly, of course, and I'll remember your promise to come back home."

Chapter 28

Early on the morning of the first work day after Christmas, Jeb knocked on the door of his boss. "Mr. Gibbs?"

Gibbs looked up from his desk. "Yes, Jeb, come in and have a seat." He leaned back in his chair.

Jeb took off his cap as he entered the office. He sat down, twiddling his cap in front of his knees. "Mr. Gibbs, I want to let you know that I may be called up to active duty with the Army soon. Rumor has it that our company could be called up as early as February. We could be gone a year."

"I've heard that rumor, too. Jeb, we've been extremely pleased with your work. You're a good employee, one of our best. You're a hard worker, and you're smart. You treat our customers well, and they all seem to like you."

"Thanks, Mr. Gibbs."

"Your going off to active duty with the Guard might cause us some complications here, but we're proud that you're serving. I hope you and Company O don't get called up, but if you do, we'll hold a job here for you when you return."

"Thanks, Mr. Gibbs. That's very kind. I'm really enjoying working here. Everyone has been great to work with, and I think I've learned a lot. I'd like to come back to work after we return."

"There'll be a job waiting for you."

"I'll let you know as soon as we get the official word about the call-up."

Chapter 29

Early 1941

Three weeks later the official word came. On January 20, the War Department issued an order for Company O to assemble at the armory in Halesford on February 3 for mobilization before deploying to Fort Meade, an Army post located in Maryland, between Washington, D.C. and Baltimore. The entire 29th Infantry Division was to deploy there in February to begin one year of intense, active-duty training.

Over the next several days, the men of Company O were given physical exams. A few failed and were released from service. Some new members were recruited. On February 3, the men of Company O assembled at the armory and were officially inducted into the U.S. Army. For the next ten days, they slept in the armory, went on long marches, engaged in drills and maneuvers, and ate in local restaurants, their meals paid for by the Army.

The townspeople were kind, supportive, and proud of their local boys. On the evening of the first Saturday of February, the community held a parade for Company O, followed by a party and dance at the high school. The mayor spoke, praising the men of Company O, and Captain Harrison thanked the community for its support. Jeb and Cal, dressed neatly in their uniforms, stood along the edge of the dance floor like wallflowers, until a couple of girls in the high school senior class took pity on them and asked them to dance.

Then on February 21, in the early dawn, the men assembled at the armory in the courthouse. They were in uniform and carried duffle bags full of extra uniforms and personal items.

Helen had driven Jeb to the courthouse, as most other parents had done with their sons. A few of the men were married, and their wives had driven them. The soldiers began to assemble inside the armory, while the parents, wives, other relatives, and friends stood outside, waiting for the men to come out and board the Army trucks parked along the street.

Finally, the men began to file out of the courthouse basement. Jeb spotted his mother and went over to her. "Goodbye, Mother. I'll write once I get to Fort Meade."

Helen hugged her son, while dabbing at a tear. "I'll write you, too, and let you know what's happening here."

Master Sergeant Buck shouted, "Fall in!"

Helen leaned up and kissed Jeb on the cheek. "Take care, Son."

Jeb turned and walked briskly to where the men were forming. They assembled by platoons and loaded themselves and their gear onto the trucks.

As the trucks pulled away, tears ran down Helen's cheeks. She walked to her pickup truck and got in. Alone, inside the cab, feeling lonelier than she had since her husband had died, she sobbed.

After several minutes, she took a deep breath, wiped her eyes with a handkerchief, and whispered aloud a short prayer, "Dear Lord, keep my son safe and bring him home." Then she turned on the ignition and drove home. When she walked through the front door, the house felt cold and empty.

Chapter 30

Fort Meade, Maryland

After a 45-minute truck ride to the train station in Bedford and several hours aboard a train headed north to Maryland, Company O arrived at Fort Meade. The men, joined by other companies of the 29th Infantry Division, marched from the train station to their assigned barracks.

"I'm glad we have barracks and won't have to sleep in tents," Jeb said to Cal, as they broke from formation and headed into the buildings that would be their home for the next year.

The inside caused them to do a double take. "Holy cow," said Cal. "Now I know why they call this a barracks—bare floors, bare walls, bare everything." Metal bunk beds lined both sides of the floor, each accented with foot lockers at their ends and tall metal lockers along the wall. The latrine and showers were at the end of the barracks.

Jeb shook his head. "So this is going to be home for the next year."

"I'm afraid so. I'll flip you for the lower bunk." Cal flipped a coin and won.

Supper that evening was served in a separate building, the mess hall, located a five-minute walk from the barracks. The meal consisted of chicken, mashed potatoes, green beans, bread, pie, and iced tea or coffee.

Jeb took the last bite and put down his fork. "Not a bad meal. Not as good as my mother's cooking, but not bad."

"Don't tell my mother," said Cal, licking his lips, "but this was better than her cooking."

The next day, Company O began rigorous training. Reveille was at 5:30 a.m. The men had a half hour for the proverbial "shit, shower, and shave" and to dress. Then came a half hour of physical training, followed by breakfast in the mess hall—eggs, oatmeal, and the proverbial SOS—"shit on a shingle," the nickname for chipped beef and gravy on toast. The rest of the morning was filled with classes. The noon meal was followed by a long march to the rifle range for target practice and a march back to the barracks. After supper, the men had to polish their boots and get their uniforms and equipment ready for the next day. Lights out came early, but so, too, did reveille.

One day in their second week in camp, in early March, Company O marched out after breakfast to a field instruction area for first aid training. The officers and senior non-commissioned officers had their own special training that morning, so Company O was led by junior non-commissioned officers. The instruction area was four miles from the barracks. The last mile the men were ordered to jog.

When at last they stopped, gasping for air after jogging over the hilly, wooded terrain, the recruits started climbing up into the wooden bleachers, where they dropped, exhausted, onto the cold, dew-moistened, seats.

"Damn, it's cold, and these seats are like ice," muttered Cal, coughing from an asthma attack brought on by the cold air.

"Yeah, but at least it's not raining," said Jeb quietly. "The sun will warm things up."

"Zip it up, you two" barked the instructor who stood at the front of the bleachers, ready to lead the first aid class. He stared intently at Jeb and Cal, and a flash of recognition lit his eyes. "Well, well, look who we have here! We've got Company O and the cream of society from Halesford, Virginia—Jeb Fletcher and Cal Barton."

"Oh, my God," muttered Cal under his breath. "Dick Drumheller."

Drumheller was dressed smartly in a tight-fitting uniform, with sharp creases pressed into the trousers. His boots glistened in the morning sun. He had three chevrons on the sleeve of his field jacket, indicating he had been promoted to buck sergeant.

Jeb shook his head, reflecting on his bad luck. *So this is where Drumheller went. It looks like the Army agrees with him, and now he's a sergeant—our instruction sergeant. This could be bad.* "What are the odds?" he muttered to Cal.

"All right, Fletcher and Barton, knock off the chitchat. I've got my eyes on both of you—a couple of wiseass troublemakers. Move your asses down here to the middle of the front row. I'm gonna' keep you under my thumb. Move it! Now!"

As ordered, Jeb and Cal moved to the center of the front row. The rest of the men finished filing into the bleachers. They sat quietly huffing, as their warm breath instantly turned into clouds of mist.

Drumheller stood ramrod straight front and center before the bleachers. He looked up at the men, sneered, and shook his head. "What a bunch of pussies! You've been here three full weeks and you still run and gasp for air like a bunch of menstrual-cramping, teenage girls." Keeping his body straight forward, he pivoted his head to the right toward his assistant, Corporal Marvin Steptoe, who stood twenty feet away. "Corporal, what should we do with these girls today?'

Steptoe, a wiry little man, sneered. "Well, Sergeant, how about some snake-bite training?'

"Snake-bite training?" Drumheller held his hands, palms up, out to his side, while tilting his head, as though contemplating. Then he clasped and rubbed his hands in front of him. "Why, Corporal, that sounds like a fine idea! What do we need for snake-bite training?"

Steptoe held up a single index finger. "Well, first, how about a snake?"

"A snake? You don't mean a real, live snake, do you?" said Drumheller, in a mocking voice.

"Yes, Sergeant, a real, snake."

"Surely you don't mean a poisonous snake? Not a real, live, poisonous snake, one with venom just pouring from his fangs?"

"Yes, Sergeant. A real, live poisonous snake."

Jeb sat up even straighter. *What the hell are they doing?*

"Well, Corporal Steptoe, do you think you could actually find a poisonous snake around here?" Drumheller bent over and pretended to look at the ground around him and under the bleachers.

"Yes, Sergeant, I do. There are snakes all over Fort Meade." Steptoe hurried to the side of the bleachers, reached in under the first few rows, and pulled out a gunny sack that was tied at the top with a rope. The men anxiously watched him. He walked back to the front and center of the bleachers and dropped the sack about eight feet from where Jeb and Cal sat in the center of the front row.

Drumheller moved five feet to the side, away from the sack. "Why, what in heaven's name do you have in that sack, Corporal?"

Steptoe bent over and untied the cord. He grabbed the sack by one of the bottom corners, turned it upside down, and backed away, pulling the sack after him. Out slithered a large, brownish snake with black and yellowish markings and an almost rectangular-shaped head. Steptoe backed further away.

"Why, Corporal, you've outdone yourself this morning. That's some snake! It looks like a rattlesnake. Is it really a rattler?"

As if on cue, the snake coiled, raised its head, and shook its rattles.

Jeb, Cal, and the other men on the front row pulled in their legs and slide back as far as they could on the front-row seat.

"Why, it is a rattlesnake," said Drumheller, with a malicious laugh.

All the recruits sat quietly, their eyes transfixed on the snake.

Jeb instinctively felt in his pockets for any type of weapon, but he had none.

The snake stopped rattling its tail and lowered its head.

"All right, girls, quit staring at that damned snake and give me your full attention. Today, I may just save your worthless, sorry asses. I'm going to teach you what to do if you or one of your buddies ever gets bitten by a poisonous pit viper. We've got lots of them around here—rattlers, copperheads, and maybe even a cotton mouth or two that you boys from the South may have brought up with you in your gear." He chuckled. "So, I'm warning you to look around, especially before you sit down. We had a recruit here last year who went to the latrine, forgot to look down the hole, sat down on the crapper, and a snake bit him on the ass. The doctors had to surgically remove a big chunk of his ass. He was lucky—the snake could have bit him on the balls."

The recruits laughed, but they looked at the snake. It had not moved. The men also looked down through the bleachers to see if there were any snakes beneath them.

"All right, eyes on me," barked Drumheller. Drawing out his pronunciation, he said, "Now, let me put you in a h-y-p-o-t-h-e-t-i-c-a-l situation. Fletcher, do you know what a h-y-p-o-t-h-e-t-i-c-a-l situation is?"

"Yes, Sergeant," replied Jeb.

"You do, do you? Well, why don't you tell all of these other girls what a hypothetical situation is?"

"A hypothetical situation is a made-up situation. It's used to test something, perhaps a theory. Or it could be used as a teaching tool."

"My, my, Fletcher, I'm impressed. You're no southern Virginia cracker, are you? You're pretty damn smart. Or at least you think you are, don't you?"

Jeb did not respond.

"Well?" said Drumheller.

"Well, what, Sergeant?" Jeb asked, fighting to keep his tone neutral.

"Don't play coy with me. I asked you a question. You think you're pretty smart, don't you?"

"I know some things, Sergeant, and there are some things I don't know."

"How about your friend, here?" Drumheller looked at Cal. "Do you think you're pretty smart, too?"

Cal did not respond.

"I'm talking to you, Barton," growled Drumheller. "Answer me."

"I know some things, and some things I don't know," said Cal, echoing Jeb.

"O.K., maybe we'll let these two smart fellows help us with our training. We'll see how much they know. Corporal, fetch me a stick."

Steptoe hurried behind the bleachers and returned with a five-foot, thin but sturdy branch from which the bark had been peeled. The stick had a yoke at the bottom end. He handed it to Drumheller.

The sergeant took the stick and walked up to within five feet of the snake. "Today, girls, you're going to learn a little about snakes and how to take care of snake bites." Raising his voice for emphasis, Drumheller continued, "This is no laughing matter. As I mentioned, we've got lots of snakes out in these hills and woods. A snake generally is not looking for a fight and will try to avoid you. But when he's threatened or cornered, he'll coil up, ready to strike. A rattler can strike his victim and sink both fangs into the skin in less time than it takes you to fart. Just watch."

Holding the stick out in front of him, Drumheller took a step toward the snake. The snake turned its head defensively toward him. Drumheller shoved the stick near the snake's head, and it backed away, moving a couple of feet toward the bleachers. Drumheller took another step and poked the stick at the snake. The snake backed up further toward the bleachers.

Drumheller's driving that snake toward us, thought Jeb. Remembering something his father had taught him one summer, he slowly moved his hands to his belt buckle. He undid the brass-plated metal buckle, and, with as little movement as possible, began pulling his belt out of the loops on his pants. He held the buckle end in his left hand and the other end in his right. *If I have to use this, I sure hope it works*.

Drumheller took another step and poked again at the snake. The snake backed up again. It was now only some three feet from Jeb and Cal. The men on Jeb's left scooted to the left, trying to put some distance between the snake and them. Sensing the movement, the snake quickly turned toward the bleachers, coiled, and rattled its tail, trying to warn off the men, while preparing to strike if necessary. Drumheller took a step toward the snake, and it turned momentarily back toward him.

Jeb slowly and cautiously stood up. With empty space to his left where the men had slid away, he stretched his belt into a towel-flipping position, holding the buckle end back with his left hand and the other end out front with this right hand. With a strong, forward thrust of his right arm, he whipped the buckle end of the belt toward the snake. As the belt stretched to its fullest, it gave off a loud POP, and the buckle snapped into the snake's head. Stunned, the snake collapsed. Jeb, his adrenaline pumping, jumped with all his weight onto the snake, near its neck. With the heel of his right boot, he stomped on the snake's skull, crushing it.

The men in the bleachers broke into cheers.

"Silence," shouted Drumheller, his face red with rage. The men instantly obeyed. Drumheller advanced toward Jeb. "Fletcher, you son-of-a-bitch. You've killed my snake."

Behind him, Steptoe said, "What'll we do now, Sergeant?"

Drumheller put the toe of a boot under the snake and kicked it violently off to the side of the bleachers. "What'll we do, Corporal? We'll get on with the instruction. That's what we'll do." He turned to face the recruits.

"All right, Fletcher. Let's see just how smart you are. Now, if you were out on patrol with your buddy Barton here, and you passed a rattler's nest, and a big, old rattler bit your buddy Barton in the calf, what would you do?"

"I'd pull up his pants leg and take a look," replied Jeb. "Then, I'd use some of my canteen water to wash the wound. I'd put a tourniquet on his leg above the bite, loosening it every so often. I'd put a piece of rubber over the puncture and try to suck out the venom, dress the wound, and kill and keep the snake to try to identify it. Then I'd try to get him medical help as soon as possible."

"You think you're pretty smart, don't you, Fletcher? You must have read the manual last night, huh?"

"Yes, Sergeant. I read the manual, as we were instructed to do."

"Well, smart boy, I've got another hypothetical situation for you. What if I was leading you on a patrol through a swamp, and I put you and your buddy Barton up on point. You lead us across some mushy ground, and then you have to step into thigh-high water. Right about that time, a big old cottonmouth, with long, sharp fangs, swims up to you and your buddy Barton. The snake strikes out and bites your buddy Barton. He bites him right in the ass."

The men laughed.

Steptoe chuckled. "Hey, Fletcher, he's got you now."

Drumheller sneered. "So, smart guy, what would you do? Go ahead. I want you to tell all these boys here just what you would do to save your buddy Barton."

Jeb stood thinking. "You're leading our patrol, right, Sergeant?"

"Right. Come on, smart boy, we're all ears. Tell us what you'd do. Would you pucker up and kiss you buddy's ass?"

"Well, in that situation, I'd have Cal pull down his pants and check to make sure he had been bitten on the ass…"

Drumheller interrupted. "And once you confirmed he'd been bitten on the ass, then what would you do, smart boy?"

"Well, that would be a different situation than a bite in the calf."

"Damn straight, boy. So what would you do? You wouldn't let your buddy die, would you?"

"No, I wouldn't let him die."

"So, what would you do?"

"That would be a much more complicated situation."

"Indeed," said Drumheller. "So what would you do? Time would be running out."

"The best thing to do would be…"

"Come on, tell us," interrupted Drumheller. "Would you kiss his ass, give it a big smooch with your lips?"

"No."

"You wouldn't kiss your buddy's ass to save him? Just what the hell would you do?" demanded Drumheller.

"I'd call for the expert to do that. I'd leave that for the instructor sergeant."

The men howled.

Drumheller's face flushed. He advanced and stuck his face in Jeb's. He sputtered, "Fletcher…Fletcher…you wiseass son-of-a-bitch! You've really done it now. You've made a monumental mistake taking me on. You know the word 'nemesis,' smart boy? Well, I'm going to be your nemesis as long as you're here at Fort Meade. Your life is going to be holy hell. Your ass is going to be grass, and I'm going to be the lawnmower. Now, drop and give me twenty, and kiss the ground on every pushup, wiseass."

Chapter 31

September 1941, Richmond

Weeks and then months passed quickly, and Ginny and Liz completed their first year of nursing school. In September 1941, at the start of their second year, they began to consider what types of nursing they wanted to pursue after completing their third and final year.

One evening, as they ate supper in a small restaurant near school, they talked of the future.

"So, what do you want to do after graduation?" asked Liz, as she added three spoonfuls of sugar to her iced tea, making it Southern style.

Ginny shook her head as she watched Liz. "I don't see how you can drink that tinted glucose." Ginny hated sweetened tea. She squeezed a slice of lemon into her tea. "I think I'd like to work in a maternity ward or maybe pediatrics. I liked our time in the pediatrics ward last spring. How about you?"

Liz stirred the sugar into her tea. "This sugar gives me energy. I'm looking for action, something exciting, perhaps a hospital emergency room in a large city. Being a surgical nurse might be right up my alley."

"I could never do that. I still get queasy just watching an operation." Ginny sipped her tea. "I don't think I could do emergency medicine, especially not surgery."

"Well, we need to be flexible, to be ready to take the best job that comes along."

"Maybe we could find nursing jobs here in Richmond."

"But, Ginny, don't you think it would be fun to move to a really big city—perhaps New York or Philadelphia?"

They broke off their discussion as the waitress arrived and served them the two slices of apple pie they had ordered.

After the waitress left, Ginny took a bite of her pie. "Umm. This is good, almost as good as my mother makes.

Good Southern cooking. If we stayed in Richmond, we could rent an apartment together."

"That would be fun, having our own place." Liz took a bite of her pie. "Great apple pie, but don't you ever want to try something more exotic—maybe Key Lime Pie or Baked Alaska? Don't you want to see more of the world, see what's outside of Virginia? We could shoot for the top and try to find jobs and an apartment in Manhattan."

"But we know this area. I could take evening classes in literature and French at the university."

"Classes? Don't you think that after three years of nursing school you'll have had enough of school?"

"I really enjoy learning. If you're tired of school then, you could keep your evenings free."

"If I go into emergency medicine, I'll want to have my evenings free, so I can go out and relax and unwind. I wouldn't want the pressure of schoolwork."

"Well, we've got almost two years to think about it."

"Yes," said Liz, finishing her pie, "but I'll bet our last two years of school just fly by."

Chapter 32

December 1941, North Carolina-Virginia Border

The first week of December, 1941, Company O and the other companies of the 29th Infantry Division conducted maneuvers in North and South Carolina. On Saturday, December 6, Company O camped near the North Carolina-Virginia border. On Sunday, the 7th, the men awoke to a relaxed day. They slept in later than usual and spent most of the morning cleaning and repairing their equipment. In the early afternoon, Jeb and Cal decided to walk a couple of miles to a nearby town to see a movie.

At the theater, they bought tickets and popcorn and settled in for the show. About half-way through the movie, the film came to an abrupt halt. Lights came on, and the manager walked out onto the stage. "I'm sorry to interrupt the movie, but I have an important announcement. We've just heard on the radio that Japanese forces have attacked the U.S. Naval Base at Pearl Harbor and other bases in Hawaii. We don't have any more details. Under the circumstances, we believe we should close the theater and everyone should go home. If you'll stop at the ticket office on your way out, we'll refund the price of your ticket. God bless the United States and our servicemen in Hawaii."

"My God!" said Jeb. "Why would the Japanese attack?"

"I don't know," replied Cal, "but it looks like we're at war."

Jeb and Cal left the theater immediately, without stopping to get their ticket refunds. They hurried back to the bivouac area.

The leaders of Company O had learned of the Japanese attack and had ordered preparations for returning to Fort Meade. Men speculated about the attack, but no one had any details. As soon as their gear was loaded, the men climbed into their trucks for the long drive back to their base.

On Monday morning, training intensified, as rumors spread among the men about the Japanese attack and how the United States would respond. That evening, the men huddled around radios to hear reports of President Roosevelt's address to Congress, asking for a declaration of war against Japan. After the radios were shut off, the men talked about what all this meant, for America, for the military, and for Company O.

"Well, we're going to be on active duty for the duration of the war," said Jeb.

"You think so?" said Cal. "Maybe they'll release us when our year is up in February and call up men who haven't served."

Jeb shook his head. "Are you kidding? They'll call up those who haven't served, but they're not going to release those of us who are already trained."

Cal nodded. "I suppose you're right."

On December 11, news came that Germany and Italy had declared war on the United States. Shortly after came official announcements that proved Jeb right—they would serve in the Army for the war's duration and slightly beyond.

A couple of weeks later, Company O deployed to the coast of the Delaware-Maryland-Virginia peninsula. Their job was to defend against any German invaders, especially reconnaissance units or spies who might cross the Atlantic and try to land on the coast.

Company O bivouacked near a small Virginia coastal town. The men patrolled the roads and beaches and manned lookout posts, braving the cold December winds. They were welcomed by the town's residents. In the evenings, many of the townspeople invited soldiers to their homes for home-cooked meals.

Within weeks, however, as authorities reevaluated the risk of a German attack and concluded that the odds were slim, soldiers from a less-ready unit were deployed to the peninsula to replace Company O. The unit that replaced the Virginia boys of Company O was from New Jersey, and the townspeople were heard to mutter about once again being invaded by "damn Yankees." The Virginia boys returned to Fort Meade for intensive training.

For the next many months, Company O conducted maneuvers in the Carolinas and then deployed to Florida.

In early September 1942, the 29th Infantry Division received orders to prepare for deployment. Only the senior officers knew their destination, and they were not sharing the information. Rumors of their destination were rampant—mostly the Pacific Theater, the European Theater, or Alaska. Company O returned to Fort Meade in preparation for the deployment. Finally, word spread that they were headed to Camp Kilmer, New Jersey. The men agreed that Europe was their likely destination.

Chapter 33

Richmond

On the Saturday before Christmas, less than two weeks after the shocking attack on Pearl Harbor, Ginny and Liz talked at breakfast before leaving Richmond to return to their homes for the holidays.

"I've been doing some thinking," said Liz. "I want to join the Army Nurse Corps."

Ginny chuckled, nervously. "Really? I've been thinking a little about that myself. I guess we've become such good friends that we've even started to think alike."

"And if you could modernize that hair style of yours and glamorize your wardrobe, we could even start to look alike." Liz laughed.

"Well, there's 'nouveau chic'…"

"There you go again with your French."

Ginny patted her hair and straightened her blouse. "As I was saying, there's 'nouveau chic' and then there's…uh…, what should I say…uh…'class.'"

The two women burst out laughing.

Liz assumed a serious tone. "I'm thinking about signing up for the Nurse Corps soon."

"You mean now?"

"Yes, now."

" But, Liz, we have a year and a half of school left."

"I know, but our military is going to need nurses."

"That's true, but we're not nurses yet. I doubt if the Army would take us."

"We've had a year-and-a-half of training."

"But we'd have so much more to offer if we were fully trained."

"Why don't we go talk to someone from the Army?"

Ginny took a sip of coffee and sat back. "Well, I guess it wouldn't hurt to talk to someone. They should be able to advise us, you know, about whether it's better to complete our schooling."

"I agree. I just think that by becoming Army nurses, we could help our soldiers and have some adventure, too. I'll bet the male-to-female ratio in the Army is phenomenal."

Ginny smiled. "You are adventuresome, aren't you?"

"The Army could be a real adventure. I wonder what kind of nursing jobs they have. I'm sure there are lots of emergency and surgery jobs, which I'm interested in. You, however, aren't interested in that."

"The Army must also need lots of nurses for the type of routine care that interests me. I suppose, of course, if the men can face being maimed and even dying, in an emergency I might be able to overcome my skittishness and help in an operating room, but I'm not sure."

"When we get back from the holidays, why don't we go talk to someone from the Army? We can see what they can tell us."

"O. K. It can't hurt to ask. Even if they advise us to finish school, we'll learn something that may be useful later."

"Don't you think we'd look spiffy in those chic Army uniforms?" Liz straightened her back and struck a formal pose.

At the thought of wearing masculine Army nurse uniforms, the two young women broke out laughing. They laughed until tears rolled down their cheeks. Then they grew quiet, as the seriousness of possibly becoming Army nurses sunk in.

Chapter 34

Halesford

Ginny spent Christmas vacation at home in Halesford. She
agonized over telling her parents that she was thinking of
joining the Army Nurse Corps. She knew they would object,
regardless of whether she might join at the end of the next
semester or wait until after graduation.

She decided to wait until Christmas Day and the family's
usual mid-afternoon holiday feast. Her parents would be
relaxed and in good humor then. So as not to spoil the
dinner, which her mother would work hours preparing, she
would wait until dessert.

On Christmas Day, Ginny fidgeted throughout dinner.
She waited until her mother had cut a piece of mincemeat pie
for everyone, added whipped cream, and served the pieces.
"Mom and Dad, I have something to tell you."

Her mother, sensing something important, put down the
fork she had just picked up. "Yes, dear. What is it?"

"Liz and I've been thinking about what kind of nursing
jobs we might want to apply for."

Her father nodded his head approvingly. "Good. With
your nursing degrees, there should be a world of opportunity
open to you. You know, Ginny, I had reservations when you
first said you wanted to go into nursing. Now, however, as
I've followed you through your first year and a half of
schooling, I've changed my mind. I think this will be a
wonderful career for you."

Her mother reached over and put her hand atop Ginny's
hand, which rested on the table. "Yes, we're proud of you
wanting to help others. And, as your father says, nursing
should afford you many opportunities. You could probably
get a job at a hospital somewhere around this area—not too
far from home—or perhaps in a local school as a school
nurse."

Ginny looked down at her pie, took a small bite, chewed, and swallowed. "Well, with the war on, we've actually been thinking about joining the Army Nurse Corps."

Her father's fork fell onto his plate with a loud clatter. The noise caused Ginny to jump in her seat.

"What? The Army Nurse Corps?" Randolph slowly picked up his fork.

Ruth looked at Randolph and then at Ginny. "That's certainly a surprise."

Ginny wiped her mouth with her napkin, pausing for time. "It would be just while the war is on."

Randolph put his fork down and looked at his daughter. "Why in the world would you want to join the Army? Is this your idea, or someone else's? Has the Army been to your school recruiting nurses?"

Ginny took a deep breath. "No, Dad. Liz and I started thinking about this right after the Japanese attacked Pearl Harbor and the Germans and Italians declared war on us. Lots of young men are being drafted. We thought we should do something to contribute, especially to help those who will be doing the fighting."

"How much do you know about being an Army nurse?"

Ginny looked down and cut a bite of pie. "We don't know very much." She put the bite in her mouth.

"You know that I served in the Army in 1917 and 1918, don't you?"

"Yes, of course."

"Well, the Army's a rough organization, especially in the field. All sorts of men are being drafted. It's not a safe environment for a young woman. You'd be exposed to a lot of coarse men and situations. You know I was wounded, don't you?"

"Yes, but you never told me much about it."

"Well, I got to see quite a bit of Army medicine. If you were assigned to a hospital you'd have to bathe and take care of personal hygiene for a lot of men. If you were assigned to a field hospital, the number of men you'd have to take care of and the type of wounds you'd have to treat could be overwhelming."

"Dad, we're exposed to a lot of that in nursing school."

"I'm sure what you see in school or a civilian hospital in Richmond is a lot different than what you'd see in the Army, especially an Army hospital treating the wounded. There are also all kinds of diseases that you'd be exposed to, compared to what you might come across in a civilian hospital here in the United States. And it could be dangerous, too. You could be sent overseas and possibly into a combat area."

"We've thought of some of those things. There are lots of Army bases here in the United States."

"Ginny," said Ruth, "ever since you were born, we've tried to protect you and keep you safe. Your father makes a lot of good points, and you should think seriously about all this." She looked at Randolph, who nodded.

"I know, Mother."

"Well," said Ruth, "while our first reaction is to think of your safety, I believe it's noble of you and Liz to think about becoming Army nurses. If I were younger, I might think of serving in some way. I'm doing what I can to volunteer here with the Red Cross, but our armed forces will surely need lots of doctors and nurses as the war continues."

Ginny and her mother exchanged faint smiles.

Randolph cut off a large bite of pie and jammed it in his mouth.

"I'm proud of you, Sis," said Tim.

"Look, Ginny," said Randolph, swallowing his pie. "I admire your interest in serving our country, but I think this is a mistake. I suggest that you and Liz check things out thoroughly and not make any rash decisions. You need to be very cautious."

Ginny looked at her father. "You volunteered for the Army in 1917, didn't you, Dad?"

"I did, and so I speak from experience. I think you should be very cautious." He took a sip of coffee.

Ginny smiled at her father. "When you were wounded, what did you think of Army nurses?"

Randolph sat back in his chair and hesitated, as though thinking back almost twenty-five years. A slight smile came across his face. "The nurses I came across were very caring toward me, without exception. Some of them were even very nice."

"Randolph, you never told me about the Army nurses," Ruth said, smiling.

"Look, I admire Army nurses and what they do, but military life, especially in wartime, is a rough existence, and our Army has all kinds of people in it. Military service can also be very dangerous."

Ginny looked at her father and then her mother. "Liz and I plan to talk to the Army after the holidays, to check things out. We'll ask lots of questions."

Randolph slid forward in his chair. "What do you mean after the holidays? You have a year-and-a-half of school left."

"We just want to learn what types of jobs there are for nurses in the Army."

"Ginny, you know that your mother and I are extremely proud of you. You've accomplished quite a bit in your young life. All we ask is that you approach this very carefully."

"Yes, dear," said her mother. "We understand how you feel. We'll stand by you, no matter what decision you make."

"Thanks. I'll definitely think seriously about what you've said, and I'll share it with Liz. We'll be careful." Ginny took an extra large bite of pie, sat back, and savored it.

Chapter 35

January 1942, Richmond and Camp Lee, Virginia

When Ginny and Liz returned to Richmond after the
holidays, they discussed how their parents had reacted when
they broached the idea of becoming Army nurses. Liz's
parents had reacted much the same as Ginny's.

Through the nursing school staff, they found a phone
number for the Army Nurse Corps in nearby Camp Lee, 25
miles south of Richmond. They made an appointment and
arranged to borrow a friend's car to drive to the camp the
next day.

They were excited and talked non-stop during the entire
trip. As they neared the base, Liz, who was driving,
exclaimed, "Look, there's the sign for Camp Lee."

Ginny peered out the window. "It looks big, doesn't it?"

Liz made a left turn and drove through the gate of the
camp. "Well, it's a lot bigger than our campus." Liz stopped
the car to let a company of soldiers march by in front of
them. "And look at all those men."

"They look pretty impressive in their uniforms, don't
they?"

"Indeed, they do. They're all so fit and trim." Liz drove
ahead. "The building should be down this road."

A minute later, Ginny said, "There it is—'Medical
Recruiting Section.'"

Liz pulled the car into a parking space, turned off the
engine, and picked up her purse.

"Well, I guess this is it," said Ginny, sitting still.

"Yep, this is it." Liz opened the car door. "Let's go show
them God's gifts to the U.S. Army."

Inside the building was an office with several young
women in Army uniforms working behind desks. A woman
at the front desk stood up and greeted them.

Liz introduced herself and Ginny and said, "We have an appointment with Captain Pollard."

"Just a moment, please," said the young woman, who turned and walked to a room in the back of the large office. She returned in seconds, led Liz and Ginny to the back room, and introduced them to Captain Pollard, the unit's commanding officer.

Pollard was a tall woman who looked to be in her late 30s or early 40s. On the lapels of her uniform jacket were the insignia of the U.S. Army Nurse Corps. "Welcome to Camp Lee," she said. "Please have a seat."

Liz and Ginny sat down in two chairs facing Pollard's desk.

"Thanks for making the drive down from Richmond. On the phone you said you wanted to learn more about the Army Nurse Corps and that you might be interested in joining us, is that right?"

"Yes," said Liz. "We're in nursing school in Richmond, and we'd like to find out about becoming Army nurses."

"We want to get some information, before we make any decisions," said Ginny.

"Of course," said Pollard. "That's the wise thing to do. Let me begin by saying that, as you probably know, the Army is growing, and, consequently, so is the Army Nurse Corps. We need many young nurses to help care for our increasing number of troops. This is a great opportunity for qualified young women to serve our country and to help our troops."

"We want to serve our country," said Liz.

"Yes," agreed Ginny, in a low voice.

"I think everyone does," said Pollard. "This is a critical period for the United States."

"Yes," said Liz.

"What can you tell us about the process of joining the Army Nurse Corps and what types of jobs we might have?" asked Ginny.

"Once you have graduated, you'd need to apply, and then...."

"You mean we'd need to graduate first?" asked Liz.

"Oh, yes, you'd need to wait until May or June. You are in your third year, aren't you?"

"Not really," said Liz. "We're actually just starting the second half of our second year."

"Oh," said Pollard. "You're so far along with your schooling that we'd want you to finish all three years, to graduate. That would benefit both you and us the most. You could join us in a medical support role with only limited schooling, but we could use you best if you're fully-qualified nurses."

"Could you tell us what would happen if we apply around the time we graduate," asked Ginny.

"Sure. First, you'd have to take a physical exam. Assuming you pass the physical, you'd undergo four weeks of training, and then you'd be enrolled as commissioned officers, as second lieutenants."

"What type of training would we receive?" asked Ginny.

"You'd learn about the Army in general and, more specifically, about Army nursing." Pollard provided more details about training.

"What kind of assignments might we get after completing our training?" asked Liz.

"We have quite a range of possible assignments, ranging from administrative office positions, to work in base hospitals, to emergency medical positions in field units."

"I'm interested in emergency medicine," said Liz.

"Good," said Pollard. "We're going to need a lot of emergency medicine nurses as this war heats up. After your training, when it comes time for your first assignments, the assignment officers would look at the needs of the Army at the time and at your preferences and see if a match can be found. Speaking personally, I have found that it's best to be flexible. A nurse may not always get her preferred assignment at first, but as time goes by things seem to work out so there is a good fit between the Army's needs and personal preferences. There's a lot of personal interaction, and things generally seem to work out. At least, that's my experience."

"That's good to know," said Ginny.

"As a second lieutenant, you'd receive a base pay of $140 a month, plus a little over $37 for a subsistence allowance."

"If we want to join, what do we need to do next?" asked Liz.

"Well, next year, in early May, as you're preparing for graduation, call me, and I'll arrange for you to come back here to take your physicals. If you pass those, we could then work out a date—maybe a week or two after your graduation—for you to report here to begin your training."

"As simple as that?" asked Liz.

"As simple as that."

Ginny and Liz thanked Pollard and headed for the car.

On the drive back to Richmond, Liz was first to speak. "I'm excited. I'll be ready to make that call next year in May."

"Captain Pollard was very helpful," said Ginny. "She's impressive—very professional."

"I agree."

"I'm going to talk to my parents," said Ginny, "but I think I'll be ready to make that call, too."

For the rest of the trip, Liz and Ginny talked about what it might be like to be Army nurses.

Chapter 36

August 1942, Eastern Coast of U.S.

In August 1942, while Company O was still training in Florida, Captain Harrison, the company commander, who was 43 years old, was promoted to major and assigned to a staff position with the 29th Infantry Division. First Lieutenant Robert Dooley, a vigorous 28-year-old platoon leader in Company O, was promoted to captain and given command of the company.

In September, 1942, Company O and other elements of its parent 29th Infantry Division received deployment orders. They soon boarded trains that took them to Camp Kilmer, New Jersey, in preparation for deployment to Great Britain. In late September, the men and their gear were trucked from Camp Kilmer to Hoboken, New Jersey. Each man lugged along a large duffle bag, containing his clothing and personal items, and his combat gear.

From a dock in Hoboken, Jeb, Cal, and the other men looked across the wide Hudson River and saw New York City. None of the men had ever been to New York. Most had never been outside Virginia until they joined the Army.

"Wow, look at that!" said Jeb, gazing across the river and shielding his eyes from the bright noon-day sun.

"Yeah, look at all the buildings," said Cal, squinting. "They look small from here, but they must be really tall."

"They're all squeezed together."

"I always wondered if I'd ever get to see New York City."

"Well, I think we're about to. I guess this is a fringe benefit of being in the Army."

The men loaded onto a ferry, and Jeb and Cal hurried for a spot on the forward railing. As the ferry made its way toward the city, Jeb was mesmerized. "The buildings are getting taller."

"Yeah. Hard to believe anyone could build such tall buildings," said Cal. "Do you suppose we'll get to stay in a high-rise hotel?"

"I have no idea. It sure would be fun to see some of the sights of New York."

"We might even meet a couple of big-city girls," said Cal, with a laugh.

"Wow! Look at that big ship ahead of us."

"That must be what they call an ocean liner."

"We seem to be headed for the dock area next to it."

Indeed, the ferries pulled up beside the large ship. The men debarked from the ferries, and the unit leaders assembled the men by platoons and companies on the dock.

Captain Dooley addressed Company O, which stood in ranks, at ease. "All right, men. This big ship behind me is going to be your home for a while."

Jeb took a closer look at the ship. *Well, we won't be staying in a high-rise hotel, but maybe we can still get off the ship and see some of the sights of New York.*

Dooley continued. "This is the Queen Mary. You may have heard about this ship. I've been told she belongs to our ally Great Britain and is manned by British seamen. She's been converted from a civilian luxury liner to a troop transport ship. She can now carry 15,000 troops. All of our company, indeed maybe our entire 29th Infantry Division, will be aboard the ship. We're going to march aboard soon. We'll be directed to that part of the ship where we have been assigned berths. We'll get more instructions once we're aboard. Any questions?"

Cal spoke up. "Captain, how long will we be in New York and will we be permitted to leave the ship to look around the city?"

"As soon as all the units are aboard, the ship will depart," said Dooley.

So much for seeing New York. "Captain," said Jeb, "where are we headed, and how long will it take us to get there?"

"I'm not at liberty to tell you that right now, Fletcher," replied Dooley. "You'll be told more once the ship is underway."

About a half hour later, Company O marched up the ramp and onto the *Queen Mary*. Jeb and Cal stowed their gear in their assigned area and hurried top side where they found a place at the railing looking out over New York.

"Well," said Cal, looking at the tall buildings of New York, "so much for a tour of New York City."

"Maybe when we get back," said Jeb.

"Right. Where do you think we're headed?"

"Europe, I would guess. It could be North Africa, but probably Europe."

"That's what I think, too, but where?"

"If it's Europe, it's got to be Great Britain. That's about the only place the Germans and Italians haven't taken over."

They watched the last units board the ship. The ramps were removed, and tugboats moved in.

"Look," said Cal, "we're starting to move."

They looked down from the stern as the water between the dock and the ship began to expand.

After several minutes watching the New York skyline recede, Jeb asked, "How long do you think we'll be gone?"

"A year, maybe."

"Maybe two," said Jeb.

The *Queen Mary* moved down the Hudson River and eastward into the Atlantic. She could steam at 28 knots, far faster than German U-boats and any Allied ships that might escort her. She crossed the Atlantic unescorted, zigzagging every eight minutes as an extra precaution.

On board, the men learned that the ship was headed to Great Britain and that the crossing would take five days.

The late September weather was warm, and over the next several days Jeb and Cal spent as much time as they could on the deck looking at the ocean. Some of the men preferred to stay below deck playing cards or reading.

On the fifth day, as the *Queen Mary* approached Scotland and the port of Greenock, an area where she would be more vulnerable to German U-boats and German aircraft, the Royal Navy sent seven ships to help escort her to port. While Jeb and Cal stood at the deck rails watching the escorts, the British cruiser HMS *Curacao*, which was crossing back and forth in front of the *Queen Mary* to provide air defense, cut closely across the path of the ocean liner.

"My, God," exclaimed Jeb, "we're going to hit that ship!"

The crew on the *Queen Mary's* bridge blew the steam whistles as a warning and turned to port to try to miss the *Curacao*, which was coming from starboard.

"Hold on," shouted Cal. "It looks like our ship won't be able to turn in time, and that other ship can't get out of the way. We're going to collide!"

The *Queen Mary* ran over the *Curacao*.

"Holy cow! We cut that ship in half," said Jeb.

Cal pointed to starboard. "Look at all the men in the water!"

The Queen Mary continued ahead, not slowing.

Jeb leaned out over the railing. "Aren't we going to stop and help rescue those men?"

"It would probably take too long for this big ship to stop and turn around," said Cal. "It looks like some of those smaller ships are going to the rescue."

"You're probably right. Our captain also may not want to stop and put this ship and the 15,000 soldiers aboard at risk."

This was the first time Jeb, Cal, and the men of Company O had seen men killed.

"This is not a good omen," said Cal.

"No, it's not."

Jeb, Cal, and the other soldiers were not told how many sailors from the *Curacao* perished. Indeed, they were ordered not to talk about the incident for the rest of the war, so as to prevent the enemy from learning details about Allied operations. The Admiralty, however, learned that ninety-seven of the men aboard the *Curacao* were rescued, but some 300 perished.

For the men who had been on the deck that day, the accident was an event they would never be able to erase from their memories.

The *Queen Mary* continued on without further incident to Scotland and docked at Greenock.

Chapter 37

September 1942, Great Britain

At Greenock, the men debarked from the *Queen Mary* and boarded trains heading south for England.

Captain Dooley came back from a meeting of officers aboard the train and informed the men of Company O of their destination. "We're headed to a place called Tidworth Barracks. It's been a British cavalry facility, and the British are going to let us be based there. In fact, our whole 29th Infantry Division will be based there. It's located about 80 miles west of the center of London. Are there any questions?"

"Captain, will we be sleeping in the horse stables?" asked Private Wright. The men laughed.

"No, I've been told we'll be in barracks, but if you'd prefer the stables, Wright, I'll see what I can arrange. Any other questions?"

"Sir, we didn't get to see much of New York. Will we be able to go to London?" asked another soldier.

"I don't know. If we do well enough in our training, we might get some time off to do a little sightseeing. We'll have to see how things go."

Company O and the other 29th Infantry Division units were based at Tidworth Barracks for seven months. During this time, the men were given permission to travel to London, and most of them took advantage of the opportunity.

Their mail was censored, and they could not tell their families back home where they were based or about their trips to London. For some of the men, there was no way they would have told their families about what went on during their trips to London, even if there were no censorship.

At the end of seven months, in May 1943, the 29th Infantry Division was moved from Tidworth Barracks and scattered in southwestern England in Cornwall and Devon Counties. Company O and its parent battalion deployed to a location near the small, quaint town of Rockpool, less than ten miles from the English Channel.

The men were smitten with Rockpool. With its small town center surrounded by residential areas, the town reminded many of Halesford, their hometown. For Jeb, the town would turn out to be only one of the attractions he would find in southwestern England.

Chapter 38

Spring 1943, Rockpool, U.K.

Shortly after arriving in Rockpool, Jeb wrote his mother a letter. Censorship rules prevented him from telling exactly where he was or what he was doing militarily. An officer reviewed all outgoing letters to ensure that nothing in the letters might help the enemy should the letters fall into unfriendly hands. Jeb's first letters home from England were relatively long, but as weeks and months passed, he found there was less to say. In his first letter home after arriving in Rockpool, he wrote:

Dear Mother,

I want to let you know that I'm well and hope you are, too.

We've moved, but I can't tell you where to. I can say that I've had a chance to see some of the countryside and this place is almost as beautiful as Virginia. I miss Virginia's mountains, however.

The weather here seems cold and damp almost all the time. I hope the weather back home is warm and sunny. Here, we have had lots of rain since we arrived. I've been wearing my long underwear, even though it's spring.

We live in a hut, called a Nissen Hut. Someone told me the name comes from a Canadian military engineer who designed the hut in the Great War. It's not luxurious, but it

sure beats sleeping in a tent. There
are 24 of us in the hut. We each have
a bed, actually a cot and mattress, and
we keep warm with an iron stove.

We have no privacy, and it's
difficult to read or write letters
because of the poor lighting and all
the activity and chatter going on in
the hut.

The other men are getting ready
to turn the lights out, so I must stop
now.

Please tell Uncle Jonah I said
hello and will write him soon.
Love,
Jeb

Helen wrote Jeb almost every day. The letters were sent
via "V-Mail," in which a letter was photocopied onto
microfilm, which was then transported across the ocean, and
then printed out in smaller form onto paper and delivered in
an envelope to the addressee. Helen also began to mail Jeb
packages of home-baked cookies and store-bought candy.
One letter read:

Dearest Son,

I am a happy person today, as I
received a letter from you this
morning, the first since you arrived at
your new location.

I thank God that you arrived
safely and are well.

I enjoyed reading what you
could tell me about the weather and
your living conditions. Here, it's been
sunny and warm, a nice spring.

Folks in Halesford are busy with all sorts of volunteer projects to help with the war effort and support for you and our other servicemen and servicewomen. I go to the library on Tuesday evenings to prepare military surgical dressings under the direction of the American Red Cross. We have as many as a dozen or more women and teenage girls come. We take sheets of gauze, cut them into large square sheets several inches on a side, and then fold them seven times to make a thick pad a couple of inches in size. We're told they'll be used in surgical procedures by military doctors to soak up fluids. We all pray they will never have to be used.

It gives us a good feeling to be doing something to help. As we womenfolk are prone to do, we chat the entire time, so I am up on all the latest gossip. Those of us with sons in the military tell what we know about what our sons are doing, but I'm afraid none of us knows much. We ladies do have a good time together. One night, Rodney Thoms brought us free ice cream from his drug store. That was a treat!

I'm sending some cookies. Let me know when you receive them.

Please take care of yourself. I miss you.

With all of my love,
Mother

Jeb wrote his Uncle Jonah a letter about life in the military:

Dear Uncle Jonah,

How are you? I hope you're O.K. and that things on the farm are going well.

As mother may have told you, things over here are O.K.

I live in a Nissen hut with 23 other men. It gets pretty noisy and heated in here in the evenings after supper. The men in my unit are about evenly divided between southerners and northerners, or, as some would say, Rebels and Yankees.

We were all from Halesford when my company left home in February 1941, but as our unit has grown and some of our good southern men have been promoted or left for other good reasons, we have picked up a lot of replacements from the North.

In the evenings, many of the men in our hut argue about the War Between the States. The Yankees call it the "Civil War," while some of our southern boys call it "The War of Northern Aggression." They argue over the origins of the war—was it fought primarily because of slavery or because of states' rights?

They argue about whether the North won because of vastly superior resources or because of its political and military leadership. They argue grand military strategy—especially whether the South might not have had to surrender if it had pursued a more defensive strategy. They argue over whose military leaders were better— Grant, Sherman, and Sheridan or Lee, Jackson, and Overstreet. They even argue tactics, especially those used at Gettysburg and in Jackson's Shenandoah Valley campaign.

Many of the men had grandfathers who fought in that war. They're proud of their ancestors and their military heritage. Some of the men from the South close their arguments by stating that they wished their grandfathers had killed more Damn Yankees during the war, while some from the North say they wished their grandfathers had killed more Rebels.

I have friends on both sides of the arguments, so I usually stay neutral by taking a walk until the debaters run out of steam.

Well, it's about time for lights out, so I must end.

Love,
Jeb

In another letter, Jeb's mother told more of what was happening in Halesford.

My Dearest Son Jeb,

A nice surprise came today! The postman delivered three letters.

You are a dear son to write as much as you do, with all the things I can only imagine you are doing.

The community has stepped up its support for the war effort. The Boy Scouts are collecting newspapers and all types of metal. We're told that the materials will be used for the war effort. I gave the boys two old pots that were just about worn out.

I have saved up some money and bought a war bond. The bond cost me $18.75, and I'll get $25.00 back when the bond matures and I cash it in. The newspaper says that the $18.75 raised from sale of one war bond is enough for the government to buy three bayonets. I like to think that I am helping at least a little in making sure you and our other boys in the service have the equipment you need.

Last week the Lions Club held an auction to sell bonds. People in the community donated items to be auctioned off, and then people bid on the items. Each winning bidder had to buy war bonds in the amount of the bid. So those who won the bids would be out of their money only until the bonds matured and they cashed them in, and then they would not only get their money back but also earn interest to boot. The bids, thus, were really high. One pair of donated women's nylon stockings brought a bid of $3,000! Can you believe that?

I've started growing a Victory Garden in the back yard. The more food I can grow for myself, the more there will be for you and our other boys and girls in the military. I may even have enough to share with some of our neighbors.

I must get to bed, as I'm tired after working all day at the factory and then digging in the garden this evening for an hour after supper.

Take care, son.
With all my love,
Mother

P.S. I'm sending more cookies.

Jeb's letters tended to get shorter as time passed.

Dear Mother,

Thanks so much for the cookies. The men in my hut always look forward to your packages, which I share with them. Thanks also for the letters. I had not received any for several days, but I got five today.

We've been very busy, and I've got to get to bed.

Love,
Jeb

Chapter 39

Jeb could not write home about the training that Company O was undergoing. The men were preparing for an invasion. They went on long marches, often in cold, rainy conditions. They camped out for a week or more at a time. The Nissen hut was a luxury compared to sleeping in cold tents, which often leaked.

The men frequently went to rifle ranges and fired their weapons. They also practiced small unit tactical operations, especially fire and maneuver, in which one element of a squad would lay down covering fire against the enemy while other elements of the squad maneuvered to get closer to the enemy soldiers or outflank them. They also loaded onto troop transport ships from which they climbed into small landing craft, known as "Higgins boats" or the British equivalent "landing craft assault." These smaller craft carried some 30 troops and were used to practice landings on British beaches, in preparation for landings at some other unknown destinations.

In the evenings, while deployed at their base near Rockpool, the men could relax by going to the movies, recreation facilities, or some of the pubs in the small town. Some of the men bought used bicycles to give them more mobility in the evenings and on weekends.

The men also talked among themselves in the evenings. In addition to bantering about the Civil War, some of the men liked to debate religious issues. They debated whether killing German soldiers would violate the commandment "thou shall not kill." Those who read the Bible frequently pointed to Biblical stories which appeared to justify killing, either by man or God. Most agreed that the United States was defending itself and other countries from attack and death by Germany, Italy, and Japan, and that action taken in self-defense was not breaking a commandment.

They also addressed why God allowed good people to be killed. Some argued that maybe God was not all-knowing, all-present, and all-powerful. Others argued that God had given man free will and would not intervene to save even good people. There was little consensus, as was the case for most issues the men debated.

Jeb and Cal went to the movies together about once a week, and they went to a pub every couple of weeks. They exchanged information from back home in Halesford.

"I got a letter from my mother today," Jeb said one day.

"How is she?"

"Oh, she's fine, but she says the rationing is getting stricter. She's planted a Victory Garden and hopes to grow enough to feed herself and some of the neighbors."

"Yeah, my parents have planted a garden, too," said Cal. "My mother goes once a week to the library to prepare surgical dressings. My dad's a district air warden, and they practice for air raids."

"My mother is making surgical dressings, too," said Jeb. "She feels that at least she's doing something to help those of us in the military. She worries a lot about me. Last week she wrote that my cousin Thomas Sutton was injured fighting in Italy. His wounds are putting him out of action, and he's being sent back to America."

"Sorry to hear he was wounded," said Cal, "but, you know, if he's being sent home he may be one of the lucky ones."

"I was thinking the same thing," said Jeb.

Chapter 40

May-June 1943, Richmond

By early May 1943, as they prepared to graduate, Ginny and Liz firmed up their plans to join the Army Nurse Corps. They had already had heated discussions with their parents and had worn them down to the point that the parents, with reluctance, were prepared to see their daughters join the Army.

Liz called the nurse's unit at Camp Lee and made arrangements for Ginny and her to take their physical exams. They again borrowed a car and drove to the camp. At the end of their exams, the administering nurse informed them that they had passed and asked if they wanted to enroll.

Liz turned to Ginny. "Let's do it."

Ginny nodded. "Let's do."

They were enrolled and told to report for the beginning of training ten days after they graduated.

Their parents drove to Richmond for their graduation. The Class of 1943 was the first class of nurses to graduate wearing stylish, navy-blue capes over their white dresses.

Ginny and Liz returned to their respective family homes for a short vacation. Ten days later their parents drove them to Camp Lee. The fathers had arranged for extra rations of gasoline for the military-related trip.

The two families arrived at the base nearly at the same time and drove to the area where the candidate nurses were to report. The Jackson and Hawkins families again greeted each other and exchanged pleasantries, as they had on several occasions at the nursing school.

In a reception building, a woman in uniform pointed out the candidate nurses' barracks, and the two fathers and Tim helped the young women carry their civilian clothes and personal items to the barracks.

The mothers, who were lagging behind, stepped into the barracks and almost simultaneously exclaimed, "Oh, my."

The barracks was a typical Army barracks—dark, Spartan, crowded, lacking in privacy, and in need of painting.

Ginny and Liz glanced at each other, trying not to let their parents see their dismay.

"Well, this is going to be home, sweet home," said Ginny, with a resigned smile, "but only for the next four weeks."

"I'll bet the time will go fast," said Liz.

"I sure hope so," Ginny muttered quietly.

Other candidate nurses and their families began arriving. They began greeting one another.

"I guess it's time for us to head home and let you girls get acquainted with your new friends," said Randolph. He thought back to his experiences in the Army in meeting fellow soldiers. *The girls will meet many new friends here, but they'll probably never see most of them again after their training.*

Ginny and Liz walked their families to their cars, and the families began to say their goodbyes. The mothers had tears in their eyes, and the fathers struggled to suppress their emotions.

Ruth faced her daughter and put both her hands on Ginny's upper arms. "I thought it was hard saying good-bye when we dropped you off in Richmond for the first time, but this is much harder. I never thought my daughter would be serving in the Army and going who knows where."

"I'll be fine, Mother."

Tears began rolling down the older woman's cheeks as she stepped forward and embraced her daughter. "Write to us and let us know if you need anything," she said quietly.

"I will." Ginny felt a catch in her throat but no tears came as she stepped back.

"Take care, Sis," said Tim, patting Ginny on the shoulder.

"I will. You take care of Mom and Dad." Ginny reached up and ruffled his hair. "If you want my room, you can have it. I think I'm really flying the nest this time."

Randolph gave Ginny a hug and whispered in a voice that was breaking, "We're all proud of you, Ginny." He abruptly turned and walked to the car, dabbing at his eyes. Ruth and Tim followed.

As Ginny watched her family depart, she was joined by Liz, who had said goodbye to her family. They waved as the cars pulled away. The two young women then hurried into the barracks to meet their new friends.

The next four weeks were designed to introduce the forty candidate nurses to Army life and Army nursing. Reveille was at 5:30 a.m. The young women had to be dressed and ready for breakfast by 6:30 a.m. After breakfast, they had drill practice, then the first class of the day, followed by calisthenics, another class, lunch, another class, more drill, and a final class. They were taught military courtesy and customs, uniform regulations, and organization of the Army and its medical units. They marched, and they drilled. They took long road marches, loaded down with heavy packs. They even learned how to protect themselves against chemical attack.

Most of their classes focused on military medicine, including first aid, field sanitation, control of communicable diseases, triage, hospital procedures, and ward management. After supper, they had to study, shower, prepare their uniforms, and shine their shoes and boots for the next day. The physical and mental activities were demanding, and all the women were ready for sleep by 9:30 p.m.

On the weekends, Ginny and Liz slept in, looked around Petersburg, and occasionally went back to Richmond. They were invited to dances at the post officers' club. They had a few dates with young officers but nothing serious developed.

They wrote their parents about twice a week telling them about their training. Their mothers sent newsy letters from home.

At the end of their four-week basic training, they were to be commissioned and take oaths as second lieutenants in the United States Army. They invited their parents, but the best each family could do, given the rationing of gasoline and tires, was to send them cards of congratulations, expressing pride in their daughters and hopes for their safety.

One of the last requirements of their training, a sobering one, was to make out a will and power of attorney.

As the young women neared completion of their training, school officials informed Ginny and Liz that their high marks in the classroom had earned them top choices for their first assignments as Army nurses.

They discussed their options. "I'd like to be stationed somewhere on the East Coast," said Ginny, "perhaps here in Virginia."

"Virginia?" said Liz, placing her hands on her hips. "We've seen Virginia. How about California?"

"California would be neat, but I guess I'm an Easterner by heart."

"Well, I guess if we stay on the East Coast, we might get sent to Europe. I'd love to see Europe. That would be much better than some of those God-forsaken islands in the Pacific."

"Whoa, Liz," said Ginny, pretending to pull back the reins on a horse. "I thought the personnel people told us we'd be stationed in the United States."

"Yes, for our first assignment, but they said we could volunteer later for an assignment overseas."

"Right, but we wouldn't be sent overseas unless we volunteered."

"Correct, but wouldn't you like to see London, perhaps eventually Paris, and who knows, maybe even Berlin?"

"Liz, let's focus on our first assignment."

"O.K. Let's request somewhere near a big city in the East, say, New York City, Philadelphia, or Boston."

"That'd be fine."

They submitted their request. The Army, in its infinite wisdom, sent them to the base hospital at Fort Dix, located in the New Jersey countryside.

Chapter 41

May 1943, Rockpool, UK

In May 1943, Jeb and Cal were both promoted from private first class to corporal. During an intense field training exercise in which Jeb's sergeant was injured, Jeb stepped up and led his unit in a successful seizure of their objective. His actions impressed his immediate superiors—platoon sergeant Staff Sergeant Tucker, platoon leader Second Lieutenant Howard Stockton, and company commander Captain Robert Dooley. They already knew Jeb to be bright and energetic. With Jeb's actions in the training exercise, they saw that he had the ability to lead others and take the initiative. They noticed that Jeb's fellow soldiers trusted him and were ready to follow his lead.

Two weeks after the exercise, a runner came to summon Jeb to report immediately to Captain Dooley's office. He had never before been ordered to report to the captain. As he walked to Dooley's office, his mind buzzed with questions. *Why would the captain want to see me? Has something happened to my mother? Have I somehow gotten into trouble?*

When he walked into the outer office, the company clerk, a staff sergeant, sat typing. The clerk looked up. "Go on in, Fletcher. They're expecting you."

They? Who're they? This could be serious. Jeb cleared his throat, walked to the entrance of the inner office, and knocked on the door frame.

"Come in, Fletcher," called Captain Dooley, who was sitting behind his desk.

As Jeb stepped into the office he saw Lieutenant Stockton and Sergeant Tucker, sitting in chairs off to the side.

Jeb approached the captain's desk and came to attention. "Corporal Fletcher reporting, sir."

"At ease," said the captain.

Jeb spread his legs apart and locked his arms behind him, the formal at-ease position.

"We've been talking about you, Fletcher."

Not good, thought Jeb, *but at least it's about me and not some bad news about my mother.*

Dooley continued. "We've been impressed with how you've conducted yourself. You're a good soldier, and you seem to have an instinct for leading." The captain paused.

Jeb thought the pause was intended to allow him to respond, but he couldn't think of anything to say.

"Your squad leader, Sergeant Rankin, is being promoted and moved to a support position with the battalion. Lieutenant Stockton and Sergeant Tucker have recommended that you be promoted to sergeant and that you lead your squad." Again Dooley paused, and again Jeb said nothing.

"I'm accepting that recommendation. Congratulations, Sergeant Fletcher."

Sergeant Fletcher, Jeb said to himself. *I like the sound of that. But what all will that mean?*

Dooley smiled and came around his desk to shake Jeb's hand.

Jeb, with only a hint of a smile, said, "Thank you, sir."

Both Stockton and Tucker approached, offered their congratulations, and also shook Jeb's hand.

"Now, Sergeant Fletcher," said Dooley, "you may think we've been training hard. Well, we have. But our training is about to intensify. We'll be fighting Germans before long. For the sake of our mission and for the sake of your men, it's now up to you to make sure that each and every man in your squad is in the best physical condition possible, fully trained, and combat ready. Is that clear?"

"Yes, sir." *That's a heavy responsibility.*

"All right. Now go with Lieutenant Stockton and Sergeant Tucker, and they'll announce my decision to your squad."

"Yes, sir."

The three men walked to the hut where Jeb's squad lived. Squad members were relaxing after lunch. When Tucker called the men out for formation, they lined up, standing at attention, facing Stockton, Tucker, and Jeb. Jeb felt embarrassed.

"At ease, men," ordered Stockton. "You may have heard that Sergeant Rankin is being promoted and moved to a battalion support position. To replace Rankin, upon my recommendation and with the support of Staff Sergeant Tucker, Captain Dooley has just promoted Corporal Fletcher to sergeant and made him the leader of this squad. This is effective immediately. Your squad is one of the best in Company O. I will expect you to get even better." The lieutenant turned to Jeb. "Sergeant Fletcher, carry on."

"Yes, sir." Jeb called the squad to attention and saluted the lieutenant. Stockton returned the salute, and he and Tucker headed back toward the company office.

Jeb was left with what was now his squad. "At ease," he ordered.

"Sergeant Fletcher," said Corporal Frank Smith, emphasizing the title "Sergeant." "What did you have to do to get that promotion?"

"Knock it off, Smitty," said Cal.

"Yeah, Smitty," said another.

Jeb looked at the men and cleared his throat. "I'm not sure why I was selected. Each of you could lead this squad just as well. I've accepted the position, and I'll do everything I can to make sure we're prepared and equipped for our mission, and I'll look out for your welfare. I can't promise or offer anything more than that. Any questions?"

"Congratulations, Jeb," said Cal, as he and the others came forward to extend their congratulations and shake his hand.

Jeb then called the squad back to attention and dismissed them.

Cal lingered behind to talk to Jeb as the others left. "Well, damn, now I have to take orders from you," said Cal, with a grin that seemed to Jeb not fully genuine. "I thought it might come to this one day."

"Hey, Cal, we'll always be best buddies, right?"

"I hope so, Jeb, but we both now know that what we may want and what the Army wants are usually two different things."

Chapter 42

Summer and Fall 1943, Camp Lee and Fort Dix

In early July, Ginny and Liz arranged for a military sedan to take them from Camp Lee to nearby Petersburg, where they boarded a northbound train. As the train crossed a bridge over the Potomac River, Ginny said softly, "Goodbye, Virginia. We'll miss you, but we'll be back."

"Yes," said Liz with a laugh. "Goodbye old girl. We're off to see Washington, Fort Dix, New York City, and who knows where else in the world."

As the train passed through Washington, D.C., they looked out the window, searching for some of the famous sights in the nation's capital. They got a glimpse only of the tall Capitol Building. At Union Station, they transferred to a train headed toward New York that would stop at Fort Dix. When they arrived at the base a few hours later, a private met them at the station and drove them to their quarters. He unloaded their duffle bags at the front door of the nurses' quarters, saying he was not allowed to carry them inside.

Ginny and Liz picked up their heavy duffle bags and struggled into the building. A female private at the front desk checked them in, explained where the room was that they were to share, and gave them each a key.

"What luck we're having, getting to share a room," said Ginny as they walked down the hall toward their new accommodations. She unlocked the door and made a sweeping gesture for Liz to enter first.

Liz surveyed the room. "Not too bad. Much better than the group barracks at Camp Lee." Inside were two steel, single beds, two dressers, two desks, and a window with a blind and curtains.

"Rank does have its privileges," said Ginny, as she began unpacking her things.

"Yeah," said Liz, "what rank we have. This status of 'relative rank' stinks, I tell you. We're second lieutenants, but we don't really rank salutes from those of lesser rank." Liz opened her duffle bag. "Its discrimination, I tell you."

"Well, things are getting better. At least we're now getting the same pay as males, not just half pay as was the case a year or so ago."

"That's at least a first step."

"Yes, it is. After being in school for so long and having no income, it's really great to be earning my own money."

"I agree. Let's hurry and unpack and then go look around Fort Dix."

What they found that day and in the ensuing weeks was an extremely active military post. Thousands of men were being processed at Fort Dix before being deployed to Europe.

Ginny and Liz, wearing freshly-laundered, neatly-pressed, white dress uniforms with the insignia of second lieutenant nurses, spent most days taking medical histories of soldiers and giving shots to prevent illness. Many of the men seemed young to the nurses, and, indeed, many of those being drafted were now only eighteen.

The social life of nurses at the post was not what the two young women had hoped. Most of the men were just passing through and did so rather quickly. However, just as the number of nurses at Fort Dix was growing, so was the number of doctors.

Liz started dating a surgeon, a captain in his late thirties, who took her to dinner and dancing in New York City. She was increasingly attracted to him—until she found out from another nurse, who knew of him in civilian life back in their hometown in the Mid-West, that he was married.

Ginny met Ronald Wright at a dance at the officers' club. He, too, was a surgeon with the rank of captain.

Late one evening in September, after Ginny had returned to their quarters from a date with Captain Wright and Liz had returned from a date with an officer she had met recently, the two women chatted as they prepared for bed. Liz asked "So,

Lieutenant Jackson, tell me, is Captain Wright also Mr. Right?"

"Where in the world did that question come from?"

"And your answer is?"

"His name is 'W-r-i-g-h-t,' with a 'W.' We have lots of fun. He's a good dancer and talker."

"Does he have a surgeon's deft hands?" Liz asked, laughing.

"Will you stop that?"

"Oooh. Sounds like this has the potential to get serious. I might just be hitting a nerve."

"I'm not telling you one more thing, until you promise to stop," said Ginny with an exaggerated scowl, which quickly turned into a smile and then laughter.

"I'm caught in a dilemma," Liz said, spreading her arms and holding her hands up in mock puzzlement. "Should I continue to tease my roommate mercilessly, or should I stop teasing so I can learn more about Mr. Right, which will give me more fodder for teasing later?"

"You're skilled at dealing with dilemmas, aren't you? Tell me some more about your doctor friend."

"My doctor friend?"

"Yes," Ginny said with a broad smile, "you know, the one that is married."

"Ouch! O.K., you win. I'll behave," laughed Liz. "I'd sure hate to be in an alley fight with you."

"I've learned a lot from you, Liz."

"Can I be serious for a minute?"

"Sure, but you're not going to ask me again about Mr. Right again, are you?"

"That's right. I mean that's correct. I've been thinking. We've been here at Fort Dix for several months. It's been an interesting assignment, but I'd like to do more."

"Such as?"

"I'd like to go to England. We've been helping all these young men prepare to ship out to England, and the Army seems to be building up for an invasion into Western Europe.

I think we ought to be part of that, rather than just sitting here at Fort Dix."

"That's amazing. I've been thinking the same thing. We've been together so long we're even starting to think alike."

"What about Captain Wright?"

"Ronald's nice, but he's not Mr. Right. I've nothing to keep me here at Fort Dix."

"Well, I finally wormed the information out of you, about Mr. Right, and it only cost me a deployment to England."

They both laughed heartily and then grew quiet.

"I hope we know what we're doing," said Ginny.

"It's the right thing—I mean the correct thing—to do."

Ginny held up her index finger, signaling an afterthought. "If we're accepted for overseas duty, we won't tell our parents that we volunteered, will we?"

"No way."

They submitted requests for transfers and a few weeks later received orders to report in late December to a U.S. Army hospital near Portsmouth, England, in the southwest corner of the country near the English Channel.

Chapter 43

September 1943, Rockpool, UK

On a hot day in September 1943, during a training session, a runner once again came to Jeb with a message to report to Captain Dooley.

What could this be about? Jeb thought, as he hurried to the company's office. He hadn't been summoned to see the captain since he had been promoted three months earlier.

The clerk greeted him and motioned him toward the captain's office. The captain sat at his desk doing paperwork, unaware of Jeb's arrival.

Jeb knocked on the door frame. "Good morning, sir."

Dooley put his pen down and looked up. "Oh, Sergeant Fletcher. Come in and have a seat."

Jeb entered and sat down in a chair in front of the captain's desk. He placed his cap on his leg and sat quietly as Dooley finished writing on a paper.

Dooley dropped the paper in an out box and looked at Jeb. "General Gerhardt has asked each company commander in our division to nominate one or two men per company whom the general might consider appointing to OCS, Officer Candidate School." Dooley paused.

Jeb's mind raced ahead, but he said nothing. *Was the captain going to ask him to suggest a candidate—or might the captain actually be thinking of him?*

"I've been watching how you handle your squad. You know how to focus on the mission and get the job done. You also know how to take care of your men. You're a fast learner. You seem to have had no problems with your squad after you were elevated from within to be squad leader. If there were any problems, you must have handled them, without causing them to be brought to my attention." Dooley again paused.

Jeb again said nothing, but his mind jumped ahead. *So the captain was thinking of him, but did he really want to become an officer?*

"We've got a lot of good men in our company. I might nominate one of the senior noncoms, but I need them to help me run the unit. Anyone selected for OCS will probably not come back to this company."

I'd hate to leave Company O, Jeb thought. He wanted to ask, *If I don't come back here, where in the world might I be assigned?* He remained silent.

"You've now got over three years of military experience in the ranks—not too little, and not too much. I want to nominate you for OCS."

Once again, Jeb said nothing.

"I won't nominate you unless you agree to be nominated. It's your decision. Becoming an officer involves a lot of responsibility. You're responsible for your mission and for the lives of your men. I won't hide from you the fact that junior officers in combat have a high mortality rate, compared to many other ranks. Becoming an officer, however, can provide you a chance for greater leadership and influence. Those selected for training will be sent back to Fort Benning, Georgia, for nine weeks of training. There would probably be an opportunity for a few days of leave at home after you complete your schooling. Where you would be assigned after that would depend on the needs of the Army."

The reference to home leave caught Jeb's attention. *I might be able to see Mother. It's been a long time, and I miss her.*

"I don't want to pressure you, but I need an answer now. The general wants the nominations by tomorrow morning. If you won't agree to be nominated, I need to find someone else. So, what's your decision?"

Jeb looked down at the floor for a few seconds as thoughts whirled around in his head. Then he looked up.

"I'm not sure I'm the best qualified man in the company, sir."

"That's not your judgment to make, Sergeant, and it's not an answer to my question. Just give me a 'yes' or a 'no.'"

"Yes, sir, I'll agree to being nominated." *Oh, man, I've gone and done it now.*

"Good. You're the best man available."

* * * * * * * *

A week later Jeb was aboard an almost empty troop ship headed back to America. He arrived in New York and caught a train to Atlanta. From Atlanta, he took a train to Columbus, Georgia, and from there caught a ride on one of the many Army trucks shuttling back and forth from the Columbus train station to Fort Benning.

At the Army's Officer Candidate School, much of the training was similar to that which he had received as an enlisted man, but the training was now focused on being the leader of a platoon of 40 or so men in combat.

During the classroom instruction and conversing over meals in the mess hall or over beer later in the evenings, the men spent much of their time trying to find out what made a good military leader. They concluded that in essence it was accomplishing the mission while also caring for one's men. Those being led wanted their commander to know his job, have confidence in himself, and lead by example. They wanted their leader to know them and care about them, to explain their mission and to keep them informed, to share their hardships, and to not eat until all their men had been served. Any element of kindness and even some sense of humor were merely bonuses.

At the end of nine weeks, Jeb was commissioned as a second lieutenant. He felt proud when a single gold bar was pinned atop each shoulder. He found it strange to have noncommissioned soldiers salute him as they passed.

He received orders to return to Great Britain, but with five days of leave before having to board a trans-Atlantic troop ship in New York.

When he had arrived in New York more than two months earlier, Jeb had sent his mother a telegram telling her that he was back in the United States and that he hoped to visit her in a couple of months. From Fort Benning, he now sent her a telegram announcing that indeed he would be paying a visit. He gave the date and time of his estimated arrival in Bedford.

A couple of days later, as the train neared Bedford in the late afternoon, Jeb grew excited at the prospect of seeing his mother. He fidgeted in his seat and kept putting down the magazine he was reading and then picking it back up. When the train pulled into the Bedford station, he saw his mother on the platform. She was scanning the windows of each railcar, looking for him. She seemed thinner and older than Jeb remembered. When the train finally stopped, Jeb picked up his duffle bag, made his way to the railcar door, and hopped down onto the station platform.

Helen Fletcher saw him alight and rushed toward him. Mother and son hugged, kissed one another on the cheek, and held on for almost half a minute. As they broke from their hug, Helen took a step backward. "Let me see you! Oh, my! You've filled out, and you're so handsome in your uniform. And an officer, too, with gold bars!"

Jeb blushed, as other people on the platform looked at him and his mother and smiled. "It's great to see you, Mother. It's good to be home."

"And I'm so glad to have you back, even if for only a short time. Now let's get home. I've got your favorite meal in the oven."

They walked to the green pickup truck. "Would you like to drive, Jeb?"

"You bet." Jeb opened the passenger door for his mother and then hurried around to the other side and climbed in. As he pulled away, he said, "It feels strange driving. I haven't driven for months."

Jeb and his mother talked all the way home and then at home over supper and late into the night. During Jeb's three day visit, they continued to talk and to eat. Helen fixed Jeb his favorite dishes. Uncle Jonah joined them for a couple of meals.

Without the military censor, and with his mother promising not to tell, Jeb was able to share with her where he had been stationed and what he had been doing.

As they were finishing their last meal before Jeb was to leave, Helen bowed her head, and a tear rolled down her cheek. "I have missed your father so much all these years, and now I miss you."

"I know, Mother, and I miss you, too."

"I don't want to end up an old woman, all alone." More tears fell down her cheeks. "I just want you to come back home, find a nice girl to marry, and give me a grandchild that I can spoil."

Jeb reached across the table and took his mother's hand. "That's what I want, too. Don't worry, Mother. You won't be alone much longer. I'll be coming home."

Helen dried her tears with her napkin and looked directly into Jeb's eyes. "Have I told you how proud I am of you?"

Jeb looked down, swallowed, and then looked at his mother. "Thanks."

Helen accompanied Jeb back to Bedford so he could catch the train to New York, where he would board a troop ship for the return trip to Great Britain.

At the station, Helen hugged her son. "Take care of yourself, Jeb."

"I will, and don't worry, Mother." He jumped on the train and saw his mother dabbing at her eyes as the train pulled away, leaving her at the station, all alone.

Chapter 44

December 1943, Waterbridge, UK

When the ship from New York arrived in Scotland, Army officials informed Jeb that his old unit in the 29th Infantry Division had no vacant officer slots at the time and that he would be sent to the 4th Infantry Division, specifically Company N of the 1st Battalion, to replace an officer who had fallen gravely ill.

Jeb traveled by train and truck to the 4th Infantry Division's area and was dropped off in the Company N area late in the morning. He asked for directions to the company commander's office and headed that way, lugging his duffle bag and other gear. The closer he got, the more nervous he became. *I don't know a sole in this unit, I'm a wet-behind-the-ears second lieutenant, and I have no idea what I'm getting into here.*

When he walked into the office, the company clerk was hunched over his desk, busy with paperwork. To get the clerk's attention, Jeb said, "Sergeant."

The sergeant frowned at the interruption and looked up. When he saw that Jeb was an officer, he immediately stood. "Yes, sir. Sorry, sir. I was engrossed in what I was doing. I'm Staff Sergeant Davis. May I help you?"

Jeb realized that he would have to get used to the new power and authority of being an officer. "I'm Second Lieutenant Jebidiah Fletcher. I have orders assigning me to Company N."

"Oh, yes, Lieutenant Fletcher, we've been expecting you. Captain Looper just returned. Let me tell the captain you're here."

Davis walked to Looper's door. "Sir, Lieutenant Fletcher just arrived, and he's here to see you."

"Send him in."

Davis stepped back and motioned Jeb inside.

Jeb approached the captain's desk and came to attention. "Sir, Second Lieutenant Jebidiah Fletcher reporting for duty."

Looper looked up from his paperwork, stood, and stretched his arm across his desk to shake hands. "Ah, Lieutenant Fletcher. Welcome. I'm very glad you're here. We're shorthanded."

"Thank you, sir. I'm glad to be here."

"We're assigning you as platoon leader for Second Platoon. Your predecessor, Lieutenant Hall, has taken ill. I'm afraid part of his illness is psychological. Some of the men in Second Platoon can be a problem. To be frank, they wore him down. I want you to shape that platoon up." Looper looked at his watch. "I've got to run to a meeting now." He walked around the side of his desk and headed for the door. He stopped and turned back toward Jeb. "Any questions?"

Jeb felt a knot form in his stomach. *What in hell is this? I've got a hundred questions, the first of which is what am I walking into with the problem platoon.* To Looper he said, "No, sir, no questions. At least at this time."

"Good," said Looper. "Sergeant Davis can tell you how to find Second Platoon. I've got to run now." Looper grabbed his cap from a peg on the wall and hurried out the door.

Jeb went back out into the outer office. "Sergeant Davis, can you tell me how to get to the Second Platoon area? And Sergeant Davis, just between the two of us, what can you tell me about the men in Second Platoon?"

A half hour later, Jeb left Sergeant Davis and, with his gear, walked over to the Second Platoon's area.

Davis had told him he would probably find the Second Platoon sergeant, Staff Sergeant Alvin Bricker, in the mess tent. Jeb found the sergeant alone in the tent, except for some men who were washing dishes behind the serving area. Jeb approached Bricker, who was sitting and drinking coffee. "Sergeant Bricker? I'm Second Lieutenant Jebidiah Fletcher, the new leader of Second Platoon." Bricker stood, and they shook hands. "I'd like you to form the men up. I want to speak to them."

"But, sir, the men just had lunch, and they're in the barracks relaxing. Why don't you wait a couple of hours, and then...."

Jeb immediately felt adrenalin kick in and a burning sensation rise up from his stomach. Never in his more than three years with Company O had he ever heard anyone question an order. From what Captain Looper had implied and Sergeant Davis had told him, Second Platoon was a problem, and this was his first test.

Trying to control his anger but use it at the same time, Jeb cut Bricker off in mid-sentence. "Sergeant, in case you didn't understand me, that was an order. Don't you ever question one of my orders again. If you think I'm about to make a major mistake—one that will prevent us from accomplishing our mission or unnecessarily risk the lives of our men—then you say 'Permission to speak frankly, sir.' I'll then decide whether or not to grant you that permission. Otherwise, I'll expect you to follow my orders, and follow them immediately."

Bricker stiffened and reddened.

Jeb glowered at him and took a step forward. "I assume you know the consequences of not following a lawful order of a superior officer. If you don't, let me know right now. Do you understand me?"

"Yes, sir!" barked Bricker, who then wheeled about and headed to the barracks.

As soon as Bricker had formed the men, Jeb walked out front and center of the formation. "Men, I'm Second Lieutenant Fletcher, your new platoon leader."

From the back row in a low but distinctive voice came, "And a little child shall lead them." There were several snickers.

Jeb took a deep breath, as the adrenalin and rage returned. He fought to maintain his composure. "Sergeant Bricker, form this platoon again in fifteen minutes, with full field packs. We're going on a forced march. Anyone late to formation will complete a second forced march tonight, which you, Sergeant Bricker, will lead. Is there anyone here who does not understand the consequences of disobeying a lawful military order of a superior officer? If so, speak now."

Jeb waited. He let fifteen seconds of heavy silence pass. "All right, carry on. Fifteen minutes, Sergeant Bricker." Jeb strode off to where he had left his gear. He picked it up and hurried to his quarters, which Sergeant Davis had identified for him.

Jeb quickly changed into his field uniform, boots, and helmet, strapped on a pack, filled his canteen, and walked out to where Sergeant Bricker was forming Second Platoon. Jeb had missed the noon meal, but his adrenalin alone would carry him through the march.

Chapter 45

January 1944, at Sea

Shortly before Christmas, Ginny and Liz, armed with orders assigning them to England, boarded a military bus at Fort Dix for the trip to New York City, where they were to embark on the *Queen Elizabeth*, along with other medical personnel and some 15,000 troops.

The nurses were loaded down with personal gear, almost too much to carry. Each had a Class A suitcase and a Class B duffel bag. They carried duty and dress uniforms; an overcoat; a navy-blue cape with a red lining; special clothing to wear in case of a gas-attack; two canvass musette bags, the size of extra-large, strapped purses, one filled with clothing and the other with cosmetics and toiletries; a bedroll; two blankets rolled tightly; a canvass belt on which hung a mess kit, a canteen, and a drinking cup; and a steel helmet with helmet liner. Soldiers helped them with their suitcases and duffel bags, but they still struggled to climb up the gangplank.

Ginny and Liz, along with forty other women, were segregated in an area of the ship that was marked off limits to the men. They were to sleep on bunk beds three units high. The quarters were cramped, and they had to stow most of their gear under the beds.

The women were allowed to go topside to watch the ship steam out of New York Harbor. Even their section of the outside deck was blocked off from the male troops. The women marveled at the New York skyline as it receded in the distance and were thrilled to see the Statue of Liberty as the ship steamed toward the sea.

As evening fell, the nurses returned to their quarters and soon were escorted to a dining area reserved for officers. They were served by British stewards.

Ginny and Liz ate together. "When you were back in Halesford, did you ever think you'd take a cruise across the Atlantic?" asked Liz.

"Not in my wildest imagination, and especially not aboard the *Queen Elizabeth*. The pictures of the ship I've seen in *Life Magazine* don't do her justice."

"The food is quite good, unlike rumors I've heard about British cuisine." Liz took a second helping of shepherd's pie.

When the women finished their supper, they returned to their quarters. They changed into nightgowns and climbed into their bunks, where they lay talking. Soon, everyone was asleep.

Around midnight, a storm struck. As the ship began to pitch and roll, the women awoke. "Oh, my God," cried out one woman, "are we going to sink?" Another struggled out of her bunk as the ship rolled beneath her. She cried, "Where's the toilet?" and then vomited onto the floor. Three others, moved by the power of suggestion, quickly climbed out of their bunks and vomited. Those in the top bunks felt trapped. They were sure they could feel the pitch and sway more than the others, and it took longer for them to reach the floor. As the odor permeated the area, more rose and ran to the head, seeking the toilets, all of which were soon engaged. Some of the women found mops and buckets and began cleaning up the mess. No one slept.

The storm and the women's misery continued for a second day. Some of the women made jokes about the pleasures of cruising the Atlantic, but few laughed. On the third day the storm abated, and the last two days of the crossing were uneventful.

When the ship landed in Scotland, Ginny and Liz were directed to a train headed south. As the train chugged along, Liz leaned back in her seat and looked out the window. "I'm really glad to be off that ship and onto solid ground."

"Me, too," said Ginny. "I don't ever want to get on a ship again."

"Doesn't this countryside, with its hills, remind you of Virginia?"

"It does. It makes me miss Virginia and my family."

"Me, too, but we're going to have quite an adventure here. I can just feel it."

With several changes of trains, they eventually made their way to the south of England and the seaport of Portsmouth, located on the English Channel. A military car and driver picked them up at the train station and took them to the U.S. Army general hospital.

They were assigned quarters, given an orientation tour, and soon put to work. They found the work to be more demanding than at Fort Dix, but their patient load was moderate. Most of their patients were men injured in training accidents and men suffering general illnesses.

They made friends with the other nurses, doctors, and staff of the hospital. They frequently went on dates with American officers stationed at facilities around Portsmouth. On a couple of occasions, they were invited for a meal at a local British home. The workload at the hospital was slow enough that they also received a three-day pass to London. They enthusiastically took in the sights—Buckingham Palace, Westminster Abbey, Trafalgar Square, Piccadilly Circus, Parliament, and Big Ben. They met some Army officers and had dinner with them.

Life at the hospital in Portsmouth was good, but the pace would soon change as Allied forces intensified their training for the invasion across the English Channel.

Chapter 46

January 1944, Waterbridge, UK

One Friday afternoon a couple of weeks after Jeb had joined
Company N, Lieutenant Ross Millan, a fellow platoon leader
in Company N, pulled Jeb aside after a meeting of the unit's
officers. "Hey, Jeb, how would you like to go into
Waterbridge tonight? We can get something to eat and drink,
and I'll show you the town. What do you say?"

"Thanks. Sounds like fun. I haven't had a chance to see
Waterbridge yet."

"Waterbridge has a couple of nice pubs where we can get
a beer and a little something to eat. There's also a dance hall.
I've seen some pretty good looking girls there. Their accents
are fascinating."

"Sounds even more interesting."

"Most of the girls are friendly, but some aren't. It doesn't
take long to find out which are which."

Ross and Jeb left the base at 6 p.m. and hiked the mile to
Waterbridge. In the center of the town, Ross pointed toward
a building ahead. "Let's try the Black Swan. It's the best of
the pubs."

The Black Swan was crowded with local clientele from
the town and soldiers from the American base. The two
officers found an empty table. A young woman, wearing an
apron, headed in their direction.

Jeb noticed that all of the soldiers nearby grew quiet and
directed their attention toward the young woman, whom he
thought was overweight and overly made up to offset her
less than average looks. The locals paid her no attention and
carried on their conversations.

"Good evening, gentlemen. May I get you something to
drink?"

"Good evening," said Ross. "Could we get a couple of
beers to start with, please, and can you tell us what's the best

meal the pub has to offer tonight? This is my friend's first visit here. I'm sure it won't be his last."

The woman looked at Jeb and smiled. "I hope we'll get to see a lot more of you, Lieutenant. It looks like you could use a little meat on those bones of yours. We're limited in what we can serve, with all the rationing. I'd recommend you try the fish and chips."

"That sounds fine," said Jeb, looking briefly at the woman and then looking down, when she stared at him.

"I'll have the fish and chips, too," said Ross.

"I'll be right back with your beer."

After the woman had left, Ross said, with a big grin, "I think she likes you."

Jeb chuckled. "Oh, sure. I have to beat the women off with a stick."

After they finished their meal, Ross led Jeb out of the pub and down the street to the dance hall.

The old, brick building had a wooden dance floor that could accommodate fifty couples easily and perhaps twice that number in a squeeze. The room was dimly lit, most of the light coming from a spot light focused on a rotating, mirrored ball hanging from the ceiling. This night, the dance floor and the surrounding areas were crowded, with two hundred or more people. The men—mostly American GIs— outnumbered the young and not-so-young English women by three or four to one. There were only a few British soldiers present.

Ross spotted a young woman he had met before. She was momentarily standing alone, and he rushed over to ask her to dance before someone else did.

Jeb stood to the side taking in the whole scene.

Ross returned from his dance. "What's the matter, Jeb? Pickin's too slim for you?"

"No, I'm just watching now. I'll find someone to dance with later." At his high school dances, Jeb had mostly stood off to the side watching others dance.

Ross went off to ask another woman to dance.

Jeb continued to watch the activity, enjoying the music and the novelty of being in an English dance hall. A few minutes later he noticed two young women arrive through the front entrance and pause to pay the entry fee. One was a blond, the other a brunette. Jeb focused on the prettier, the brunette. As she was closing her purse, after paying the fee, Jeb noticed something white fall from her purse to the floor. Neither the woman nor anyone else appeared to have seen it fall. The two women proceeded into the dance hall, found an empty table, and sat down.

Jeb headed toward the front door, spotted the white object—a folded piece of paper, apparently a note—and picked it up. Without reading it, he walked toward the table the two women had taken. As he approached and got a closer look at the brunette, he was struck by her beauty. Her auburn hair, neatly brushed, was the first thing he noticed, followed by her brown eyes that sparkled in the reflected light. She wore red lipstick and a hint of rouge. Her dress revealed a modest amount of cleavage. He felt his heart rate increase. "Excuse me, miss."

The young woman looked up and politely cut him off. "Sorry, but no thanks."

"But…" Jeb replied.

"Sorry, you Yanks are off limits for my friend and me."

"But…"

"Seriously—off limits," she said louder and more firmly.

People at the next table looked at him.

Jeb felt his face begin to flush. He held out the piece of paper and said, with a hint of anger, "You dropped this."

The woman shook her head and held up her right hand with the palm facing Jeb. "I said 'no.'"

Jeb grasped her wrist and turned her palm up. The warmth and softness of her skin sent a wave of excitement through him.

"Stop," she said, trying to pull her arm back.

"Let her go," said the blonde, in a voice loud enough to attract the attention of more people at the adjacent tables. A man in civilian clothes stood up at one of the tables, as if ready to come to the young woman's aid.

Jeb placed the paper in her hand. "This is yours. You dropped it when you came in." He released her hand, turned, and walked away.

"What was that all about?" asked the blonde.

"Some ruse about a piece of paper." The brunette looked at the paper. She started to toss it on the floor but then hesitated and unfolded it.

"What is it?"

"Oh, my. It's a note someone gave me at work. It must have fallen out of my purse when we paid the entrance fee."

"Well, that's a relief," said the blonde. "I thought maybe he was going to mug you."

"I feel foolish."

"You didn't know the paper was yours."

"I was rude, and I'm sure I embarrassed him."

"He'll get over it."

"I'm going to apologize."

"You can't be serious."

The brunette looked around the room, spotted Jeb, who was sitting at a table by himself across the room, and stood.

"Katherine, you really shouldn't," said the blonde.

Katherine started across the dance floor toward Jeb.

Jeb saw her walking in his direction. He looked to the side but kept her in his peripheral vision. Her walk was graceful and poised. He looked down and took a sip of beer.

She came up to his table. "Excuse me."

Jeb looked up at her and then stood.

"That was my paper," she said, with a chastened smile.

"I know. I saw you drop it."

"Well, thank you for being kind."

"I…" Jeb hesitated, trying to think of something to say.

"I was rude to you," she said. "Will you accept my apology?"

Jeb hesitated. "Yes, of course. Oh, but there's one condition."

"A condition? What condition?"

"Will you dance with me?"

"Oh, I really can't."

"I promise not to step on your toes just to get even," he said, smiling.

"Well,…"

"Just one dance."

"I guess one dance won't hurt. I do owe you."

"My name is Jeb, Jeb Fletcher."

"I'm Katherine, Katherine Tefford."

As they walked onto the dance floor, Katherine looked over at her friend, who was shaking her head.

The band was playing a slow tune. Katherine turned toward Jeb. He took her right hand with his left and placed his right hand on the small of her back. He felt his heart beat faster. He hadn't touched a girl since he graduated from high school three and a half years earlier. They began to dance.

"Why did you say we Yanks are off limits?"

"My father doesn't want me to have anything to do with you American soldiers."

"Really? Why's that?"

"Well, he says that we British are grateful that America is now involved in the war, but, as the saying goes, there's one thing, perhaps three things, wrong with you Americans."

"What's that?" asked Jeb.

"Well, as the saying goes, you Yanks are over-paid, over-sexed, and over here."

Jeb blushed, and then he laughed. "I think I'd like your father."

"I'm not so sure you would."

When the song ended, Jeb escorted Katherine back to her table, which was empty. Katherine's girlfriend was standing on the dance floor with a British soldier.

"Could we sit and talk for a while?" asked Jeb.

"Well, I guess there's no problem with talking," Katherine said as they sat down at the table.

The girlfriend, Anne, returned, and Katherine introduced Jeb to her. They sat and talked, and other men came to dance with Anne. Ross came over, and Jeb introduced him to the two women. Ross then continued making the circuit.

Jeb and Katherine sat talking and danced several more dances during the rest of the evening. During the last dance, Jeb asked, "May I walk you home?"

"Thanks, but no. I came with Anne, and I need to leave with her."

"May I see you again?"

"Well, I don't know."

"How about meeting here at the dance next Friday?"

"I can't make any promises. We'll see."

Chapter 47

The next Friday evening, Jeb and Ross again walked into Waterbridge and stopped at the Black Swan.

Sipping a beer, Jeb glanced at his watch as they waited for the waitress to serve their meals. "I've been looking forward to this evening all week."

Ross arched his eyebrows and smiled. "Really? I can think of only three reasons. First, you think the food at this pub is great, in which case you need to have your taste buds tested. Second, you're smitten with the waitress, in which case you need to have your eyes examined. Or, third, you think some girl you met at the dance hall might be, even in the slightest way, interested in seeing you again, in which case you need a serious ego check."

Jeb laughed. "Wrong on all accounts. I just wanted to sit in a pub and listen to your sterling wit all evening."

"You could do a lot worse, pal, and maybe you will."

They both laughed. The waitress brought them their food, and they ordered more beer to wash it down.

Jeb glanced at his watch a couple of times while they ate. When they had finished, he said, "It's after eight. Maybe we should head on over to the dance hall."

"Anxious, are we?"

They paid their bill and left the pub.

As soon as they entered the dance hall, Jeb looked for Katherine. He didn't see her. He circled the perimeter of the dance floor, to no avail, and returned to where Ross was standing.

"What's the matter? Did she stand you up?"

"She was noncommittal last week. I just hoped she might be here."

"There are other fish in the sea. Maybe you'll hook one."

Jeb and Ross found a table and ordered a couple of beers.

Fifteen minutes later, Jeb saw Katherine and Anne come in the front entrance. His pulse quickened. "There she is."

Ross looked over at the women. "Well, well. I guess I should never again underestimate the charms of a Virginia gentleman. I presume you're going to abandon me, your faithful American comrade-in-arms, for the wiles of the English."

"I certainly hope so, if she'll have me. The English are our allies, you know." Jeb left the table and walked toward Katherine and Anne.

The two women had their backs to Jeb as he approached.

"Good evening, ladies."

They turned to face him. "Hello, Jeb," said Katherine, with a warm smile.

"Hello," said Anne, coolly.

"I have a table on the far side. Would you like to join me?"

"That would be nice," said Katherine.

Ross had left the table and was talking with a couple of young women standing at the bar.

Jeb held the chairs for Katherine and Anne as they sat down. "May I get you something from the bar?"

The women expressed their preferences, and Jeb left to get the drinks.

"He's seems more handsome tonight than he did last week," said Anne, "but you're headed for trouble, Katherine. You know how strongly your dad feels about the Yanks."

"Don't worry, Anne. I can handle it."

Jeb returned with the drinks, and the three sat and chatted for a while. Jeb asked Katherine to dance, and they stepped onto the dance floor for a slow Glenn Miller tune. "I had begun to think you might not come tonight."

"I had to think about it, but I'm glad I'm here."

"Me, too."

They danced to several songs, all slow. Jeb inhaled the sweet scent of her perfume. *Dancing with a beautiful girl, with perfume—what a contrast to the musty smells and coarse life of the Army.*

When they returned to the table, Anne said something quietly to Katherine and left to sit with some other friends.

After a couple of hours of talking and dancing, Jeb asked, "May I walk you home?"

"I'd like that. Anne has made other plans."

They left the dance hall and strolled slowly through the streets of the quaint town. The blackout was in effect, and black curtains covered the windows of the houses. The streetlights were not lit, but a full moon cast a romantic glow over the town. Jeb and Katherine chatted about their lives. After nearly a half hour, they stopped in front of a modest row house, a two story brick building, whose façade had two windows on the second floor and a large window and door on the first. The houses on each side were similar in design.

"This is where I live. Would you like to come in for a few minutes?"

"That would be nice."

"We'll have to be quiet. My parents are asleep upstairs." Katherine unlocked the door, and they stepped inside.

Katherine turned on a lamp in the living room. The room had a sofa, two chairs, and two small tables. Blackout curtains covered the windows.

Katherine sat on one end of the sofa and invited Jeb to sit on the other end. She spoke in a low voice, and they chatted quietly about the dance and their lives.

After some fifteen minutes, a deep voice from upstairs called down, "Katherine, it's time to come to bed."

Katherine blushed and called back, "All right, Dad. I'll be up in a minute." She looked at Jeb, shrugged her shoulders, and smiled. "I guess it's time for you to leave." She stood and walked Jeb to the door. She stepped outside, and Jeb followed. She closed the door behind her, and they stood together on the stoop near the door.

"Good night, Jeb. I had a nice time."

"So did I." He slipped his arms around her and kissed her.

She returned the kiss lightly and then broke away. "I have to go."

Jeb took her hand. "Next Friday?"

"Next Friday," she replied, smiling shyly as she went inside.

Chapter 48

The following morning when Katherine came down for breakfast with her parents, her father put down his newspaper and looked at her. "Who brought you home last night?"

Katherine picked up a piece of toast and began spreading some jam on it. "A friend I met at the dance."

"I thought I heard an American accent."

"He is an American." Katherine looked down and bit off a piece of toast.

"Katherine, look at me."

Katherine put down the toast and looked at him.

"I thought I warned you to stay away from the Americans."

"You did," said Katherine, glancing at her mother, "but…"

He cut his daughter off in mid-sentence. "Those Americans can be trouble."

"Henry, please let the girl finish what she was going to say," said Sarah Tefford.

"All right, Sarah, I'll let her finish. So, what do you have to say for yourself, Katherine?"

"I met him at the dance hall. He was kind and did me a favor. I was returning the favor."

"What kind of favor did he do for you?" asked Sarah.

"I unwittingly dropped a note from the office out of my purse. He saw it fall on the floor. He retrieved the note and brought it to me."

"So," said her father, frowning, "you consider something so insignificant as that as a reason to disregard my warning?"

"That's not all. When he brought the paper to me, I thought he was making something up in order to meet me. I remembered your warning, Dad. I was very rude to him and embarrassed him in front of others. After he left the table, I looked at the paper, and, indeed, it was mine and had fallen from my purse."

"Oh, dear," said Sarah, taking a sip of tea.

"I felt bad about being so rude, so, I went over and apologized."

"That was the right thing to do," said Sarah, nodding.

"What happened next?" asked Henry, sipping his tea.

"He said he would accept my apology if I would dance one dance with him."

Henry put his tea cup down noisily. "Those Americans are slick. Can't you see that?"

"He's actually very nice."

"Where's he from? I'll bet he's one of those slick New Yorkers."

"He's from a small rural town in Virginia."

"What's his name?" asked Sarah.

"Jeb. Jeb Fletcher."

"'Fletcher' sounds like a good English name, don't you think, Henry?" said Sarah.

"Well, 'Jeb' sounds to me like he's named after that wild general from the South in the American Civil War—Jeb Stuart," said Henry.

"He told me that 'Jeb' is his nickname, and that his real name is 'Jebidiah,' which is a mixture of Jedidiah in the Bible and Jeb Stuart."

Henry shook his head. "Those Americans. Why would anyone invent a name, when there are so many good names already available? Sounds like a mongrel to me."

Sarah poured her husband some more tea. "Henry, I share your concerns about all these young American men over here, but they've come to help us, and we shouldn't be rude to them. It doesn't sound like this young man can be all bad. He must have English roots, with the name Fletcher and living in Virginia. And it sounds like his people are good, Bible-reading Christians."

"Look, Katherine," said Henry, "you're a grown girl, but I want to warn you again about these Americans. I know they're our allies, and some of them can be very nice, even charming. But let me be frank. These boys are a long way from home. They don't have their parents and the people in their communities watching them. They're young men, with certain urges and desires."

"Henry," interrupted Sarah, shaking her head.

"Let me finish. These young men are attracted to young women—our young women here in Britain. They know they'll likely be going into combat before long, and they know there's a chance they'll be killed. Some of them may want to experience life and all its pleasures now."

"Henry, really!" interjected Sarah again.

"These men know that once they leave England, they'll probably never return, never have to face the consequences of any of their actions here. Even if your American soldier friend is the utmost gentlemen, the bottom line, Katherine, is that if you become friendly with him, he may be killed or badly wounded before the war is over. If he survives, he won't come back to England. He'll return to America and his family and settle down there and marry an American girl. Getting involved with an American can only mean heartbreak and trouble."

"Your father makes some excellent points, dear."

"Thank you both," said Katherine, looking up from her breakfast. "You've given me a lot to think about, and I know you have my best interests at heart." She glanced at her watch, took a last sip of her tea, and stood up. "I hate to run, but I'm meeting Anne in a half hour to go shopping and have lunch. I'll see you this afternoon."

* * * * * * * *

For the next several Friday and Saturday nights, Katherine and Jeb met at the dance hall and later walked to the Tefford home. As they talked, Jeb was fascinated with Katherine's English accent, the way she said "lahnd" for "land" and "jawhb" for "job." Katherine was equally charmed with Jeb's Virginia drawl and his use of American idioms.

When Jeb took Katherine home after the dances, her parents never came downstairs to meet him, and there were no more calls from upstairs. Katherine and Jeb spent more and more time sitting on the couch, talking, kissing, and becoming increasingly intimate.

Chapter 49

April 1944, Slapton Sands, UK

By the spring of 1944, Jeb had whipped his platoon into shape. The men were now disciplined, responsive to orders, physically fit, and well trained.

Captain Looper, however, said nothing to Jeb about what he, as a brand new lieutenant, had accomplished.

In preparation for the invasion of France, Company N was scheduled to take part in a major training exercise in southern England. The location was a beach on the English Channel, an area known as Slapton Sands, where the geography resembled the beaches across the Channel in Normandy.

On April 27, the men of Company N and other companies loaded onto large transport ships, each known as an LST, or Landing Ship Tank, to practice an over-the-beach landing. Company N was together on one ship, below the main deck.

As the naval craft approached Slapton Sands, German E-boats, similar to American patrol or PT boats, suddenly appeared and attacked the transport craft.

A torpedo, launched from one of the E-boats, struck the ship carrying Company N. The explosion rocked the craft and dazed the men. Smoke began filling the compartments.

Captain Looper yelled, "Up the ladders, men." As the men began climbing out, fire appeared at the top of the ladders. Looper yelled for the men to move back down, away from the ladders and back to midships.

Jeb hurried over to Looper. "Sir, give me a second to check out what's at the top of the ladders. We need to get out of here quickly."

"Didn't you see the fire up there?" shouted Looper. "We've got to move back now." He took off running through the men. "Move! Back to midships!"

Jeb grabbed Sergeant Bricker by the arm. "Let the other platoons go first in following Captain Looper. Hold Second Platoon here until I can check out the ladder. I don't like the idea of moving the men to midships."

As the other platoons began moving back into a corridor, Jeb climbed one of the ladders. As he approached the top, the fire disappeared. He peered out onto the deck and saw a burning tarpaulin that had slid to one side. He climbed back down and shouted to Bricker, "Get Second Platoon up the ladders. I'll try to get the rest of the company to reverse course and come back to these ladders."

As Bricker directed Second Platoon up the ladders, Jeb ran down the corridor after the rest of the company. Another explosion, this one at midships, rocked the boat and threw Jeb against a wall. Fire erupted ahead, and the corridor between him and the rest of Company N was now blocked. Jeb ran back to one of the ladders, reaching it as the last few men of Second Platoon began climbing. Bricker and Jeb were the last two out. Jeb ordered the men to inflate their lifesaver belts and jump overboard. Minutes later, the ship sank.

Jeb's platoon, picked up within an hour by other Allied ships, survived, but over 500 soldiers, including Captain Looper and the majority of Company N, and nearly 200 sailors were killed in the attack. Many others were wounded. Survivors were ordered to keep the incident secret.

* * * * * * *

The survivors of Company N were to be dispersed to other units. Captain Dooley of Company O heard of Jeb's fate. One of his platoon leaders had just been seriously injured in training. Dooley put in a by-name request for Jeb to be assigned to Company O. If the request were granted, Jeb would be back with his old company, this time as a platoon leader.

Chapter 50

May 1944, Portsmouth, UK

The staff of Portsmouth Army Hospital got a real taste of combat medicine as the survivors of the attack at Slapton Sands were rushed to their hospital. The first day of receiving and treating hundreds of wounded was near chaos. The staff felt exhausted but relieved at the end of the day when the stream of incoming casualties stopped. Some of the men had been injured in the initial blasts of the torpedoes, others had been shot, and many had been burned.

When the casualties arrived by ambulance, Ginny helped move ten of the men into her unit. None of her patients were burn victims; those were taken to a special ward.

The senior man among the ten new patients was Captain Warren Langford, an infantry company commander. Langford was a graduate of the U.S. Military Academy at West Point and a career Army officer. He was over six feet tall, tanned, and handsome.

Once the men had been settled into her unit, Ginny began to introduce herself, starting with the senior man, Langford. In a bright and cheery voice, she said, "Good morning, Captain. I'm Second Lieutenant Virginia Jackson. I'll be the chief nurse in this unit."

Langford, who was medicated but not so much that he could not appreciate Ginny's good looks, said, "Well, hello. Have I died and gone to heaven?"

Ginny smiled. "No, Captain. Just to Portsmouth Army Hospital. Welcome."

"Thanks. I'm Warren Langford. You may call me Warren."

"Sorry, sir, but hospital policy is to call all superior officers by their rank and last name."

"What can I call you?"

"'Lieutenant Jackson' or 'Nurse Jackson.'"

"I call all my subordinate officers by their first names."

Ginny smiled. "I'm not one of your subordinate officers." She turned and walked across the room toward another patient.

Langford, raising his voice, called to her, "Oh, Virginia, when you come back could you please bring me a glass of water?"

The other men, who had been listening to the exchange, laughed. One of them, in a voice lower than Langford's but still loud enough for everyone to hear, said, "'Virginia,' huh? I once had a girl friend named 'Virginia.' I called her 'Virgin' for short, but not for long."

The rest of the men roared with laughter. Langford started to laugh. Then he saw Ginny flush with embarrassment, and he stopped. In a voice loud enough to be heard over the dying laughter, he said, "Lieutenant Jackson, could I please speak with you for a moment?"

Ginny glowered at Langford. She picked up a pitcher of ice water from a stand and walked to Langford's bed. She stood holding the pitcher, hesitating, as if contemplating what to do with the contents.

In almost a whisper, which the men couldn't hear, Langford said, "I'm sorry. I apologize. I was being a horse's ass, if you'll excuse the expression. I set a bad example."

Ginny picked up a glass from the night stand next to Langford's bed, poured him a glass, handed him the water, and walked away.

Langford said, loud enough for the others to hear, "Thank you, Lieutenant Jackson."

* * * * * * * *

Several days later, after one of the several surgeries Langford would require, he awoke, in a private recovery room, to find Ginny sitting beside him. "Hello," he said. "This is a nice surprise, to wake up and find you here."

"I'm off duty, and I just wanted to see how your surgery went."

"Have you been here long?"

"About half an hour. I came by to check on you. I decided to stay a while after you called out."

"I called out? What did I call out?"

"You called out what happens to be my nickname."

"I did? What's your nickname—'Lieutenant'?"

Ginny laughed. "It's 'Ginny,' short for 'Virginia.'"

"So, I called out 'Ginny'?"

"Yes, I tried to rouse you, but you were still under the anesthesia. So, is there a Ginny in your life?"

"No. At least not yet...but one can always hope."

Ginny laughed. "Well, I've got to go. You need to rest. Take care."

"Come back tomorrow," he said, pausing and then adding, "please."

"We'll see."

"I'll let you see my scars," he said with a wide grin.

Ginny laughed. "Nothing I haven't seen before."

"Really?"

"Really, and as scars go, yours aren't much to talk about." She turned and walked out the door.

Langford burst out laughing and then winced as his guffaws pulled his stitches.

Chapter 51

May 1944, Waterbridge

After the Slapton Sands attack, Jeb felt shaken. He had come close to death. He was certain that the actual invasion would be much worse than the disastrous practice run. He began to wonder if he would survive the invasion, let alone the war. He knew that the infantry was the most exposed of the ground combat forces. He also knew that, among the infantry ranks, second lieutenants were rumored to have the lowest survival odds.

He drew strength from thinking of Katherine. She had become his hope, his main reason to live. His mother and Halesford seemed far away.

He knew that when the survivors of Company N were dispersed to other units, he might be assigned to some area away from Waterbridge and Katherine.

The next Friday evening, Jeb again met Katherine at the dance hall and walked her home. As they sat on the couch kissing, Jeb pulled away.

Katherine looked at him, knitting her brow. "What's the matter, Jeb?"

He took her hand and looked into her eyes. "Katherine, I love you."

She smiled. "I love you, too, Jeb."

They kissed, and then Jeb pulled away. He smiled for a second and then the smile disappeared. "Could we try to get away, just the two of us?"

"Get away? What do you mean?"

"I think I'm going to be transferred before long. Our evenings may be coming to an end."

"Where would we go? When?"

"I have a pass for next weekend. We could go to London."

Katherine did not respond immediately.

Jeb looked down. "It was only an idea."

"You mean overnight?"

"Yes, but if you don't...."

Katherine reached out and touched his cheek. "We could try."

Jeb took Katherine in his arms and kissed her hard. She returned the kiss.

They began planning the trip to London.

* * * * * * * *

A week later, early on Saturday morning, Jeb and Katherine arrived separately at the train station in Waterbridge at the agreed time. They kept apart and made only furtive visual contact. Each purchased a ticket to London, and they sat apart on separate benches in the station. When the train arrived, they let others from the town get on first. Then they stepped aboard the last car, which no one else from Waterbridge had entered. Once on the train, they sat together and began talking about London.

Reaching the city, they took a cab from the train station to an intersection near a hotel that a fellow officer had recommended. Jeb and Katherine had agreed that they should not be seen together in the hotel, so Katherine waited on a park bench while Jeb walked to the hotel and reserved a room. After dropping his bag in his room, he returned to the park. Katherine then left Jeb sitting on the bench while she walked to the hotel, reserved a separate room, and dropped her bag in her room. When she returned to Jeb in the park, it was shortly after noon.

Jeb stood and took her hand. "Let's get something to eat and then see London."

"Sounds like fun."

They stopped at a restaurant and then walked around central London in the early afternoon, looking at the sights and browsing in the windows. By four o'clock, they had had enough of sightseeing.

Jeb took Katherine's hand. "Let's go back to the hotel."

"I could use a rest," she said, squeezing his hand.

As they approached the hotel, Jeb suggested that Katherine go in first. He would follow a few minutes later. He would go to his room and then come to hers.

In her room, Katherine unpacked and freshened up.

Jeb went to his room and in a couple of minutes stepped out into the hall. A couple was walking toward him. He clicked his fingers and said, "Oh, darn," as though he had forgotten something, and went back into his room.

A half minute later, he opened his door and stuck his head out. The hall was clear. He hurried to the stairs and climbed, two steps at a time, to the third floor. He went to Room 322 and knocked. Katherine opened the door, and he quickly stepped in, while she shut the door behind him.

He took her in his arms. "We're finally alone."

"Finally," said Katherine, pulling him closer to her.

They kissed, but then Jeb pulled away. He looked intently at Katherine, whose eyes were now wide with confusion. "Are you sure you want to do this?" he said. "It's O.K. if you don't."

"I'm sure," she said with a slight smile, as she moved back into Jeb's arms.

They kissed again. Then they began helping each other undress. Their hearts raced, but they took time to look at each other's bodies, in this first-time experience for each.

Katherine pulled back the bedspread and slipped in under the covers. She patted the place next to her. Jeb climbed in under the covers beside her, and they began a journey of which each had dreamed. At first they kissed tenderly. Then their kisses became increasingly passionate, and they began exploring and fondling each other.

"Just a minute," said Jeb, as he paused and sat up on the edge of the bed.

"Are you all right?" asked Katherine.

"I just need a moment." Jeb reached for a condom that he had placed on the nightstand and put it on.

He slid back under the covers and again embraced Katherine. They kissed deeply, and then he pushed himself up and was atop her.

"Gently," she said.

He tried to be gentle as they became one. They moved slowly, savoring the new, long-awaited feeling. They soon moved faster, their breathing and pulses quickening. Then they were racing rhythmically, breathing hard, and calling out, until they lost themselves in orgasmic ecstasy. Fulfilled, they collapsed and lay back, awash with pleasure.

They pulled the sheet and blanket up over their perspiring bodies and lay there, cuddling. They fell asleep and slept for more than an hour. When they awoke, they were famished. They freshened up, got dressed, and went out in search of something to eat. They returned to the hotel at 10:00 p.m. and were in bed, naked, by 10:03. Not until midnight did they again fall asleep. They slept satisfied and exhausted the rest of the night, except for a brief interlude of lovemaking around 5:00 a.m.

Later in the morning, Jeb and Katherine checked out of the hotel separately, had breakfast in a nearby restaurant, and caught a cab to the train station. They bought return tickets and headed separately to the departure platform for the train that would take them to Waterbridge. As they had agreed, they climbed into the last train car and sat at opposite ends. They could at least look at one another. Katherine saw some people she thought she recognized who lived in Waterbridge, so she shook her head to indicate to Jeb that they should remain seated apart. They longed for each other, to at least hold hands, but they felt compelled to keep apart for appearances sake.

When they reached Waterbridge, several passengers got off. One, an acquaintance of Katherine, greeted her. Katherine glanced back at Jeb, and they nodded goodbye to each other. Then Katherine walked home alone, while Jeb hiked out to his camp in the countryside.

Chapter 52

May 1944, Portsmouth

Jeb's hunches about a transfer were correct. He received orders to report in two days to his old company in the 29ᵗʰ Infantry Division, Company O. He made a date with Katherine for the next evening. He also decided to make one last visit to the Company N survivors of Slapton Sands, who were recuperating at the Army hospital in Portsmouth. He had visited twice before. He borrowed a jeep and drove to the hospital.

As he was walking down the hall, he passed a nurse, who was reading a chart on a clipboard as she walked. He stopped, turned around as she continued walking down the hall, and called, "Ginny?"

The nurse stopped and turned toward him. "Yes?" she said, looking up from her chart and expecting to see someone from the hospital staff. She didn't recognize him at first. It had been four years since they had seen each other at their high school graduation. "Jeb? Jeb Fletcher, is that really you?"

"It's me, Ginny. Gee, it's good to see you—to see a familiar face from back home." *She's even prettier than she was in high school—a more mature beauty.*

"I almost didn't recognize you, Jeb. You've changed." *Is this really Jeb Fletcher? He's no longer the young-looking teenager. He's taller and quite handsome, with that dark hair. An officer, too.*

"I guess the Army can do that to you. You haven't changed much, Ginny. I would have recognized you anywhere."

"I hope that's a compliment."

"Oh, most definitely."

"What are you doing here, Jeb? I heard from my folks that you were in the Army, but I didn't know where."

"Have you got a few minutes to talk? Maybe over a cup of coffee?"

"Sure. I'm just getting off duty. There's a canteen down the hall. I'll drop off this clipboard on our way."

They chatted as they walked to the canteen and as they sat and drank coffee.

"I'm here to say good-bye to some of the men in my company who were injured recently."

"At Slapton Sands?"

"Yes."

"There's a lot of them here. That was tragic."

"Yes, we were lucky to have any survivors."

"Were you there?"

"I'm one of the lucky ones. I only got wet when we abandoned the ship."

"We're doing the best we can for them."

"I'm sure you are. My mother said in one of her letters that you had joined the Army Nurse Corps, but I had no idea where you were stationed. How long have you been in the Army?"

"It's been almost a year now, since last June when I finished nursing school."

"You went to school in Richmond, didn't you? I tried to keep track of you—and, of course, other classmates—but then things got busy."

"Yes. After school in Richmond, I joined the Army Nurse Corps at Camp Lee and then was stationed at Fort Dix before coming here in January. So, bring me up to speed on what all you've been doing since graduation."

"Well, I went to work at Gibbs Lumber Yard, and then Cal Barton and I joined the Guard with Company O."

"Cal Barton. Where's he now?"

"He's in Company O here in England."

"Gee, it's a small world—three of us from the Class of 1940 here in the Army in England. Where else have you been?"

"Well, we got called up to active duty in February 1941. We trained at Fort Meade in Maryland, in the Carolinas, and in Florida. We arrived over here in October 1942 and have been training ever since. I went back to Fort Benning, in Georgia, for Officer Candidate School last summer. When I came back to England after OCS, I was assigned to the 4th Infantry Division. Now I just got orders transferring me back to my old company, Company O, in the 29th Infantry Division."

"Is anyone else from Halesford over here?"

"Yes. Dick Drumheller's in our battalion."

"Dick Drumheller. *It seems like ages since I've seen Dick. I'd like to know what happened to him, but I don't think I want to inquire further.* Well, I guess that makes four of us over here from the Class of 1940. Please tell Cal and Dick 'hello' for me when you see them."

"I will." Jeb finished his coffee. "I'd better get going. I've got to be back at base in two hours, and I want to visit several of the men here. It's been wonderful seeing you, Ginny."

"You, too, Jeb."

Ginny wrote her parents that night, being careful not to include things that might get her in trouble with the military censors:

> Dear Mother and Dad,
>
> Thanks for your letters. I'm proud that you both are involved in so many volunteer projects to help the war effort. What the folks back home are doing is very important for us over here.
>
> Liz and I have been able to do some sightseeing. We haven't been able to see much, but what we've seen is beautiful. Spring here is almost as

pretty as back home, but I miss spring in Virginia—my favorite time of the year.

I'm sorry I haven't written more often, but we've been busy.

I miss you both dearly. I wish I could come home for a visit or you could come here for a visit, but, of course, that's impossible.

We've been taking care of men who have become ill or injured in training accidents. I can't say much, but now I'm really beginning to feel that I'm making a contribution.

In case you have any worries, I'm perfectly safe here. It's almost like being back home in Virginia.

I met an officer today. He's actually a patient of mine. He gave me a hard time at first. I think he's pretty full of himself, but he later apologized. He's quite handsome, and I think he can be charming when he wants to be.

Oh, you'll never guess who came to the hospital today—Jeb Fletcher. He came to visit some men in his unit who are hospitalized here. We just happened to run into each other in the hall. He's changed a lot from how I remembered him in high school. He seems more mature. He's a nice-looking young man. We had a good chat. He said that Cal Barton and Dick Drumheller are over here, too. It seems like ages since we were all in high school together.

I must get to bed now. It's been
a long day. I love you both and miss
you.

       Love,
       Ginny

Chapter 53

With Warren being assigned to Ginny's ward, the two saw each other every day. As he improved, he received passes to leave the hospital for half days and then full days, but he had to return at night. One day he invited Ginny out for dinner and a movie. At the theater, they sat in the last row and held hands. On the way back to the hospital, while strolling through a park, he kissed her.

One Friday in early May, after several dates, Warren again asked Ginny to go out to dinner with him. During the meal, she thought he seemed unusually serious. As they were finishing dessert, Warren took her hand. "I received orders today. I'm to return to my unit tomorrow."

Ginny's brow wrinkled, and she squeezed his hand. "So soon?"

"I'm afraid so. Will you write me?"

"Of course."

"Ginny, we haven't known each other for long, but I know you're special. I'd like to look for you when this is over."

"I'll be waiting," she replied. She had never felt about any other man as she felt about Warren. She thought she was really falling in love for the first time in her life.

They took out pens and paper and exchanged the addresses of their military units and the homes of their parents back in America. Then they strolled back to the hospital in silence, holding hands. They kissed in an alcove of the hospital until two nurses came along. Warren was gone the next morning.

* * * * * * * *

In mid-May, the nurses at the Portsmouth hospital received a notice calling for volunteers to fill vacancies in an Army evacuation hospital. The evacuation hospital would be deployed onto the European continent shortly after the invasion, whenever that might be, and would treat seriously injured soldiers until they could be flown or transported by ship back to Britain. Additional nurses were needed to bring the unit to maximum strength. Ginny and Liz discussed the notice over a cup of coffee during a break.

"What do you think, Ginny?" asked Liz.

Ginny did not respond immediately.

"If we go to France," said Liz, sipping her coffee, "we'll be part of the real action. We might actually save lives, rather than merely caring for those who have been stabilized."

Ginny stared at her coffee. "I don't know. The notice says the evacuation hospital would be only a few miles behind the front lines. It would be a lot more dangerous than remaining here in England."

"Well, evacuation hospitals are still miles behind the front lines. It's not like the field hospitals, which are much closer to the actual fighting. I think we'd be safe. Even if we stay here in England, we might get hit by one of those German buzz bombs or rockets." She smiled and added, "Or we might even get hit by one of those crazy Army truck drivers."

"Yes, but here at least we have the entire English Channel separating us from the Germans."

"True, but don't you think the seriously wounded should have the best nurses to care for them as quickly as possible? And we're the best, aren't we?" Liz said with a smile.

"Were you ever on a debate team, Liz? You've almost convinced me—almost."

Liz took a last sip of coffee and pushed her cup away. "Don't you think that Warren's unit will be one of the first to go up against the Germans?"

"That's hitting below the belt, Liz."

"I'm only stating the obvious. He's in the infantry."

Ginny sat still, quietly thinking. Then, in a barely audible voice, she said, "O.K."

"O.K.? O.K. what?"

"O.K., let's volunteer." Ginny sighed. *I really don't have a good feeling about this. Just what are we getting ourselves into?*

Chapter 54

Early the next day, the chief nurse of the Portsmouth Army Hospital came to the ward where Ginny and Liz were working. She handed each of them a paper. "Your orders just arrived."

"Already?" Ginny took the orders and started reading them.

"That's really fast," said Liz, merely glancing at the paper.

"The Army can move fast when it wants to. As you can see, you're to report to the evacuation hospital this afternoon. It's temporarily located just outside Portsmouth. I'll get someone to take over your shift, and then I'll find you a car and driver to take you there. You'd better say your goodbyes and go pack. You'll need to change from your whites to your field uniforms."

"Thanks for all your help," said Liz. Ginny added her concurrence.

The chief nurse shook their hands. "We'll miss you both around here. Part of me wishes I was going with you, but part of me doesn't. I think I'm too old for where you're going. Take care of yourselves and take good care of the boys you'll be sending back to us."

Shortly after lunch, an Army car arrived to take them to the evacuation hospital. The driver helped load their gear into the trunk and then drove out into the countryside. After twenty minutes, he pulled the car to a stop on the side of the road next to a large field. "Here you are, lieutenants," said the driver, jumping out and opening the back door.

"But this is just a muddy field," said Liz, not moving from the car.

"Yes, with just a few tents and a lot of trucks," said Ginny. "Are you sure this is where we're supposed to go?"

"Yes, ma'am. This is the place. I was told that your unit just arrived a few hours ago. They're still setting up. I think you may be in time to help."

"Where exactly are we to go?" asked Ginny.

"Oh, they're expecting you. Here comes a jeep now, probably coming to pick you up." The driver pointed to a jeep approaching from across the field. As the jeep neared, he unloaded their gear onto the ground. "Good luck." He climbed into the car and drove away.

Rain began to fall as the two nurses waited for the jeep. The rain was light at first but then turned heavy.

"It's miserable out here," said Liz, wiping the rain from her face.

Ginny looked down at her uniform, which was turning darker and darker as it absorbed more and more of the rain. "And we gave up that nice, dry hospital for this?"

The jeep pulled up, and the driver, a corporal, climbed out. "Welcome to the 52nd Evacuation Hospital. Lieutenants Jackson and Hawkins, right? I'm Joe Giardi." He held out his hand.

Ginny and Liz shook hands with him.

"Sorry about this rain," said Giardi, loading their gear into the jeep. "If you'll climb in, we'll head for some cover."

They climbed in, and Giardi turned the jeep around and headed toward the tents. The rain pelted everyone in the topless jeep as Giardi drove across the field. "I don't know whether you'll want to change into something dry or not. We have a five-mile hike tonight after supper."

"A five-mile hike—at night and in the rain? You aren't serious, are you?" asked Ginny, shaking slightly from the cold rain.

"I'm afraid so. The colonel has really been busting our butts in the last couple of weeks. We've gone on four hikes and moved twice. This morning, he had us take down our tents and pack everything up on the trucks. We drove only five miles to this location. We're still setting up the tents and getting the equipment ready. He's getting us ready for something, but he's not saying what."

Giardi pulled the jeep up to one of the tents and hopped out. "This is your luxury suite. You'll share it with a couple of the other nurses. I'll take your gear to the tent door, but you'll have to take it inside. For some reason, nurses' tents are 'off limits' to us GIs." He grinned as he unloaded the gear.

Ginny glanced around the area. "Joe, where are the latrines?"

"Well, right now, the ladies room is down that avenue." He pointed down a muddy path toward the woods. "All we've had time to do so far is dig a slit trench. We'll try to put a tarp up around it to give you some privacy, but first we have to finish setting up the rest of the tents." Giardi climbed back into the jeep, calling out before he pulled away, "Chow's at 1730, the hike at 1900."

"Thanks, Joe," the two women called out almost in unison.

Liz picked up her duffel bag. "Let's get our things in out of this miserable rain."

Ginny followed. "Everything is probably soaked already. I know I'm soaked to the skin. And we're supposed to go on a hike tonight in this rain?"

The tent was empty except for four cots. Two of the cots were made up and had some gear on top of them, apparently already taken by the two other nurses.

Ginny started to take off her jacket. "Let's change into dry uniforms."

"Hold your horses," said Liz. "We don't have a lot of clothing. While we're wet, we ought to go outside and look for others. We'll need to report in, and they may want us to help set up the hospital."

Ginny began buttoning up her jacket. "You're right. But first, I've got to pee. Let's go find the latrine."

They walked down the muddy path until they came to the slit trench.

"This is it?" Ginny said, shaking her head.

"Ugh! Well, it looks like what Joe described."

The trench was about a foot wide, six feet long, and two feet deep. Dirt was piled off to the side, with a shovel stuck upright in it. The rain was soaking the freshly dug soil, muddying the whole area. On a two-foot-high stake was a roll of toilet paper, covered with a tin can. The trench was completely out in the open.

"Can you at least stand here and give me a little cover?" asked Ginny, as she started unbuttoning her pants.

Liz took off her jacket and stretched it out as Ginny straddled the trench, dropped her pants, squatted, and peed.

"My turn," said Liz, as the two women changed positions. As she squatted, Liz looked up at Ginny and smiled. "Well, we're looking for adventure, aren't we?"

Chapter 55

May and June, 1944, Waterbridge, Rockpool

The evening before he was to depart for Company O, Jeb took Katherine to dinner. He told her he would try to see her the following weekend but could make no promises. There were rumors that training would intensify, and finding transportation from Company O to Waterbridge would be a problem.

When Jeb reported in to Company O near Rockpool, he found that the men were engaged heavily in combat training. Captain Dooley and others welcomed him back. Dooley asked about his experience at Officer Candidate School, and several men asked about his visit to their hometown of Halesford, but everyone was so busy that there was little time for small talk.

Jeb saw Cal, and they chatted briefly. Cal asked how Jeb's mother was, and Jeb instantly regretted that he had not gone to visit Cal's family while he was home in Halesford. Hoping to reestablish their close ties, Jeb said, "Hey, why don't we go into Rockpool some evening and have dinner and a beer or two?"

Cal smiled but shook his head. "That would be nice, but I don't think it'll be possible. The training has really picked up, and everyone is exhausted by the end of the day. And, of course, you're now an officer, and I'm not."

Jeb grimaced. "Well, let's get together and catch up some more on what's been happening in our lives."

Jeb went to find the Second Platoon, which he was to lead. The unit was in the midst of a series of strenuous training exercises. Jeb found the platoon sergeant, Sergeant Hubbard, and immediately took command.

That evening after supper, he sat down to write Katherine and his mother. He informed Katherine that all weekend passes had been cancelled, so he would not get to see her soon. He wrote how he often thought of the weekend they had spent together in London. He said he missed her and felt her absence, especially at night when the activity of the day no longer preoccupied him.

He also wrote his mother a short note:

> Dear Mother,
>
> Thanks for all your letters. I'm sorry I haven't written you as much, but we've been very busy, and by the evening when I have some free time, I'm usually too tired to write.
>
> You know how you always say "It's a small world"? Well, it really is. I visited a hospital recently and bumped into Ginny Jackson. In her nurse's uniform, she's even prettier than I remembered her from high school.
>
> I want to let you know that I'm back in my old unit, the one I left Halesford with. I'm really glad to be back. I think Captain Dooley pulled some strings.
>
> I'm a platoon leader in our company, which I regard as an honor. I just hope I make good decisions and can return all the men back home safely.
>
> Please tell Uncle Jonah hello for me.
>
> Love,
> Jeb

Jeb thought about mentioning Katherine in his letter but decided against it. *I can't tell my mother everything, and she probably wouldn't approve of some things.*

At the end of May, Company O and other units were trucked from their camps to areas near ports in southern England. These areas were fenced and displayed on new Army maps as long ovals, gaining the nickname "sausages." Once inside the fence, the men could not leave. Military police and other guards were posted to ensure that the men were isolated from the population. General Eisenhower's command, the Supreme Headquarters Allied Expeditionary Force, did not want word to leak out that the Allies were preparing for the invasion of France. The Germans knew an invasion was coming, but they didn't know exactly when or where.

On June 2, Jeb and other officers in the 29th Infantry Division were ordered to attend a briefing. Major General Gerhardt, the division commander, addressed the group. Then a staff officer presented what he called "the big picture."

Allied forces, including the 29th Infantry Division, would cross the English Channel and land on the beaches of Normandy on June 5. The immediate mission was to secure a toehold along the coast of France to allow Allied reinforcements to pour into France and then move inland. To the best knowledge of Allied intelligence officers, the Germans believed that the Allies were not ready for the invasion and that when it did come it would be launched across the narrowest part of the English Channel, south of London and Dover, into the Pas de Calais region of France. Partly to surprise the Germans, the Allies planned to invade further west into Normandy.

The assault would be supported by over 5,000 ships and other naval craft and over 11,000 aircraft, including heavy and medium bombers, fighter aircraft, transports, gliders, and other planes. Allied aerial and naval bombardment would soften up the German defenses along the beaches. Then nine Allied divisions—five American, three British, and one Canadian—would invade by sea and air. Six of the divisions would be infantry divisions, which would deploy by sea. The other three would be airborne, including paratroopers and glider forces. There would be over 150,000 troops and nearly 20,000 airborne forces in all.

The six infantry divisions would attack into areas the Allies had designated as codenamed beaches. A British division would attack the easternmost beach, Sword Beach. A Canadian division would attack just to the west on Juno Beach. Another British division would attack in the center on Gold Beach. To the west of Gold Beach was Omaha Beach, which would be attacked by both the U.S. First Infantry Division and the 29th Infantry Division. Finally, on the far west, the 4th Infantry Division would attack onto Utah Beach. The three airborne divisions would land behind the beaches.

Following presentation of this "big picture," the officers were divided into smaller groups. Here, they were briefed on specific plans for their units. Jeb and other officers in his battalion were informed that Company O and its sister companies were assigned to attack sectors of Omaha Beach. Company O would be the first company to land in its designated sector. It would land at low tide, when the obstacles the Germans had planted on the beaches— obstacles designed to rip out the bottoms of boats or blow them up—would be exposed. Landing at low tide, however, meant that the men of Company O and other units would have to cross some 400 yards of sand before they could find cover behind the seawall or natural, elevated land features.

The briefing officers went into detail on the location of German gun emplacements, the location of German mines and obstacles, the draws to follow to get off the beaches, and the bluffs behind the beaches. They passed out maps and answered questions.

Then all the officers of the division were reassembled. Major General Gerhardt asked in a loud, deep voice, "Are you ready?"

The men, in unison, shouted back, "29, Let's Go!," the motto of their division.

Jeb and the other officers returned to Company O's area where Captain Dooley briefed Jeb and the other platoon leaders on their specific assignments.

Jeb then went to the Second Platoon area and had Sergeant Hubbard assemble the men. Jeb briefed the men on the scope of the invasion and on Second Platoon's assignment. Concluding, he said, "Men, this is what we have all been training for here in England for 20 months. We're well trained and equipped. Our air and naval forces will be pounding the German positions for hours before we land. Our task is an important one. It won't be easy. I'll do my best to see that we achieve our mission and keep our platoon intact. Are there any questions?" There were none.

Late that evening, the men of Company O sat or lay talking. Some talked, and some tried to sleep. No longer did they banter about the Civil War. Now, they talked about what they were fighting for, and about courage and fear. None of the men had been in combat, so the discussion was a theoretical one, with many theories expressed.

"We're fighting to keep our country free and to defeat the Nazis," said one man.

"I'm fighting to get this damn war over and get home to my wife and family," said a second man.

"You can say that again," said a third.

"Sure, those are good motives on a grand scale, but when the shooting starts, we're fighting for each other, for the guy right beside you," said a fourth soldier. "If any one of us shirks his duty, we'll all get killed."

"Right," said another. "We're a team. We've trained as a team, and we'll fight as a team."

"Yep," said another, "and we fight so as not to disgrace ourselves, to maintain our self-respect. I sure wouldn't want to let you guys down, and I don't want to let myself down. I just pray that God will give me courage for what I need to do."

"We also fight to make our parents, our wives if we have them, and our friends back home proud of us. We don't want to be a disgrace to our families and friends," said yet another man. "I know my parents want me to come home safely, but they also want to be proud that I did my duty."

"Right," said another. "We're probably all going to have some fear when the shooting starts—fear of being killed or wounded, of being a coward, and of failing as a soldier or as a human being. We've just got to keep focused on our mission and on supporting each other, while remembering our training."

Finally, a large, burly man, who was lying down with his eyes closed, spoke. "If you guys don't knock it off so I can get some sleep, I'll come over there and really put some fear in you."

On June 3 and 4, the men moved from the sausage holding areas to various ports along the Channel and onto transport ships. Many of the ships carried landing craft which could be lowered into the sea, each filled with some 30 soldiers or more. Aboard these landing craft, the men would head to the beaches. They would soon be able to test the theories they had debated. The invasion was planned for June 5.

Chapter 56

June 3, 1944, Halesford

The people of Halesford tried as best they could to keep up with developments in the war and to share news about their young men and women in the military. They believed that the county's former National Guard unit, Company O, and its parent division, the 29th Infantry Division, were probably in England and would be part of the anticipated invasion into continental Western Europe, but they were not certain and had no details.

Helen Fletcher had run into Ruth Jackson at the grocery store in late May. They had shared the news in the letters they had received, including the fact that Jeb and Jenny had met, wherever it was they were. Both mothers were concerned for the safety of their children, as well as for the safety of all those serving in the military from Halesford.

On Saturday afternoon, June 3, Helen was relaxing in her living room, reading the newspaper and listening to music on the radio. Shortly after 4:30 p.m., an announcer interrupted the music to say: "We interrupt this program to report that we have just received a flash announcement from London. General Eisenhower's Headquarters has announced that Allied forces have landed on the coast of France. We have no further information at this time but will keep you informed as we receive further reports. We now return you to regular programming."

Helen was overcome with emotion. She was thrilled that the invasion had begun, an invasion deemed necessary for ending the war and bringing Jeb back home, but, at the same time, she feared that Jeb might be part of the invasion force and that his safety might be at risk.

As she sat trying to deal with all the thoughts going through her head, the announcer came back on the radio. "Ladies and Gentlemen, we apologize for once again interrupting this program. We have now been informed that the report I read a couple of minutes ago about Allied forces landing on the coast of France is a mistake. That information is said to be erroneous. We regret the error. We now return you to the regular programming."

"What's going on?" Helen asked aloud. She retrieved a pen and paper and started a letter to Jeb to tell him about the announcements.

Helen found the answer to her question several days later in the *Halesford Bulletin*, which relayed a story from the *New York Times*. A 22-year-old British teletype operator working for the London Bureau of the Associated Press had been practicing June 3 on what she thought was a disconnected teletype machine. In reality, the machine was not disconnected, and it contained a previously-prepared recorded message about Allied landings in France. Somehow, the young woman caused the message to be sent to North America and Latin America. It was picked up and broadcast by 450-500 radio stations in the United States. A "kill" message was sent two minutes later when the mistake was noticed, but it was not received until after many radio stations had broadcast the first announcement.

The newspaper reported that the Germans appeared not to take the announcement seriously, with Berlin Radio reporting on June 3 that "the invasion is nowhere near."

Not reported in the media was the reaction of General Eisenhower's staff, which had worked diligently to maintain the secrecy of plans for the upcoming invasion, including the timing. The staff had been greatly upset when the erroneous report was broadcast and later greatly relieved by the German broadcast that the invasion was not near. They would have been even more relieved if they had known that Field Marshall Erwin Rommel, who was in charge of the German defenses along the English Channel, had traveled to Berlin to spend a few days there celebrating his wife's birthday and seeing Adolf Hitler.

Chapter 57

June 5 and 6, 1944, English Channel

Bad weather and choppy seas predicted for June 5 caused General Eisenhower to postpone the invasion. When the meteorologist predicted a break in the bad weather on June 6, Eisenhower gave the go-ahead. The swells in the English Channel would be only three to four feet, not the five to six feet of June 5 which might well have sunk many of the landing craft.

The outcome of the invasion was uncertain. The weather was questionable, German military intelligence and preparedness were in many respects unknown, and the adequacy of Allied planning was yet to be tested. After giving the go-ahead, Eisenhower wrote a contingency statement accepting full responsibility should the invasion fail.

Company O had been aboard a troop transport ship for two days. The men were tired and anxious. At 2:00 a.m. on June 6, they were awakened and fed breakfast.

After eating, Jeb went up on deck. He saw Cal standing by the rail, looking toward France. Jeb moved in beside him. "Hey, Cal. Well, I guess this is it."

"Yeah, Jeb, but I don't have a good feeling about it. Something in my gut just tells me we may not make it through all this."

Jeb put his hand on Cal's shoulder. "You've just got the jitters. We all do." *I have a bad premonition, too,* thought Jeb, *but I'm keeping it to myself.*

"I feel responsible for getting us involved in all this, for pressing you to join the National Guard with me."

"Don't feel responsible. We'd have been drafted anyway, and we wouldn't be nearly as well trained. We could even be fighting on some forsaken island in the Pacific."

"Maybe." Cal pulled a white envelope out of his jacket. "I've written a letter to my parents, in case I don't make it through this. If you make it and I don't, will you see that it gets mailed to them?" He slid the envelope back inside a waterproof bag stuffed inside his jacket.

"Sure. But we're going to make it through this, Cal."

The conversation was interrupted by an announcement over the ship's loud speakers. "Now hear this! Now hear this! An announcement from the Supreme Commander, Allied Expeditionary Force, General Dwight D. Eisenhower." Then came Eisenhower's voice.

Soldier, Sailors and Airmen of the Allied Expeditionary Force!

You are about to embark upon the Great Crusade, toward which we have striven these many months. The eyes of the world are upon you. The hopes and prayers of liberty-loving people everywhere march with you. In company with our brave Allies and brothers-in-arms on other Fronts, you will bring about the destruction of the German war machine, the elimination of Nazi tyranny over the oppressed peoples of Europe, and security for ourselves in a free world.

Your task will not be an easy one. Your enemy is well trained, well equipped and battle-hardened. He will fight savagely.

But this is the year 1944! Much has happened since the Nazi triumphs of 1940-1941. The United Nations have inflicted upon the Germans great defeats, in open battle, man-to-man. Our air offensive has seriously reduced their strength in the air and their capacity to wage war on the ground. Our Home fronts have given us an overwhelming superiority in weapons and munitions of war and placed at our disposal great reserves of trained fighting men. The tide has turned! The free men of the world are marching together to Victory!

I have full confidence in your courage, devotion to duty and skill in battle. We will accept nothing less than full victory!

Good luck! And let us all beseech the blessing of Almighty God upon this great and noble undertaking.

As Eisenhower's order of the day was being broadcast over the loud speakers, sailors walked around handing out paper copies to the troops. Jeb took a copy, folded it in quarters, and stuffed it in a waterproof bag inside his jacket.

He turned to Cal and held out his hand. "Good luck, Cal."

Cal shook Jeb's hand. "Good luck to you, too, Jeb. I think we'll need it."

Chapter 58

The two friends returned to Company O's area of the ship. Before long, bosons' whistles began blowing, and then an announcement came over the ship's loudspeakers: "Now hear this! Now hear this! All assault troops proceed to your debarkation areas."

The command came as a jolt. Jeb swallowed, tugged on his web belt, tightened the straps on his 60-pound backpack, and patted down his ammunition to make sure it was secure.

This was the moment the men had been preparing for, intensively for months, less intensively for years. Jeb recalled the months of training when Company O was a National Guard unit in Halesford and then the training at various military camps during summer training exercises, the intensified training when Company O had been called up to active duty in February 1941, the ratcheting up of the training after the attack on Pearl Harbor, and the further intensity when Company O arrived in Great Britain. Company O was as well trained as it could be. Now, the company would see how well it could perform and how much courage its men had.

Sailors scurried to their posts. Moments later came a second command. "Man the boats."

Captain Dooley shouted, "Company O, load up!" Jeb gave the command for his platoon, "Second Platoon, load up." He heard the waver in his voice and wished he had shouted louder. He hoped it was just the coolness of the morning. His knees and torso shook, from either the cold or the anxiety he felt, or perhaps both. His feet and hands hadn't been warm the entire time he had been in England. Maybe France would be warmer.

Nearly 200 men in Company O, minus the cooks and some others who would deploy later, climbed into six landing craft hanging from davits alongside the transport ship. They were lowered into the dark sea. The landing craft,

operated by British sailors, moved into a line formation and
began circling, while other craft were lowered into the sea.
Overhead, they heard the roar of bombers flying across the
Channel toward Normandy. Soon they saw flashes from
bombs falling on the Normandy coasts and the German
defenders.

The landing craft continued to circle. They were waiting
for the bombers and warships to pulverize the German
defenses. They were waiting for the light of dawn and for the
order to head for the beaches.

Around 5:30 a.m., the Allied battleships, cruisers, and
destroyers began firing their heavy guns, bombarding the
coast. Smaller Allied naval craft fired streams of rockets.
The noise was deafening. With each shell and rocket fired,
flashes of light lit up the darkness. The noise, the light, the
smell of gunpowder and smoke, and the pitching sea were
almost enough to overcome one's senses. Jeb felt he was in
the middle of hell. His only consolation was knowing that
the Germans were on the receiving end.

As the Second Platoon's landing craft pitched, rolled, and
yawed in the dark waves, many of the men became seasick.

"Damn, you're shaking like a wet dog," one man said to
another.

"Can't control it." muttered the second man in a weak
voice, his head bent down. "Wish I could, but I can't."

"It's pretty cold, especially for June."

"Yeah, I'm cold, but I'm sick at my stomach, too, and I'm
scared," said the shaking man, half-slumping against the side
of the boat.

A wave hit, bouncing the men into the air. The men
reached for the gunwales to steady themselves.

The shaking man bent over and vomited his breakfast
onto the floor of the boat. Men nearby started to retch and
tried to move away as best they could.

Jeb, standing next to the man, already felt queasy, and the
sight of the man vomiting was more than he could handle.
He didn't want to vomit in front of the men, but now,

involuntarily, he felt his breakfast start to come up. He turned his back to the men, hoping they wouldn't see him. He pulled out a brown paper bag each man had been issued and vomited into it. He threw the bag overboard. He was surprised how much better he felt after surrendering his breakfast. Not wanting more men to vomit into the boat, Jeb called out, in a voice that was little more than audible, "If you're going to be sick, use the bags you've been given and throw them overboard."

Another of the soldiers began retching.

"Use the damned bags," Jeb shouted.

Confirming the power of suggestion, two men immediately complied, puking their breakfast into their paper bags.

One of the men said, "I don't know what awaits us on that beach, but I'd sure like to get off this damned bucking bronco before all its rivets pop and we drown."

"You can say that again," croaked a man who had just vomited. "It's bad enough to be scared, without also being seasick. You don't seem to be scared."

"Believe me, every man here is scared."

The landing craft circled for nearly an hour before moving into an assault formation. The coxswains maneuvered the six landing craft so they would assault the beach side-by-side and land simultaneously on Omaha Beach at the scheduled time of 6:30 a.m.

Suddenly, Sergeant Hubbard shouted in an excited voice from the front of the landing craft, "Lieutenant Fletcher, we're taking on water." His voice barely carried through the deafening thunder of naval gunfire that continued to come from further out in the Channel. Water was coming in from the right front corner of the craft near the ramp and had begun to flood the deck with an inch of saltwater.

"I see it," yelled Jeb. He turned to the coxswain who stood beside him steering from the rear of the craft. "What's the problem, Yeoman?"

"I don't know, sir. We may have opened a hole when we bumped another boat as we were lowered, or we may have hit something the Jerries have planted out here. It's even possible that all this slamming up and down by the waves has ripped something apart."

"It's coming in faster," yelled Hubbard, as the water rose a couple more inches inside the boat.

"Damn, that water's cold," shouted one of the soldiers, shivering even harder.

Jeb knew that the water was 56 degrees, but he had not shared that with the men. The air was about the same. The darkness, the overcast sky, and the 12 knot wind made it seem even colder.

Jeb looked out at the five other landing craft of Company O running alongside them, then at the Allied ships behind them in the Channel. He looked at the Normandy beaches ahead and the bluffs behind the beaches. German heavy guns were firing into the Channel. He glanced down at the deck, where the water had risen to half a foot. "How far out are we?"

"Probably a thousand yards, sir," said the coxswain.

"Can we make the beach?"

"I don't know, sir. We're taking on a lot of water—and fast."

Hubbard made his way to the back of the boat. "Sir, the water's pouring in. We're in trouble. Should we warn the men—remind them how to inflate their life preserver belts?"

Jeb took a deep breath, trying to control the shiver he felt in his knees and which was threatening to rise to his chest. "All right, listen up, men," he shouted. He was embarrassed that his voice sounded high-pitched, at least to his ear. "With the water we're taking on, we don't know if we can make it to the beach. We're going to try. If we make it, you know what to do. We've trained for this for months. But in case we can't make the beach, Sergeant Hubbard is going to refresh you on how to inflate your life preserver belts. If the boat sinks, inflate your belts and stick together. One of the landing craft coming back from the beach will pick us up."

As Hubbard reminded the men how to inflate their safety devices, water continued to pour into the boat. The water was now a foot deep and increasing. Their boat was falling behind the other landing craft that continued to move toward the beach.

"It's not looking good, sir," shouted the coxswain.

"Get us in as far as you can," Jeb ordered. *After all our amphibious assault training, here we are sinking in the Channel—damn.*

The boat started to founder under the weight of the water and troops. It proceeded another fifty yards, ground to a halt, and began sinking from under the men.

"Inflate your life belts," shouted Jeb.

The men found the water rising up to their wastes and then their necks. They dropped their rifles and began trying to get the 60-pound packs off their backs. They helped each other, some cutting the straps of the packs with their knives.

Then they couldn't feel any bottom. The radio operator, who had a 70-pound radio strapped to his back, sank and was not seen again. The others, who had inflated their life belts, began treading water. Some began to pray they would be rescued.

They floated in the cold water for two hours, many of the men approaching severe hypothermia. Finally, a landing craft coming back from the beach spotted them. It stopped and picked up the 29 survivors.

The boat took them back to the transport ship. Jeb was the first off the landing craft and onto the transport. He found a division staff officer and explained what had happened. Jeb then gave instructions to Sergeant Hubbard. "We need to get the men dry clothes, new equipment and arms, and return them to Company O on Omaha Beach as soon as possible. It may require going back to England for a few days. You take charge of the men."

"Where are you going, sir?" asked Hubbard.

"I'm catching a ride to the beach. I'll see you and the men in Normandy, just as soon as you can get there," he shouted, climbing down a net toward a landing craft almost filled with men and ready to pull away.

Chapter 59

June 6, 1944, Omaha Beach

Company O, minus Jeb's Second Platoon, was the first company to land in its sector of Omaha Beach. Sister companies landed simultaneously on adjacent sectors, and other companies were scheduled to land at intervals following these initial landings.

As Jeb approached the beach aboard the landing craft on which he had hitched a ride, he saw carnage everywhere. Bodies and equipment floated in the water and lay in the sand. *These men didn't have a chance. They didn't get off the beach, and some didn't even get to the beach.*

The coxswain lowered the ramp, and Jeb and the others waded into waist-high water. Gunfire sounded from the bluffs and inland, amidst the nearly deafening fire that continued from Allied naval guns in the Channel.

The men emerged from the water and began running across the beach. Sporadic German rifle and machine-gun fire hit near them, spitting up sand, hitting some of the men. Jeb dove for cover behind the seawall. *This is the real thing—it's not training anymore.* He saw a carbine and picked it up. At least he now had a weapon.

A medical team nearby was helping the wounded. "Where's Company O?" Jeb shouted.

"They got shot up pretty bad, lieutenant," a medic shouted back, continuing to work on the injured. "What's left of them should be somewhere through that draw." He pointed to a path leading away from the beach through some small hills.

Jeb raised his head above the seawall. A bullet whizzed by, and he crouched back down below the concrete. *I can't just hunker down here. I've got to get over the wall and find Company O.* He took a deep breath and bounded up onto the seawall and then rolled over it. He ran for cover into the draw.

He proceeded down the draw for several minutes.
Rounding a bend, he saw three GIs taking cover some ten
yards away in a large hole. The hole was probably the result
of an Allied bomb or naval gun shell. One of the men stood
up, and Jeb saw movement off in the distance to the right. A
German machine gunner was turning his gun toward the
American. Jeb raced forward and hit the GI with a flying
tackle, driving both of them into the bottom of the hole, just
as bullets from the machine gun sprayed above them.

"Damn," cried the man lying on his back. "What the hell
are you doing?"

Jeb rolled off the man, staying low. The other man's voice
seemed somehow familiar.

"He just saved your life, Dick," said one of the men, as
bullets continued to fly overhead.

"Yeah," said the second man, "at great risk."

Jeb looked at the man who was still lying on his back. It
was Dick Drumheller.

"Dick, it's me, Jeb Fletcher."

Drumheller sat up and looked at Jeb. "Well, I'll be
damned."

"What unit are you men with?" Jeb asked.

"We're part of division staff," one said. "We got
separated from the others in the landing."

The German machine gunner continued to fire
sporadically over their heads.

Jeb picked up his carbine, which he had pitched into the
hole just before making the tackle. *The safest thing to do is
hunker down in this hole, but I'm expected to lead, and I
know from training what needs to be done.* "We can't stay
pinned down here. You three lay down some covering fire.
I'll try to work my way around behind that machine gun."

As the three spread out in the hole and took turns popping
up and firing toward the machine gunner, Jeb climbed out of
the hole and ran back into the draw, crouching low as he ran.
He turned left and headed around behind the machine
gunner. Reaching some bushes, he paused. Twenty yards in

front of him were the machine gunner and an assistant. The gunner fired toward the hole and waited, fired and waited. Jeb unhooked a hand grenade clipped to the front strap of his backpack, pulled the pin, and heaved it toward the Germans. The grenade exploded, killing both enemy soldiers. He hurried back down into the draw and then to the hole where the GIs waited. "I got 'em. Let's get out of here."

They began moving further inland, with Jeb in the lead. The path from the beach ran to a road. As they reached the road, rifle fire erupted from behind some trees. The four dived into the ditch alongside the road. They saw a German run from the trees in their direction and start to heave something toward them. Jeb shot the man before he could throw the projectile. The projectile fell at the man's feet and exploded, spraying dirt into the area. The Americans fired several other shots into the woods.

Minutes later, Drumheller, kneeling in the ditch a couple of yards from Jeb, yelled "Watch out!"

Jeb turned and saw another German starting to heave something toward them. Jeb shot the German, but not before he had made his throw. The projectile rolled into the ditch between Jeb and Drumheller. They could see that it was a "potato masher," a stick with a grenade on the end of it. Drumheller and Jeb glanced at each other for a split second, and then Drumheller suddenly leapt onto the grenade.

The explosion stunned Jeb. He lay there for a few seconds, trying to concentrate on where he was and what he had just seen. His ears rang. He glanced down at his body and saw no damage. He crawled over to Drumheller and rolled him over. Blood was everywhere. There were wounds to the chest and legs. A wave of nausea swept over Jeb, and he struggled not to gag. He had seen animals slaughtered on the farm, and he had seen some injuries during training, but this was different.

One of the other men crawled over. "Oh, my God."

Drumheller was unconscious.

Jeb tried to rouse him, but there was no response. "He saved my life and probably sacrificed his."

"We're you close friends?" asked one man.

"No, but we went to school together."

"Why'd he do it? Why'd he leap on that grenade?"

"I don't know. I can't explain it."

"Maybe he thought he owed you one—for tackling him and saving his life earlier," said the second man.

"Maybe," said Jeb.

"It was a hell of a thing to do," said the first man.

"Yes, it was." Jeb lay still for a moment. German gunfire raked the area around the ditch. *My God, I'm not going to survive even this morning.* He took a deep breath, and thought back to his training. "I'm going to try to get around behind those woods." Pointing to the first man, he said, "You give me some covering fire." To the second, he said, "You give Dick first aid. See if you can save him."

Jeb crawled down the ditch. His knees were shaking. When the first GI fired into the woods where they had seen gun flashes, Jeb took a deep breath, bolted out of the ditch, and ran in a crouch to the far left of where the fire was coming. He dropped down behind a fallen tree and looked around. A path led into the woods. He ran to the opening of the path and, once in the woods, carefully made his way toward the source of the gunfire. After forty yards or so he spotted two German soldiers. They had their backs to him and were firing toward the Americans in the ditch. Taking aim, he shot one in the back, then the other. He neither saw nor heard any other Germans. He retraced his way back out of the woods.

Jeb returned to the ditch. "I shot two of them. I think they were the only ones left."

The second man said, "Dick's regaining consciousness. He's in and out."

Jeb looked at Drumheller, whose eyes were now open. "Thanks, Dick. Thanks for saving my life."

In a barely audible voice, Drumheller said, "Couldn't let you be the hero." He lapsed back into unconsciousness.

Jeb shook his head and stood. To the second man, he said, "You stay here and care for him. Try to flag down some help, maybe a medic. We're going ahead to try to catch up with Company O." To the first man he said, "Come on, follow me."

Chapter 60

Jeb led the way further down the road, alert to any German ambushers or stragglers. Fifteen minutes later, rounding a bend, Jeb spotted a large group of GIs, sitting on the ground and eating rations. He looked at his watch. So much had happened, and it was only noon.

Some of the men saw Jeb and the man with him but paid them little attention. Jeb saw a group of thirty soldiers sitting off to the side eating. Their backs were to him. He thought he recognized some of them, even from behind. He walked over. "Is this Company O?"

All of the men turned to see who had spoken.

"Lieutenant Fletcher!" exclaimed Master Sergeant Buck, jumping to his feet and extending a salute, which Jeb returned. "Yes, sir, this is Company O, or what's left of us. What happened to your platoon, sir?"

"We sank in the Channel and were taken back to the transport ship. We lost all our gear. Sergeant Hubbard will get the men reoutfitted and bring them back to the beach as soon as possible. I caught a ride back to the beach. This fellow with me is from division staff. Where's Captain Dooley?"

Buck shook his head. "He's dead, sir."

"Dead?"

"Yes, sir. A mortar round hit his boat, just before the ramp dropped."

"Damn. He didn't even make it ashore. How about Lieutenant Stockton?"

"Dead, too."

"Lieutenant Trotmeyer?"

"Dead, sir. All of the officers are dead, except you."

My God, thought Jeb. "How about Cal Barton?"

"Sorry, sir, but he didn't make it either."

One of the other men spoke. "Cal got hit just as he got to the seawall. I ran over to help, but he'd taken a round right in the chest. He was still alive." The GI pulled an envelope out of his jacket. "Cal handed this to me, and then he died. It's addressed to his parents."

Jeb shuddered and then stood still, dazed. *All the other officers and Cal dead.*

Jeb held out his hand. "Let me have the envelope. I told him I'd take care of it."

The soldier handed over the envelope.

"Sir," said Buck, "I believe you're now in command of what's left of Company O. Would you like something to eat? We've scavengered some rations from around the beach."

"Thanks. Maybe later." Jeb thought for a moment. "O.K. Give the men a few minutes to finish eating and then form them up. We're going to go see if we can find another company to link up with."

"Yes, sir." Buck called out orders to the men.

As soon as the men finished eating and formed into a file, Jeb moved up behind the tenth man in the file. From there, he could see the first third of the unit and could control all of it. "Let's go," he ordered.

The men of Company O moved out. After ten minutes, they came to a wooded area. Jeb saw a path through the woods and ordered the company to halt and kneel down. He made his way to the front of the file, kneeled behind a tree, and peered down the path.

The woods reminded him of home, yet it seemed different. He looked around, trying unsuccessfully to identify the trees. He looked down at the forest floor. The earth was black, far different from the red clay back home in Virginia. The woods and earth somehow smelled different, too, somehow foreign.

A noise down the path startled him. He dropped quietly to the ground and stretched out flat in the prone position. He lay on the damp forest floor on his stomach, his left arm stretching forward in a v-shape, supporting the carbine which was pointed down the path. For a moment, he had the strange sensation of déjà vu, first of being back home hunting, and then practicing on an Army rifle range. Another noise came from down the path, and he sensed danger. He could feel the blood pulsing through his body. This was not hunting or even rifle practice. The carbine seemed heavy and unsteady.

He lay there for a couple of minutes. Down the path, nothing moved. His shallow, rapid breaths lengthened, and he relaxed a bit. Then he saw movement, only a trace of dark gray at first. The glimpse of gray grew into a man, a man who slowly appeared from around a curve in the path about 40 yards away. The gray was the uniform of a German soldier.

Jeb sighted his carbine on the chest of the man. When the German paused and looked around, Jeb tried to hold him in his sights, but the barrel and sight seemed to move back and forth. Jeb had seen the Germans that he had killed earlier as targets, not individual men, killing two with a grenade and shooting two others in the back. Now he could distinguish the face and features of the man in his sights.

Jeb thought back to the time when he was 12, and he, his father, and Uncle Jonah had gone hunting. *He believed he remembered what had happened, but he was not certain. He thought that he had seen two birds fly up from the brush almost at the same time. One rose straight up ahead, and he had fired at the bird. Almost at the same time, another bird had flown up to the left, and a second shot had rung out. Then he had heard the terrible, deep cry that came from his father. He remembered seeing his father covered in blood, dying. Everything had happened so fast. Uncle Jonah had told the sheriff that the two shots had gone off almost simultaneously and it was too confusing to say exactly what had happened.*

As Jeb kept his carbine sighted on the German, the man leaned his rifle against a tree, unbuttoned the fly of his trousers, and relieved himself. Jeb could now see the man's face. *He looks like Mike Zimmerman's dad.* The German finished, buttoned his fly, and picked up his rifle. As he started up the path toward Jeb, he suddenly alerted. He froze in place and began raising his rifle.

Jeb's arms and hands seemed to move in slow motion. He felt the cool steel on his trigger finger as he kept his carbine sighted on the soldier's chest. When the German started to aim toward Jeb, Jeb pulled the trigger. CRACK! The German fell. *I just shot another human being face-to-face. It was a clear case of self-dense. He would have shot me.* Jeb wasn't sure that he believed this rationalization, but it would do for now. He stood up, stepped out onto the path, and motioned for the men to follow.

Chapter 61

June, 1944, UK and Normandy

The staff of the evacuation hospital had trained rigorously in late May and the beginning of June. On June 6, D-Day, they watched thousands of Allied bombers fly overhead on the way to France and later as they returned to Britain. The staff learned that the invasion of Normandy was underway. Higher headquarters sent a warning order for the hospital to be prepared to deploy to France within days.

The staff received special training in climbing down rope ladders, a skill needed to transfer from a troop ship to a landing craft.

On June 10, a transportation unit trucked the staff and their equipment to a dock in Portsmouth, where the staff boarded a troop transport ship that would carry them from southern England to Normandy.

The nurses were dressed in soldiers' uniforms, altered for size. They carried 25 pound packs and bedrolls and wore helmets. They looked like petite men. They were partitioned off from the troops while they were aboard ship.

The staff arrived off the coast of Normandy late on June 11. There were hundreds of ships in the area. Many had affixed to them barrage balloons, which flew overhead to ward off enemy aircraft. The staff, both male and female, climbed over the sides of the ship and down nets into landing craft, which took them in to Omaha Beach. Destroyed equipment lay everywhere on the beach, which was pockmarked with large shell holes.

Ginny shook her head as she and Liz looked at the destruction. "Can you imagine what our troops must have gone through when they landed here five days ago?"

"It must have been hell," Liz replied.

The staff loaded onto several trucks and drove inland. Ginny and Liz sat together in the back of one of the trucks.

Dead, bloated cattle and horses lay along the roads and in the fields. The stench was sickening. Farm houses and villages lay in ruins, and fresh graves dotted the landscape. The convoy passed a temporary military cemetery, lined with white crosses. Lying to the side were bodies awaiting burial.

"This is awful," said Liz.

Ginny could not speak.

The trucks drove through an infantry unit marching forward, with men moving along on both sides of the road. The men noticed the nurses and began to whistle and yell cat calls. Some of the nurses, even though shocked by the death and destruction they were witnessing, began to wave to the men. The whistles and yells increased. Other nurses joined in, and a few started blowing kisses. The men yelled and whistled even louder, and soon all the nurses were waving, blowing kisses, and laughing.

"Anything for the troops," said Liz, as she blew kisses.

"That's why we're here," said Ginny, smiling and waving between kisses.

Colonel Goodman ordered the convoy to deploy to a field some 15 miles behind the front lines, protocol for evacuation hospitals. Here, the hospital would receive patients sent from field hospitals deployed closer to the front lines.

The hospital was a relatively large unit, with 70 tents, 400 patient beds, 40 nurses, 38 doctors and other male officers, and over 240 enlisted men serving as litter bearers, orderlies, and technicians. With the help of a quartermaster unit, the hospital's enlisted men set up the tents for hospital operations and then tents to accommodate the staff. To help deter enemy attacks, the tops of the tents had been painted with red crosses, each lying within a white circle. Two hours after the men had erected the surgery tents, trucks began bringing the first patients. Within a few hours, the hospital had about 200 patients, half its capacity. By the second day, the hospital neared its capacity. The hospital operated around the clock, in 12-hour shifts.

When patients arrived, the staff assessed them for surgery. They treated men with chest and intestinal wounds; facial and other head wounds; injuries to the limbs, some requiring amputation; burns; and other serious injuries.

The evacuation hospital tried to stabilize all the patients and, using triage procedures, operated on the most critical, if they were up to surgery and deemed likely to survive. Once treated, the men would either be sent back to their units or moved by air or sea to Army general hospitals in Great Britain for longer-term care or more intensive care. If a man died, he was buried in the military cemetery near Omaha Beach. There was a continuous flow of men leaving the hospital and new casualties coming in.

Liz worked in surgery. Ginny performed many tasks. She helped with triage; prepared patients for surgery; cared for them after surgery, including building them up with plasma; administered shots of the new wonder drug, penicillin, to help treat infections; and cared for those who were dying.

One night at the end of the first week, Ginny and Liz lay on their cots in the tent they shared with two other nurses, who were on duty. "This has been some week," said Liz. "Physically, I'm tired, but, wow, the experiences I'm having. In a civilian hospital, I would never have seen, let alone treat, half the types of injuries we're treating. I'm learning so much, and with each operation, our team just seems to get better. If practice makes perfect, we're sure getting lots of practice."

"I have a lot of respect for these wounded soldiers," said Ginny. "Most want to make sure others are treated before they are. I know they must be scared, especially the badly injured ones, but they try not to show it."

Exhausted, Liz fell asleep and began snoring loudly.

Ginny lay awake thinking of Warren, wondering where he was and if he was safe. Soon, despite Liz's snoring, she, too, was asleep.

Chapter 62

As the fighting between the Allies and the Germans intensified, the hospital's workload increased. The nurses, doctors, and enlisted men worked longer and longer hours, with fewer and fewer breaks. They worked seven days a week. When they were not on shift duty, they were expected to help sanitize the facilities, roll bandages, repair rubber gloves and other equipment, and sharpen needles. They slept whenever they could. They grew increasingly fatigued.

Living conditions were primitive. The nurses wore GI field uniforms or coveralls, which most had to tailor to fit their smaller bodies. They had to wear their heavy helmets when outside the tents. In surgery or while caring for patients, they wore bandanas around their hair. They washed their underwear and hung it to dry in the tents in which they slept.

They often were served hot meals. Other times they ate mostly K rations, which came in a small cardboard box. Inside were crackers, a tin of meat or cheese, a fruit bar, powdered coffee, and an envelope of lemon crystals to be added to the water to mask its chlorine taste and smell. Their rations included two packs of cigarettes a week, and they could buy a small amount of liquor each month.

The latrine was the standard 12-inch-wide slit trench over which one straddled, but at least the orderlies had erected canvas sides for privacy, or near privacy. To the nurses' dismay, fighter pilots began low-level buzzing, wiggling their wings as they flew over occupied latrines.

For bathing, the nurses had to fire up wood-burning stoves in their tents, heat water in their steel helmets, and take a "bird bath" by dipping their washcloths in the hot water and cleaning themselves. As time went by, they used more and more perfume, not only to mask the odors of their own bodies but also to ward off the smells of the other staff and patients.

When it rained, the pathways between the tents turned to thick, gooey mud. The nurses got wet, and their clothes and tents seemed never to dry out.

After they completed their shifts and headed to bed, Ginny and Liz often lay on their cots talking before falling asleep.

One night, Liz said, "Guess what I dreamed last night?"

"That you were on a date with Clark Gable at a swanky restaurant in New York."

"No, even better than that. I was in a modest hotel in Paris, all alone, in a bathtub filled with hot water and bubbles, and I was guzzling champagne."

Ginny laughed. "I must say, this country living has really changed your idea of a good time."

"I'd give anything for a hot bath, even a shower."

Ginny sighed. "I had a terrible dream last night. It was a nightmare—related to one of the patients I've had."

"What'd you dream?"

"A couple of days ago, I was asked to 'special duty' a young soldier who was dying. He was nineteen. The doctors had tried everything but just couldn't save him. I sat with him overnight. He talked about his home in Michigan, about his mother and father, and about his girlfriend. I told him I was sure they all loved him very much and that to them he was a hero. He asked me to help write a letter to his parents and one to his girlfriend, which I did. The next morning, as I sat holding his hand, he opened his eyes and looked intently at me. I thought I could see in his eyes both fear and comfort that someone was with him. Then he squeezed my hand, and he was gone."

"Oh, my." Liz wiped away a tear. "We surgery nurses aren't asked to provide 'special duty,' but I've been present when some young men have died. Most of our patients, however, are anesthetized. What did you dream?"

"I dreamt I went personally to deliver the letter to his parents. They were heartbroken, absolutely crushed. Then I delivered the letter to the girlfriend, and she went to pieces.

It was awful. But one good thing is going to come out of that dream."

"What's that?"

"Somehow I'm going to find extra strength to help keep other boys from dying."

Chapter 63

Mid-June, 1944, France

The men in Jeb's Second Platoon, after sinking in the Channel and being reoutfitted in Britain, landed in Normandy in mid-June and rejoined Jeb and the remnants of Company O.

Jeb told the men of Second Platoon what had happened to the rest of the men in Company O. One of the men from Halesford told Jeb that he had learned that Dick Drumheller had survived and was in a hospital in England.

A new company commander was assigned from battalion headquarters. Additional, individual replacement officers and enlisted men took the places of those who had been killed or wounded. Jeb resumed his position as leader of Second Platoon.

With the new replacements, Company O lost the feeling of familiarity it had when it was in Halesford and even in Britain. Earlier Jeb had known everyone in Company O at least by name. Now, he knew well the men in his Second Platoon, which was still mostly intact, but he no longer knew even the names of the majority of men in the company.

For the next few weeks, Company O fought toward St. Lo, a small town in Normandy only some 20 miles from Omaha Beach. The fighting was intense as Jeb led his platoon in attacking enemy positions. He and his men shot and killed many Germans. While they killed to achieve their assigned mission, protect themselves, and help defeat the Nazi war machine and end the war, the killing was now mechanical and little thought was given to lofty goals other than survival.

Jeb saw men in his company hit by enemy rifle and machine gun fire, others by mortar and artillery fire. Some were only grazed, but others took hits in the arms or legs. The worst were the chest and head wounds. Medics treated those with minor injuries, and those men stayed with the company. The more seriously wounded were evacuated to Britain. Those who died in France instantly or after being wounded were buried near Omaha Beach.

Jeb tried to care for all of his men. He knew he wasn't as attached to the new men as he was to those from Halesford and those who had joined his platoon in Britain, which seemed a lifetime ago, and this bothered him. He wanted to treat all men fairly.

He had been in combat only a few weeks, but the war and the killing were wearing him down. Every day was a test of survival.

On June 27, he received a letter from Katherine. It was the first letter he had received from her in weeks. He thought it strange that the envelope had a London return address. Jeb had been so busy and tired in preparing for the invasion and fighting in France that he had not written to her since May. He opened the letter:

> Dear Jeb,
>
> I haven't heard from you since the two letters you sent me in mid-May.
>
> I tried to contact you before the June 6 invasion but was rebuffed by the military at each attempt. I can only believe that you have been fully committed to your duties and have not had time to write.
>
> I am not sure how to tell you this, but I guess it's best to be direct. I am pregnant. I thought we had taken precautions, but evidently things were not 100 percent foolproof. My parents are distraught, and my father has made me move to London to live with a

cousin until the baby is born. He
wants me to give the baby up for
adoption.

I'm not sure what to do. If you
receive this letter, please write as soon
as you can.

I'm sorry to add to all the worries
you must be having now with all that
is happening in France, but I thought
you would want to know, and I need
your reassurance.

I'm feeling very lonely and miss
you more than you can imagine.
                    With all my love,
                        Katherine

Jeb read the letter over and over again with mixed
emotions. He regretted causing so much trouble for
Katherine, but he was actually heartened to learn that he had
helped create new life, especially when there was so much
death and destruction around him. He would write Katherine
soon, but now he had to deal with Third Platoon and
operational plans for fighting tomorrow.

Chapter 64

July 1944, Normandy

During the push by Allied forces into the Normandy heartland in late July, the evacuation hospital stayed busy. One day Colonel Goodman sent for Ginny to come to his makeshift office in a corner of one of the large tents.

Ginny wondered why the Colonel wanted to see her. *I hope nothing is wrong at home.* She stuck her head inside the tent. "You wanted to see me, Colonel?"

"Yes, Ginny. Please come in and have a seat."

She took the empty chair opposite the crate he used as a desk.

"A nurse in one of our field hospitals has fallen ill. We need to replace her right away. If the men don't survive in the field hospitals, they won't make it here. I think you're the best nurse to replace her."

Ginny hesitated, letting the words sink in. "A field hospital? Why me, sir?"

"I've watched you with the wounded, and I've watched you with the staff. I've seen you use your initiative—which is critical in a field hospital. In a nutshell, you're the best nurse we have, one of the best I've seen. You'll be of even greater value in the field hospital than here."

Ginny blushed. "I appreciate your confidence in me, sir, but..."

Goldman interrupted her. "I won't lie to you. There's more risk there. The field hospitals are only a few miles behind the front lines. I can order you to go, but I won't. I'd like you, if you will, to volunteer for the assignment—for the sake of the wounded. If you won't volunteer, I'll have to lean hard on someone else. Will you go?"

Ginny again hesitated. Thoughts poured into her head. *I hear his praise, and that's nice, but my parents warned me to be careful. They would be devastated if something happened to me. Yet, if I don't go, he'll just pressure one of the other nurses. I know I'm here to help the troops, especially those who are up front putting their lives at risk. Then, of course, there's Warren, somewhere up on the front line.*

"What do you say, Ginny?"

"I'll go, sir."

Chapter 65

After Ginny packed her gear, she went looking for Liz, who was on duty in the operating room. During a break between patients, Ginny told her best friend about the colonel's request and her reluctant acceptance. There was time for only a quick, tearful goodbye and hug.

Ginny was to accompany Captain George O'Brien, a surgeon, who was also being assigned to the field hospital. A driver, arranged by Colonel Goodman, helped load the two officers' gear into a jeep.

As Ginny climbed into the back of the jeep, she felt as though she were going off to battle. She was outfitted in dark green trousers, a tan shirt under a khaki-colored Army field jacket, leggings, boots, and a steel helmet with liner. She carried not only a duffel bag with all her belongings but her bedding and a lantern.

When they neared the field hospital, Ginny heard a loud BOOM, followed by another, and then several more. O'Brien glanced over his shoulder, gave her a faint smile, and said, "Artillery." They were now about five miles from the front lines.

At the field hospital, the commanding officer, Lieutenant Colonel Frank Torre, came out of the surgery tent during a break to greet them. "We're mighty glad to have you here. Colonel Goodman has said lots of nice things about both of you. We're swamped and can really use your help."

"We're glad we can help, sir," said O'Brien.

"Yes, sir," said Ginny.

"The 29th Infantry Division is engaged in some horrendous action up ahead," said Torre. "Casualties are high. I'll get a couple of our men to help you to your bunk areas. Take a few minutes to freshen up, and then I'm afraid I've got to ask you to report to the surgery tent. Did I say we're swamped?" Torre called two enlisted men over and told them to help the officers.

One of the enlisted men grabbed Ginny's duffel bag and lantern, leaving Ginny to carry her other gear, and led her to her tent, dropping her gear outside the entrance. "Someone from the night shift may be sleeping, so you may want to be as quiet as possible, although it amazes me how we can sleep through all the artillery fire." Several more BOOMs of artillery rounds sounded in the distance.

"Thanks." Ginny pulled back the flap covering the entrance and stepped into the tent. Inside, two of the four cots were, indeed, occupied with sleeping nurses. Another cot had personal belongings on it. Ginny quietly placed her sleeping bag on top of the vacant cot. She retrieved her other gear and started to store the duffel bag under the cot. She stopped when she noticed that a large hole had been dug under her cot. She looked around and saw that all the cots had holes under them. She put her gear on top of her bed, quietly exited the tent, and made a stop at the latrine. When she bumped into another nurse, she introduced herself and then said, "A quick question. I noticed a hole under my cot. What's that for?"

"That's your foxhole. Don't fill it up or cover it over. If we get shelled, you'll find that hole is your best friend."

Ginny shook her head in disbelief and headed to find Lieutenant Colonel Torre. The colonel directed her to help care for the men who had just been operated on. She helped change dressings, applied casts, and placed limbs in traction. While helping two men whose jaws had been wired in place, she was quietly advised by the staff to make sure the wire cutters stayed near them in case they should become sick and have to vomit. She tried to relieve the men's pain and provide as much comfort as possible.

No patient would stay at the field hospital for more than a week or two. Most would be returned to their units for duty or moved to the evacuation hospital for further treatment. Some would die. A few of the patients were wounded German soldiers, who would eventually be sent to prisoner-of-war camps once they recovered.

After a couple of days of caring for post-operative patients, Ginny was asked to help with triage, assessing the priority for treating incoming patients according to the seriousness and immediacy of their needs and the likelihood that surgery would successfully save their lives. She had to examine and assess men injured by gunshot, artillery and mortar round fragments, land mines, and fire, as well as those suffering from trench foot. Some had lost limbs, others had their torsos ripped apart, and still others, especially tank crewmen, had been horribly burned. The worst in Ginny's mind were those whose faces were terribly disfigured.

After several days of twelve- to fourteen-hour shifts, she found it difficult to fall and stay asleep. She was haunted by faces of seriously-wounded, probably hopelessly-wounded, men—men she had helped reject for priority care, men she had probably relegated to almost certain death.

Toward the end of Ginny's first week at the field hospital, one of the surgical nurses, overcome by fatigue, passed out and collapsed on the operating tent floor. Just at that moment, Ginny happened to pass by the door of the surgical tent. Lieutenant Colonel Torre, in the midst of an operation, spotted her. "Ginny, come in here!"

Ginny entered the surgical area and saw the nurse on the floor.

"Get some help and get her out of here. Then scrub up and get back in here quickly. We need you."

Oh, my God, Ginny said to herself. *I'm not a surgical nurse.* As she ran to find help, she said a short prayer. It had been a while since she had prayed. *Dear Lord, help me, help our surgeons, and help these wounded, and, again, if you didn't hear the first time, help me.* Ginny found two stretcher bearers and had them move the nurse to her tent. Ginny checked the nurse over and then went back to the operating area to scrub up and report to Colonel Torre.

The operating room was a large tent, in the middle of which were surgical tables lit by a couple of overhead light bulbs, powered by a generator. Compared to what Ginny had seen at the evacuation hospital, the wounds here at the field hospital were fresher and dirtier. She felt nauseated by the smells—blood, dirt, sweat, alcohol, and ether.

With instruction from the doctors and other nurses, she cleansed wounds, extracting dirt, splinters, pieces of clothing, and other debris, while others worked on higher priority surgery for the patient. She watched the doctors and nurses work, and soon she was handing them instruments, swabbing fluids, and counting instruments to ensure that none of the paraphernalia was left inside the patient as he was sewn up.

When Torre asked her to hold and secure a soldier's leg that had been partially blown off below the knee, she retched as the leg was amputated. The room began to spin, but she gained her equilibrium. She repeated her prayer silently in her head, *Dear Lord, help me*, until it almost became a mantra. Five hours later, most of the critical cases had been addressed.

Torre called for a break. "Ginny, you were superb in there. I think you've found a new calling."

Ginny was overwhelmed—with the compliment, the demands of the work she had been doing, fatigue, and the surgeon's reference to a "new calling." All she could say was, "Thank you, sir."

Torre reassigned her to the surgical unit.

She found surgical nursing to be the most intense and demanding work she had ever performed, and she found herself exhausted at the end of her shifts. She was relieved, however, that at least she no longer was a triage nurse, playing God and judging whom to save and whom to abandon.

Chapter 66

July 1944, France

Jeb and Company O fought from the Normandy coast inland into France.

Late one day, Jeb finally found a few minutes to write a short letter to Katherine. He knew a censor would be reviewing it.

Dear Katherine,

I'm sorry I haven't responded sooner to your letter and your news. I wanted to write, but there's been no time.

I'm sorry for the trouble I've caused—for both you and your family.

I wish we could be together and talk this through, but that, of course, is impossible now.

I will support whatever you decide to do. All I can say is that I love you and want to be with you when the war is over.

Must go.

With all my love,
Jeb

* * * * * * * *

On July 28, late in the afternoon near a small French town as Jeb was leading his platoon on a flanking movement around a German unit, one of his men stepped on a German land mine, a "Bouncing Betty." The mine popped up several feet in the air and then exploded, blowing shrapnel in all directions.

Pieces of steel hit Jeb in the cheek, throat, side of the neck, shoulder, arm, and thigh. A medic gave him a shot of morphine and had him moved immediately by stretcher to the battalion aid station. From there, he was transported to a field hospital.

The hospital's tents were overflowing with wounded. The staff and operating facilities were overburdened, and new casualties kept arriving.

The staff examined Jeb's injuries. Using triage procedures, they placed him in the section for patients who were seriously wounded but were not candidates for successful surgery—patients who would probably die. In this section, the staff could try only to stabilize him and make him comfortable, nothing more.

Jeb lay on a cot. It was nighttime. In the dim light, he could see other seriously-wounded men lying on cots around him. Some were calling out or moaning. Because of his throat wound, Jeb could not speak. He saw that not a one of these men was being taken away to be operated on. One man tried to lift himself up, then let out a cry, fell back and was silent. A nurse checked on him, and soon two stretcher bearers removed him from the tent. Nurses and orderlies were attending to the men, but they apparently were administering only fluids and pain killers. Jeb tried to focus. *They've written me and these other guys off. They don't think they can save us, at least not with what they have to work with.*

A nurse Jeb hadn't seen before, dressed in what appeared to be a surgical smock, walked by. Using his good arm, he grabbed her smock. He brought her to a stop. He was surprised by his own strength. He held on as tight as he could and wouldn't let go.

The nurse looked down in the dim light and saw the hand clamped on her smock. She started to try to remove his hand but then hesitated. She leaned over in the dark tent, looked into his face, which was partially wrapped, and whispered in his ear, "If you let go, I'll try to get you help."

To Jeb, the nurse was a blur, but he thought he detected something in her voice that told him she could be trusted. He let go of her smock. The nurse walked away.

Fifteen minutes later, two stretcher bearers came into the tent, picked up Jeb's stretcher, and took him to a brightly-lit room. The overhead light nearly blinded him. People wearing surgical garb and masks appeared on each side. Someone behind him put a cloth over his face. He smelled a medicinal odor, and a wave of heat surged through his body. He tried to struggle and then everything went black.

Chapter 67

Late July-August 1944, UK

When Jeb regained consciousness, he found himself aboard a plane with ten other wounded soldiers and two flight nurses. One of the nurses told him they were headed for England.

When the plane landed, ambulance crews took Jeb and the others to a U.S. Army hospital in Blockford, west of Southampton, in the center of the southern British coast.

Jeb's spirits were lifted by the bright and clean hospital. After being in the field, he relished the comfortable bed and clean sheets. The attractive nurses were a bonus. He underwent several surgeries. With each operation and as the days went by, he began to feel better.

A couple of weeks after he had arrived at the hospital, he received a letter from his mother. It had been forwarded to him from Company O. There were no letters from Katherine.

> Dear Son,
>
> I think of you all the time. I know you must be very busy with little time to write. I wish you could write and tell me where you are and what you're doing, but I realize you can't. The important thing is that you stay safe.
>
> I have some sad news. Your Uncle Jonah died yesterday. He had not been feeling well for weeks. I think he knew he was dying.
>
> Last week he brought a letter to me and asked me not to open it until he passed, whenever that might be. The letter is written to you and me,

and he asked that I send it to you after I had read it.

It is certainly a bittersweet letter. Please read the enclosed letter from Uncle Jonah now, and then read my second letter to you that follows and comments on his letter.

I hope that his letter won't cause you any further distress and that, indeed, it may grant you some relief and maybe even comfort.

You are in my prayers always. I hope you are healthy and well. I wish I could be there with you now, or you could be here with me.

With all my love,
Mother

Jeb then read the letter from Uncle Jonah:

Dear Helen and Jeb,

I don't have much time left on this earth, and I feel I must unburden my soul. I do so not to win favor with my creator, who will soon judge me, but because I know I've hurt you both and know I owe you an explanation.

A decade ago, I did a most cowardly thing. I've regretted it every day since. I think I would not have done such a thing when I was a younger man, before I was injured in the Great War. I know you may think that is a weak excuse. All I can say is that being gassed and suffering as I have for so many years weighs heavy on the mind and heart and makes one cringe and shrink at the thought of further pain and suffering.

On October 18, 1934, I accidentally shot and killed Jeremiah. It was purely an accident. I never would have intended to do harm to such a loving and caring brother, a brother who helped raise me.

Jeremiah, Jeb, and I had gone to the back pasture and woods to hunt quail. We were lined up in a row, Jeremiah on the left, me in the middle, and Jeb on the right. I can see it as though it was yesterday.

Two birds suddenly flew up at the same time from the high grass in front of us. The one on the right flew straight up, and Jeb fired at it. The second bird flew low to our left.

I swung my gun to the left, tried to aim in front of the fast-flying bird, and fired.

I can still feel the surprise and anguish as I pulled the trigger and saw Jeremiah in my sights. I have had that image in my head every night for almost ten years.

If shooting my brother, even though by accident, wasn't bad enough, I then lied about the incident. I told the sheriff that things were so confused and happened so fast that I couldn't say exactly what happened.

I think the sheriff might have thought that my statement was designed to protect Jeb, as though Jeb had shot his father accidentally and I was trying to claim or share the responsibility. In fact, I was trying to protect myself, and in so doing I placed a dark cloud over Jeb's head.

I hope that in your hearts you can find a small bit of forgiveness for me. That's my fervent wish. I don't deserve it, but I sincerely wish it.

As an old bachelor, I've got no family. You two have been the only family I've had for years now, since Jeremiah's death. You've always been kind and treated me as one of your own.

To help make amends, I'm leaving you all my savings, my land, and my other earthly possessions, to be split equally between you.

My lawyer, Mr. Hastings, will contact you, Helen, at the appropriate time. He'll know how to handle things for Jeb while he's in the service.

I know it's been difficult financially for you since Jeremiah's death. I wish I could have assisted you more than I've been able to over the years. I sincerely hope that these new, far more substantial bequests will make things much easier for you.

Helen, you've done a wonderful job in raising Jeb alone.

Jeb, you're a fine young man. Your father, bless his soul, would be very proud of you, as we all are. I could not be more proud of you if you were my own flesh and blood.

I'm sorry for what I've done. I
wish both of you peace and happiness
for the future.

With deep regret and deep love,

Jonah

Tears streamed down Jeb's cheeks as he read the letter.
He was saddened by the death of his uncle, whom he had
always loved and who had been almost a surrogate father
during Jeb's teenage years. The letter made him feel only
compassion for his uncle. He felt not the least bit of anger.
He also felt a great sense of relief. He had always believed in
his heart that he had not shot his father, and now Uncle
Jonah had confirmed the facts. He lay there in bed and let out
a large, audible sigh.

Then Jeb read his mother's second letter:

Dear Son,

While it is hard, I hope that you
can find forgiveness in your heart for
Uncle Jonah. I have.

I always believed what you told
me about the accident, so Jonah's
confession was no surprise to me. I
was surprised that he confessed, but
what he confessed was no surprise.

Jonah did not have an easy life.
Your father told me in detail how
Jonah suffered from the effects of the
gas attacks. We should all pray that
gas is never again used in war. I
sincerely hope and pray that when this
war is over there will be no more
wars.

Jonah was a kind man. He helped
us out in many ways over the years.

The gifts he has bestowed upon us
from his estate further reflect his
kindness.

I will ask Mr. Hastings to invest
your share of the estate carefully until
you return.

May God bless Jonah Fletcher and
may God bless you, Jeb.

Love,
Mother

In a low voice, Jeb said, "Amen. May God bless Uncle
Jonah."

Chapter 68

August 1944, Blockford and London, UK

Over the next few weeks, Jeb healed quickly. Indeed, the doctors were amazed at the speed of his recovery. As he got better, he was given half-day passes to leave the hospital. He thought often of Katherine and began to contemplate traveling to London to find her. When he received a pass for an entire, upcoming weekend, he decided to head for London.

Early Saturday morning, he caught a train to London and checked in at a hotel—the same one where he and Katherine had stayed. He bought a map of London and then took a cab to the address that had been on Katherine's letter, presumably the address of Katherine's cousin.

At a small, brick row house, Jeb rapped on the door.

A woman in her late 30s answered. She gave him a quizzical look. "Yes?"

"My name is Jeb Fletcher. I'm looking for Katherine Tefford. Do you happen to be her cousin?"

The woman frowned. "Yes, I'm Katherine's cousin. I know who you are. You're trouble."

"I'm sorry if I've caused Katherine and her family trouble. I really am. Is she here? I'd like to speak to her."

"She's not here."

"Can you tell me where she is?"

"I shouldn't."

"I only want to talk to her. I got shipped over to France, and we haven't really been able to communicate since I last saw her. She sent me a letter."

"She's gone home for a short visit."

"You mean back to her parents in Waterbridge?"

"Yes, back to Waterbridge. I wouldn't advise you to go there, however. You're not in good odor around there, and you'll only make matters worse."

"I expect I'll be sent back to France soon. Can you please tell her that I came looking for her?" He scribbled on a piece of paper. "Here is what will probably be my military address, and here is my mother's address. My mother can forward any mail. Will you give her this?"

"I'll think about it," the woman said, as she shut the door.

Chapter 69

Mid-August, 1944, France

Jeb had recovered sufficiently that he was released from the hospital a few days later with orders to return to France. Still needing time to heal, he was assigned to light duty with a unit of officers who had been in combat and were now tasked with providing newly-arrived infantry officers insights on combat with the Germans.

After a month in this unit, Jeb received orders assigning him to the staff of the Supreme Headquarters Allied Expeditionary Force—General Eisenhower's staff.

Jeb had no idea how he happened to be selected for the SHAEF staff. He suspected that his selection had something to do with the time he happened to meet General Eisenhower, but he wasn't sure.

The chance encounter occurred shortly after D-Day. Jeb was riding in a jeep, along with a driver and an enlisted man who sat in the rear. They were driving along a back road not far from the coast. When they rounded a curve, Jeb spotted the backs of two American soldiers walking along the road some one hundred yards in front of them. The two soldiers heard the jeep and turned toward it, waiting for it to approach.

As the jeep drew closer, Jeb was astonished. "Holy cow, that looks like General Eisenhower." He ordered the driver to slow down. Even closer, Jeb could see by the uniform and rank insignia that it was Eisenhower. He looked just like his photos in *Stars and Stripes*. The other man was a major. "Pull up and stop the jeep. That's the general."

The driver stopped in front of the two men.

Jeb and the two other soldiers jumped out, came to attention, and saluted. Jeb said, "Good afternoon, sir."

Eisenhower returned the salute, as did the major. "Good afternoon, gentlemen," said the general. "We're mighty glad to see you."

"I'm Lieutenant Jeb Fletcher, sir. We're from the 116th Infantry. May we give you a ride?"

"Yes, indeed. You're just what we've been looking for. We were doing some aerial reconnaissance when a storm blew in, and we had to land our 'Grasshopper' on the beach," Eisenhower said, referring to a small, two-seater aircraft.

"If you'll take the front passenger seat, General, I think the rest of us can squeeze in back," said Jeb.

"Why don't you drive, Lieutenant Fletcher? You can tell me what your unit has been doing."

"Yes, sir."

Eisenhower settled into the front passenger seat, Jeb got in the driver's seat, and the others squeezed in the back. The major looked at a map and gave Jeb directions to a command post several miles away. Jeb put the jeep in gear and drove off.

"Where are you from, Lieutenant?" asked Eisenhower.

"Virginia, sir."

"Where in Virginia?"

"Halesford County, in the southwest, nor far from Roanoke and Lynchburg."

"I went fly fishing once near Roanoke. Beautiful country. Lots of mountains, right?"

"Yes, sir. I miss the mountains."

"Is Jeb your real name, and does it have anything to do with Jeb Stuart?"

"Jeb is a nickname, sir. My real name is Jebediah." Jeb went on to explain how he got his name.

For the rest of the drive, Eisenhower asked questions about Jeb's unit and what it had been doing recently. Jeb answered all the questions in detail. As they neared their destination, Eisenhower pulled out a pen and small notebook and began to write in it. "Tell me again how you spell your first name, Lieutenant Fletcher."

Now, almost three months after this encounter, Jeb found himself assigned to a special projects team that reported directly to Eisenhower's chief of staff, Lieutenant General Walter Bedell Smith. The commander of the special projects team, Jeb's immediate boss, was Col. Henry Runyon. Their boss, General Smith, was direct, blunt, and a hard task master, with none of Eisenhower's affability.

Serving on the special projects team would expand Jeb's perspective of the war.

Chapter 70

September 1944, Field Hospital in France

One evening in September at the field hospital, during a short lull after treating a large batch of arriving patients, a sergeant ran into the office area with news for Lieutenant Colonel Torre. Torre then call for Captain O'Brien, and the two huddled together for several minutes. Torre went back to surgery, while O'Brien went looking for Ginny. When he found her in the break area, he approached her and said quietly, "Ginny, come with me for a minute." He walked back to the office with Ginny following, mildly curious. Once inside, he said, "Sit down, please."

Ginny sat. *What's this about? Have I done something wrong?*

"I'm afraid I've got some bad news."

"Has something happened to my family?" Ginny blurted out.

"No, not your family. I'll be very direct. We just got word that the evacuation hospital, which had moved recently, was hit, probably by German long-range artillery. Several patients and staff were killed and many more wounded. I'm sorry to tell you this, but Liz is dead, and so is Colonel Goodman."

"No," Ginny cried out in disbelief. "It can't be true."

"I'm afraid it's true." O'Brien went over and put an arm on her shoulder.

Ginny pulled away. "How do you know? How can you be sure?"

"It's a reliable report."

She started shaking her head. "What happened?"

"I don't have any other details. We'll probably learn more later. I'm terribly sorry—I know you and Liz were close."

Ginny stood up. "How did you hear?"

"It came in over the field radio just minutes ago. Why don't you call it a night and go back to your tent? We can handle things here."

Ginny took a step toward the doorway. *This can't be true,* she thought. She turned back toward O'Brien. "Are you sure there's no mistake?"

"I'm sorry, but the deaths of Liz and Colonel Goodman seem confirmed. Do you want me to walk you back to your tent?"

"No, thank you. I can manage."

In a daze, Ginny walked back to her tent. The other nurses were on duty. She fell onto her cot and wept loudly. She lay there crying, remembering all the good times she and Liz had at nursing school and during their more than a year together in the Army. She thought of Liz's parents and how they would be devastated by the news. She also thought of Colonel Goodman. He had been kind to Liz and her. Then a question came to her for which she knew there was no answer: *Had Colonel Goodman, by sending her to the field hospital closer to the front, actually saved her life?*

Chapter 71

September 1944, France

The next day, Captain O'Brien drove Ginny in a jeep to a memorial service at the evacuation hospital. O'Brien had found out which other members of the staff had been killed or injured and had shared the information.

The new commanding officer of the hospital met them. "The service will start in just a few minutes, now that you're here. It'll last only fifteen minutes. We're back in operation, and casualties are starting to come in. We can't spare more time."

A chaplain from an infantry unit approached Ginny. "Lieutenant Jackson, I understand you were a close friend of Lieutenant Hawkins. Would you be willing during the service to read the 23rd Psalm from my Bible?"

Ginny hesitated. *I'm not sure I can control my emotions, and right now I don't know what I think about God.*

The chaplain placed a hand on Ginny's shoulder. "Think about it, and let me know before I begin the service."

One of the nurses approached Ginny and hugged her. "I'm so sorry about Liz. I know you were both very close."

"Thanks," said Ginny.

The nurse stepped back, as tears began to stream down her face. "They asked me to prepare Liz for burial. They didn't want the men to do it. I cleaned her wounds and washed her. Then I dressed her in her Class A uniform—it wasn't easy. I brushed her hair, even applied some lipstick. When I was through, Liz looked very neat and proper, like the first-class Army nurse she was."

Ginny reached out and hugged the nurse, as both women sobbed. After a minute, Ginny pulled away and went looking for the chaplain. "I'll read the psalm, for Liz—Lieutenant Hawkins—and also for Colonel Goodman."

The service was held under an open tent, which held the remains of ten casualties—Liz, Colonel Goodman, three members of the hospital staff, and five patients. The chaplain and Ginny stood inside the tent, while others stood outside, surrounding the tent. Ginny read the psalm during the service and found comfort in the words.

She and Captain O'Brien returned to the field hospital after the service. Ginny volunteered for the night shift. She wanted to be busy, not lying on her cot unable to sleep.

The war continued, and the days and weeks went by. Ginny remained with the field hospital as it moved with the front lines further into France and then into Belgium. The casualties continued to come in. At one point, so many wounded were brought to the hospital that the litter bearers had to fit the patients in around the edges of the tents, putting their heads and chests inside under the tent but leaving their legs outside.

Dealing with her grief, Ginny, in honor of the memory of Liz, rededicated herself to serving the wounded. She worked long hours, fought fatigue, and tried to treat each wounded soldier as she would want to be treated if she were wounded, or as Liz might have wanted to be treated.

Ginny and Warren were able to correspond with each other. Their letters were short, as they had little time to write and found that there was not much they could say that would pass the military censors. They wrote of their hopes for after the war.

* * * * * * * *

On the first day of October, during a break in surgery, Ginny sat with other nurses in the warm sun outside the main tent. Lieutenant Colonel Torre walked up. "Ginny, could I see you for a minute?" Ginny looked at him, wrinkled her brow, and stood. The other nurses looked at her. "Let's go back to my office," Torre said, turning toward his tent.

Ginny followed, as her stomach began churning.

Once in the tent, Torre said, "Have a seat. I'm afraid I have more bad news."

"Oh, no," Ginny said in a low voice, as thoughts raced through her head. *Is it my mother, my dad, or Tim? Is it Warren? I don't think I can deal with more bad news.*

"You're a friend of Captain Warren Langford, right?"

Ginny's heart sank. "Yes. Is he all right?"

"I'm sorry, but I'm afraid he's been killed."

"No!" Ginny slumped in her chair and started to sob.

Torre offered her a tissue. "I'm sorry."

After a minute, Ginny, still crying, asked, "What happened?"

"Someone at the evacuation hospital, who knew you were friends, heard from someone in his unit. Apparently, he was leading his company in an attack in Belgium, and a German artillery shell hit his command post. The only consolation is that he never knew what hit him. He died without suffering. I'm sorry, Ginny."

Ginny collapsed and almost slid to the floor before Torre caught her. He called for help and had Ginny taken to her cot in the tent she shared with others. When she did not get up the next day, Torre had her transported to a French hospital that the Army had taken over further behind the front lines. She was put to bed and stayed in bed, getting up only to use the bathroom. She ate nothing and drank little.

At the end of the third day, she had a visitor. She appeared so thin and haggard lying there in bed that he double checked the bed chart to make sure it was her. He sat on a chair beside the bed, patiently waiting while she slept. When she started to awaken, he said softly, "Hi, Ginny."

She opened her eyes and blinked a couple of times. She recognized him and smiled slightly.

He took her hand and looked into her eyes. "I hear you've had a tough time."

She looked away, took a deep breath, and sighed. "Oh, Jeb, I think it's more than I can bear."

He continued to hold her hand and sat patiently looking at her. Then he said, "Tell me about it."

Ginny looked at him and pulled her hand away. "It's not just the demands of being an Army nurse...." She paused and tears welled up in her eyes and began flowing down her cheeks.

Jeb handed her a tissue from the bedside table.

Ginny wiped the tears. "There's the daily sight of so much pain and suffering, the horrendous injuries and disfigurements which I can't get out of my mind." She began to sob again.

Jeb took her hand.

Ginny rolled onto her side facing him.

"I miss Liz, my best friend, so much, and now, I've lost Warren." Ginny's sobs turned into spasms, and she shook.

Jeb put his free hand on her shoulder and gently rubbed.

Her sobbing finally slowed and then ended. She spoke for a few minutes about Liz and Warren.

When she had finished, Jeb stood up. "Why don't you try sitting up?"

Ginny pushed herself up and dropped her legs over the side of the bed.

Jeb sat down next to her on the bed and put his arm around her. Ginny leaned into Jeb's shoulder, and then collapsed into him.

He held her for several minutes as she sobbed. When she finally grew quiet, Jeb dropped his arm but continued sitting next to her.

"How did you happen to come here today, Jeb?"

"I heard from a friend in Company O that you were over here, and I happened to be on a trip to this area. Actually, I wanted to stop and thank you, and then I heard what had happened."

Ginny reached for another tissue from the bedside table and blew her nose. "Thank me? For what?"

"I was wounded in late July, and I think you saved my life."

"What?"

He stood. "Let's go for a walk, and I'll tell you my story."

Ginny grabbed some tissues and wiped her eyes. "O.K."

"I'll wait in the hall while you get dressed. They won't let you out of here in pajamas."

After Ginny had washed her face, applied some makeup, and dressed in her uniform, she joined Jeb, and they walked around the hospital grounds.

"In late July," began Jeb, "I was wounded when a land mine exploded. I ended up in a field hospital, where they put me in what I believe was the section for men not expected to survive. The men around me were badly wounded, but no one was being taken to the operating room. I couldn't speak because of a throat and neck wound, but when a nurse walked by, I grabbed her smock."

Ginny stopped and looked directly into Jeb's eyes. "And you wouldn't let go."

"Yes. She said that if I let go, she'd try to get me help. She was good to her word. I was drugged, but I thought there was something familiar about the voice, something I could trust. Being on the SHAEF staff, I have lots of access, and I checked the roster for the field hospital. There you were."

"I had no idea that was you, Jeb. That's almost an unbelievable coincidence."

"Coincidence or providence, whatever it was, you got me into the operating room and saved my life. That's why I wanted to find and thank you."

Ginny blushed. "I'm glad I did." She took Jeb's hand, squeezed it, and then let go. "I'm hungry." Pointing to the village shops just outside the hospital's gates, she said, "Let's go see if we can find something to eat." She cradled her arm in Jeb's, and off they walked.

Jeb returned to his projects team that evening, and the next day Ginny returned to the field hospital and resumed her duties.

Chapter 72

December 1944—January 1945, Germany

On December 20, 1944, Colonel Runyon called Jeb and others on the special projects team to an urgent meeting. "Gentlemen, we have a new assignment—straight from General Smith. We're to investigate reports of a German massacre on December 17 of more than 80 captured GIs. The incident happened about four miles southeast of Malmedy, Belgium. This appears connected to the counteroffensive the Germans have launched. Reports indicate that a regiment of a German armored division ran into a lightly-armed American convoy at a crossroads. The Germans were part of a Waffen SS panzer division."

Jeb had heard of the Waffen SS, a unit of the military arm of the Schutzstaffel, an organization formed to protect Hitler and the Nazi elite and filled with men fanatical in their dedication to the Nazi cause.

"Those are mean bastards," said one of the men.

Runyon continued. "According to some eyewitness accounts, SS troops fired on and soon captured our 285th Field Artillery Observation Battalion along with some men from other units, perhaps a total of 120-140 men. The Germans rounded up survivors, lined them up in a field, and mowed them down with gunfire from the road. Then they walked around shooting individuals. More than 80 may have been killed."

"Damn," said another of the men, as they all stirred in their seats.

"Some were able to escape. Rumors of the massacre have already spread to our frontline units. Some of our unit commanders have talked of taking no SS troops alive. The site of the massacre is now beyond our lines. Until we can reach the site, we're to interview those who escaped. Once we're able to reach the site, we're to look for and record the evidence and talk to any local witnesses. General Smith wants full and careful documentation, for possible war crimes prosecution."

Runyon gave assignments to team members. Jeb was to interview some survivors who had been wounded and hospitalized.

Jeb traveled to a U.S. Army evacuation hospital in western Belgium where some of the wounded were being treated. One of men was a staff sergeant from the artillery observation battalion. Sitting down on a chair next to the man's bed, Jeb shook the man's hand and introduced himself. "Sergeant, I'm Lieutenant Jeb Fletcher. I'm assigned to a special team that works for General Smith, General Eisenhower's Chief of Staff. We're investigating the December 17 action near Malmedy, where I understand you were wounded." Jeb paused, letting the information sink in. "I'd like to ask you some questions, if you feel up to it."

"Yes, sir. I'm a little doped up for the pain, but I'm thinking pretty clearly."

Jeb wanted to put the man at ease. "Good. May I first ask where you're from?"

"I'm from Bedford, Virginia, sir. Ever hear of it?"

Jeb grinned. "Indeed! I'm from Halesford."

"Well, I'll be darned, it's a small world," said the sergeant, with a smile. "Our football team used to play Halesford every year."

"And you used to whip us almost every year. I've got scars to prove it."

Both men laughed.

"It's sure nice to see someone from home, or almost home." Jeb paused and pulled out a tablet and pen, turning serious. "Can you tell me what happened on December 17 near Malmedy?"

The sergeant hesitated, took a deep breath, and in a voice that quivered said, "Yes, sir, I'll try. But first, could I ask what happened to the other men in my unit? Many are good friends. Two are from Bedford County and another's from the next county over, Franklin County."

"We're just now starting to investigate. I'm sorry to say, but according to preliminary reports, as many as 80 or more men may have been killed."

"That's awful—80 men! Can you tell me who was killed?"

"These are just preliminary reports. I can't really give you names now. We have names of at least some of the survivors, but we're still investigating what happened to others."

"Can you at least tell me if my three buddies from Southwest Virginia survived?"

"What were their names?"

The sergeant named his friends. Jeb looked at the list of men who had escaped. "I'm sorry, but their names aren't on the list of men we definitely know survived."

Jeb paused as the sergeant looked down in silence. After a minute, he said quietly, "What can you tell me about December 17?"

The sergeant took a deep breath and sighed. "Well, we had orders to move to a new location. We were approaching Malmedy. When we got to an intersection, all of a sudden these German tanks and armored vehicles appeared. There was a mess of them. They started firing. All we had were rifles and pistols. We bailed out of our jeeps and trucks and dove into the ditches along the road. The ditches were wet, and it was really cold. Several of our men were hit—I saw them lying there. The Germans moved in, overpowering us. We surrendered. They were SS."

"How did you know they were SS? Could you identify their unit?"

"They had those double streaks of lightning on their collars—the SS insignia. I don't know what unit they were."

"Please continue."

"Well, they took our guns. They took my watch and my wallet and tried to take my high school ring, but my fingers were too swollen. They moved us to a field alongside the road and had us form a row. We expected them to take us prisoner and march us back to their lines. Instead, they opened fire, with machine gun and small arms fire. It was awful." The sergeant shook his head and stopped talking.

Jeb waited for a half minute or so. "Do you know why they started firing?"

"No, sir. We weren't firing—we were disarmed. I didn't hear any order to fire. They just started firing."

"What did you do?"

"I fell to the ground, face first, and played dead. They continued to shoot. I was hit twice in the back. Then the heavy shooting stopped. After that, some of the Germans came into the field and began shooting those still alive. While I was face down, I could still see off to the side. It was terribly cold, lying there on the ground, but I didn't move. I tried to conceal my breath, my breathing. One of our men near me started making noises. He was wounded and crying out in pain. He flipped over onto me. I could see a German with a pistol approach from the side." The sergeant again stopped talking.

Jeb reached for a pitcher. "Would you like a drink?"

"Yes, sir, please." The sergeant took a drink and then a deep breath and continued. "Standing over me, the German fired a shot into the man on top of me. The bullet must have gone through him and then hit me in the knee. It hurt like hell, but I didn't flinch."

"My, God. What happened next?"

"Well, the tanks started moving. At some point, one of our men yelled, 'Run for it.' I guess most of the Germans had moved on. I was able to get up—I was surprised I could do it—and I ran. A German officer still in the field tried to shoot me, but his pistol didn't fire. I crossed another field and hid in a shed. One of our men, who wasn't wounded, joined me in the shed. We stayed there over night. The next day we walked across a field, and a farmer motioned us toward a house. They took us in, fed us, and hid us in the attic. My clothes had stuck to my wounds, and I didn't want them to mess with it and start the bleeding again. The Germans came to the house but didn't come in. The other man wrote a note and gave it to the woman of the house. She took it next door, and a Belgian boy from next door took the note to American lines nearby. I guess at this time the area was no man's land. An Army ambulance came and rescued us."

"That's a horrific story. I'm sure glad you survived, along with many others. We'll find the bastards who did this, and, when we do, your account will be a great help in prosecuting them."

"I'm glad to help, Lieutenant. I'll be glad to testify on behalf of all my friends who have been killed."

"Thanks. I'll do my best to build the case against those responsible. We owe our soldiers that and more."

"You know, Lieutenant, I keep asking myself why I survived while my buddies died. I wondered whether maybe God protected me, but then I ask myself why would God protect me and not them. I'm no better than them, probably worse. I guess it just comes down to luck."

"There appear to be about 50 of you who survived, so you weren't alone in somehow being fortunate. Well, I'd better let you get some rest. Take care and get well soon."

"Thanks, Lieutenant. I feel better having talked about what happened, and I feel better knowing that someone is working to get those responsible."

Some three weeks later, in mid-January, Allied forces finally pushed the Germans back east of Malmedy. The American forces had been instructed to avoid the intersection where the massacre had taken place, so as to preserve it. When Jeb, other special team members, and other Army elements arrived at the intersection, they found bodies of American soldiers lying frozen in the snow and ice. The bodies had a range of wounds, some shot in the torso by machine gun fire from a distance and some shot in the head by pistol at close range. Jeb and others meticulously photographed and recorded what they saw.

"Damned Nazis," said Jeb to one of the team members. "This was a massacre, in violation of the laws of war. These men had surrendered. We need to find the SS troops who did this."

With the help of an interpreter, Jeb began looking for local Belgian witnesses. He interviewed several.

The team prepared a preliminary report on the incident at Malmedy and sent the report to General Smith for use in a possible future war crimes trial. Men from the Inspector General's and Judge Advocate General's offices would provide more detailed reports.

* * * * * * * *

In May 1945, Jeb attended a war crimes trial at Dachau, Germany, of 74 German soldiers, 30 of whom were suspected of shooting Americans in the Malmedy Massacre at the beginning of the Battle of the Bulge, as the two events came to be called. The Malmedy Massacre had resulted in the deaths of 88 Americans, including two men from Bedford County and one from Franklin County, Virginia. Fifty-four survived, including one man from Bedford County—the sergeant Jeb had interviewed. Some of the Americans were held by the Germans in a prisoners of war camp, and one died there.

Of the 74 Germans tried, nearly all were convicted, with 43 sentenced to death, 22 sentenced to life in prison, and most of the others receiving lesser sentences. In later years, Jeb would learn that none of the death sentences were carried out and that in the 1950s, in a different political environment in which Germany became a friend and ally of the United States and other Western allies, all the men who had been convicted were paroled. The infamous commander of the SS panzer regiment involved in the massacre, Lieutenant Colonel Joachim Peiffer, was sentenced to death but was released from prison in late 1956. In July 1976, when Peiffer was living in Traves, France, a group set his house on fire, killing him in the blaze. The arsonists were never caught.

Chapter 73

February 1945, Germany

In February 1945, as he was wrapping up his part of the investigation of the Malmedy Massacre, Jeb visited a frontline unit to interview another survivor who had escaped the massacre unharmed.

Allied forces were pushing the Germans back into Germany after their Battle of the Bulge counteroffensive. The weather was freezing. It had been one of the coldest winters in Europe in modern history. Snow and ice covered the fields.

After interviewing the survivor, Jeb climbed into his jeep and was about ready to leave the area when a column of men passed him. The column consisted of ten German prisoners of war, guarded by two GIs. As the men passed, Jeb noticed something different about the last prisoner. He wore the insignia of the SS. He also was wearing American combat boots. Rumors had spread that SS troops had taken the boots off American soldiers they had killed.

SS forces were responsible for the Malmedy Massacre. Jeb felt both adrenalin and anger rise inside him. He stepped out of the jeep and patted the pistol holstered on his belt, confirming its presence. "Corporal," he shouted to the American soldier leading the column of Germans.

The corporal turned, saw Jeb, and halted the column. "Sir?"

"Hold those men there." Jeb approached the group and walked back and forth along the line of Germans, inspecting their uniforms. Stopping at the last man, the one with SS insignia, he demanded in an angry, accusatory voice, "Where did you get those boots?"

The German shook his head.

Jeb pointed to the man's boots. "Where did you get those boots?"

Again, the German shook his head. "Ich spreche kein Englisch."

Jeb kicked the man in the ankle. "Those boots. Where did you get them?"

The German winced. He shook his head yet again.

"Can anyone here translate?" asked Jeb.

"Not us two," said the corporal, nodding toward the other GI. The Germans did not respond.

"Those are American boots. Give me your rifle, corporal."

"Sir?"

"Give me your rifle."

"Yes, sir." The corporal handed his rifle to Jeb.

Jeb pointed the rifle from his hip toward the German. "Now sit that man down and have him take off his boots, or you take them off him."

"But, sir, it's freezing out here."

"Corporal, those boots are the property of the U.S. Army. Get the boots off that man and give them to me."

"Is that an order, sir?"

"That's an order, Corporal. My name is Lieutenant Jebediah Fletcher. I'll cover you while you get his boots. If he fights, he's a dead man."

"Yes, sir." The corporal shoved the German to the ground and began removing the man's boots.

When the German began yelling, Jeb step closer and pointed the rifle at the man's head. The German shut up.

The corporal removed the boots and handed them to Jeb. Jeb gave him back his rifle. "Carry on, corporal," he ordered.

"Yes, sir." The corporal turned to the prisoners, swung his arm forward, and shouted, "March."

Jeb watched the two guards and the prisoners march off, the last prisoner obviously in great discomfort as he walked through the snow and ice in his stocking feet. *I can probably get court martialed for that.*

He heaved the boots deep into the woods, climbed into his jeep, and drove away.

Chapter 74

April 1945, Ohrdruf, Germany

In mid-April, Colonel Runyon called Jeb into his office. "General Patton has asked General Eisenhower, General Bradley, and General Smith to come to his temporary command headquarters to see something he's discovered. General Smith wants you and me to go along. We fly there tomorrow morning."

"Yes, sir. What has General Patton found?"

"It's something about German atrocities. He won't give any details, but he assures everyone it's extremely important."

The next day the party of Army officers flew to an airfield near Ohrdruf, Germany. General Patton met the plane, accompanied by several Army cars and jeeps to transport the visiting party. Introductions were made as necessary, and everyone shook hands. Jeb had not met Generals Omar Bradley and George Patton before.

Eisenhower turned to Patton. "So, George, what is it you want to show us that's so secretive?"

"I want you to see first-hand what those German bastards have done," said Patton. "It's revolting, shocking. I want you to experience it without any prior explanation."

"O.K., lead the way."

The men piled into the cars and jeeps, and the caravan drove away down the road. A half hour later, they pulled up to a camp surrounded by barbed wire. GIs were posted at the gate. The Americans got out of the vehicles. Even before they entered the gate, they were greeted by an overwhelming stench. Inside the camp, along the road, lay many dead, half-naked bodies. Further into the camp were shallow graves, filled with naked, emaciated bodies, not yet buried.

"Oh, my God," said Eisenhower, shaking his head.

Bradley was speechless. Patton walked off toward a building, vomited, and returned to the group.

A colonel reported to those assembled that his men had found and counted over 3,200 dead bodies, only some of which had recently been buried.

As the party prepared to leave, Eisenhower turned to Smith. "Beetle, I want this documented and publicized. Take lots of pictures, and get the correspondents in here. Likewise if we find more such camps. If we find any survivors, get them some food and medical care, and do it quickly, and start planning how we can get the survivors back to their families and homes—if they have any left. Also, start building the case for a war crimes trial. Now let's get out of here."

Smith assigned the task to Colonel Runyon and his special projects team. Shortly thereafter, American forces captured another concentration camp. This one was captured before the Germans could kill all the inmates. Runyon, Jeb, and others, accompanied by Army photographers and press correspondents, drove to the site immediately.

As they entered the camp, men in striped pajama-style clothes emerged from the buildings. They were emaciated, looking almost like skeletons with a light layer of skin over their bones.

"Most of them appear to be Jews," said an Army lieutenant colonel whose battalion had captured the camp. "There are over 5,000 prisoners here. The German guards fled just before we got here."

"What language do they speak?" asked Runyon.

"Most speak German."

"Do you have an interpreter?"

The commander called a captain forward.

"Sir, I'm Captain Schwartz. I can interpret for you."

"O.K." said Runyon, as he looked out at the prisoners and began to address them, pausing after each sentence so Schwartz could translate his remarks. "Gentlemen, I'm from Allied headquarters, from General Eisenhower's staff. Our troops liberated you yesterday from the Nazi oppressors. We are here today to observe and investigate this camp and what it represents. We will get you nourishment and medical care very soon. We will work to return you to your families and homes as soon as possible. We will also record and photograph what we see so we can let the world know what has happened here. May God bless each and every one of you."

The prisoners stood silently, making no response.

"Let's look around the camp," said Runyon.

A commander led the group to a section in the back of the camp that had shallow, mass graves. "Sir, we believe there may be over 10,000 dead prisoners in these shallow graves," said the officer.

"My, God," said Runyon.

Within days, Allied forces overran other concentration camps, including Buchenwald, Erla, Belsen, and Dachau. Investigating the camps was a gruesome task for Jeb and others. Their reports would be used later in prosecuting these Nazi war crimes. The special projects team also helped other elements of Eisenhower's staff plan for providing food and medical care for the liberated prisoners.

The work of the team was intense, and General Smith was a tough taskmaster. Jeb, however, got to see a level and scope of activity he could not have seen with an infantry unit. Some things he wished he hadn't seen. There were two Judge Advocate General officers on the team. From associating with these officers, Jeb gained an appreciation for the law and how it provided a framework for most everything, even the U.S. Army. He began to think about what he would do after the war. Law definitely was now an area of interest.

Chapter 75

Spring-Summer 1945, France and America

Weeks after Germany's surrender on May 8, 1945, Jeb, having served in the Army for four-and- a-half years, was one of the first to receive orders to return to America. He wanted to return to England to look for Katherine. He had written her several times but received no reply. The Army, however, would not authorize him to return home via England. So, in mid-July, he boarded a troop transport ship headed for New York.

Once he landed, he sent a telegram to his mother to let her know that he was in New York and would be home as soon as he mustered out at Fort Meade. After almost a week of filling out forms, turning in equipment, and being examined medically at Fort Meade, he was discharged from active duty with the Army.

Late on the afternoon of July 20, he caught a bus from Fort Meade to Washington, D.C. From Washington, he caught an evening train to Bedford, arriving at 4 a.m. He was fortunate in catching a ride to Halesford with a milkman, who dropped him off at his home at 5 a.m.

When Jeb stepped up on the front porch, some of the boards creaked. From the upstairs window, he heard his mother call through the open window, "Is that you, son?"

"Yes, Mother, it's me." He heard rapid footsteps on the stairway and then the unlocking of the front door.

Helen opened the door, yelled "Jeb," and rushed into his outstretched arms.

"Hi, Mother." They embraced warmly and kissed each other on the cheek.

"Come inside, son," said Helen as she led Jeb to the kitchen. "I want to see what you look like in the light. Oh, but it's wonderful to have you home for good. I've been looking forward to this day for over four years."

"So have I."

She looked him up and down. "You're so thin. We've got to put some weight on you. Let me fix you breakfast." She pulled out some bacon and eggs and made a pot of coffee. They ate and talked the whole morning, Jeb telling his mother about his experiences and she catching him up on the news in Halesford. They took naps in the afternoon.

That evening over supper, they started talking about Jeb's future.

"I want to go to college," said Jeb. "I think I can afford it now. I have the money Uncle Jonah left me, and I saved quite a bit of my Army pay. Also, there's a new government program to help pay for school and training for veterans, called the GI Bill."

"That'll be wonderful, Jeb," said Helen. "What college do you want to attend?"

"I'm not sure yet. I have a few in mind, but I want to check them out."

"Well, you have some of the summer left to make a decision and apply."

Jeb hesitated. "There's one other thing I haven't told you."

Helen sat up straight. "What's that, dear?"

Jeb hesitated, taking a sip of coffee. "There's a girl I met in England. Her name is Katherine, Katherine Tefford. I want to go to England to look for her."

Chapter 76

July 1945, America

Ginny also received orders to return to America. She sailed
to New York on the *Queen Mary*, along with fifty other
women and almost 15,000 soldiers. Her orders gave her
thirty days of leave. After that, she was to report to the Army
hospital at Camp Lee, Virginia. She had been in the Army
just over two years, and she thought she might be sent to the
Pacific to help prepare for the invasion of Japan.

When she arrived in New York, she found a hotel for the
night and checked the train schedules for the next day. She
sent her parents a telegram, which read: "In NYC stop Arrive
Bedford July 28, 4 pm stop Please meet stop Love Ginny."

The next day, she hopped on a train that eventually would
take her to Bedford. As the train pulled in to the Bedford
station, she saw her parents on the platform anxiously
examining each car. A soldier helped her with her bag, and
she rushed to the door of the railcar.

When she stepped out onto the platform, her parents
spotted her and rushed forward. Ginny called "Mom," and
threw herself into her mother's open arms. Her mother
smothered her with kisses as she said, "Ginny, my Ginny."
Both women were crying. Then Ginny turned to her father,
who had tears in his eyes. She had seen her father in
emotional moments turn away, but she had never before seen
him cry. "Dad," she said softly, as she embraced him with a
long hug. Her father tried to speak but couldn't. He pulled
her into him and patted her on the back.

Other people on the platform paused to watch, but quickly
looked away, either from a desire not to intrude on the
occasion or a fear that they could not control their own
emotions.

Randolph finally let go of Ginny. Recovering, he said,
"Well, I guess we should leave. We've got a good drive over

to Halesford." He picked up Ginny's bag which the soldier had left on the platform, and the three of them headed to the car.

"How's Tim?" Ginny asked as soon as they got in the car.

"We just got a letter from him yesterday," said Ruth. "He likes South Carolina and Camp LeJeune. He says he's thriving on the training and knows he made the right decision volunteering for the Marine Corps."

"I'm concerned,' said Randolph. "I fear that he'll be sent to the Pacific as soon as he completes his training. The newspapers are full of reports about the Far East. Now that the war is over in Europe, we and our Allies appear to be gearing up for an invasion of Japan."

"I may get sent to the Pacific, too," said Ginny.

"Oh, no!" said her mother. "I wish this war would be over soon."

Wanting to change the subject, Ginny asked, "So, how's everything in Halesford?"

"There's a certain sadness hanging over the community because we've lost so many of our young men," said her father.

"Yes," said Ruth. "We were especially sorry that so many of your classmates were killed."

Ginny sighed. "I've heard that we lost ten members of the Class of 1940."

"I think that's right," said Randolph. "Halesford lost several young men in the D-Day Invasion. The Bedford community lost twenty men on D-Day, which is just tragic. As tragic as D-Day was for folks around here, however, the overall losses for the whole war are much higher. I think Halesford may have lost over 100 men in the war so far, and it's not over."

"But we have good news, too," said Ruth. "The good news is that some of the boys—as well as some of the girls, including our own dear one—are starting to come home now."

"Who else has come home?"

"Well, for one," said Ruth, looking at Ginny in the back seat, "Jeb Fletcher came home last week."

Ginny smiled. "Oh, I'm glad he's home safely. How is Jeb?"

"He seems well. I saw his mother in the market on Monday. She was ecstatic to have him back. Then a couple of days ago I saw Jeb in the market. He's such a nice, polite young man."

"Yes, he is."

"Oh," said Ruth, as though she had forgotten something that might be important. "He asked about you."

"He did? What did he say?"

"He didn't say so, but I thought he appeared to be concerned about you. He said he had seen you in Europe. Maybe you should call him and let him know you're home."

Chapter 77

July 1945, Halesford

The next morning, at 11:00 o'clock, the Jackson's doorbell rang.

"Ginny, can you get that, please?" called Ruth. "I'm in the midst of putting together a dish for dinner."

"Sure, Mom." Ginny went to the door and opened it.

"Hi, Ginny," said Jeb, with a big smile. "Welcome home."

"Jeb!" She stepped forward and gave him a big hug. "How did you know I was home?"

"Oh, some little bird whistled to my mom early this morning."

"Hmm. I think I might just know that little bird."

"So, how are you, Ginny?"

"I'm well. I'm feeling much better than the last time I saw you."

"I'm glad to hear that."

From the kitchen, Ruth called, "Who is it dear?"

"Come on back to the kitchen. Mother's making something for dinner, and she'll want to say hello to you."

"Mom, it's Jeb. Are you surprised?"

Ruth turned away from the sink toward them. "Oh, Jeb, how nice to see you again."

"Good morning, Mrs. Jackson. It's good to see you again, too. I'll bet you're delighted to have Ginny home."

"Oh, yes, very glad. I'm fixing dinner—a little fried chicken—would you like to join us?"

"Well, that's very kind of you, Mrs. Jackson. Are you sure I wouldn't be intruding?"

"Not at all."

Jeb patted his stomach. "Well, I can't get enough home-cooked fried chicken."

"Randolph will be home from the office at noon, so why don't you two run off somewhere and come back at noon."

Jeb said to Ginny, "Maybe we could go for a walk."

"Sounds great."

The two young people left the Jackson home and began walking along the tree-lined streets of Halesford.

"Jeb, I'm glad we have a chance to talk. I've been wanting to thank you for visiting me at the hospital in France."

"I was glad I could be there."

"That was the lowest time of my life. I've thought about your visit many times since."

"So have I."

"Before your visit, I couldn't get out of bed or talk to anyone. I really didn't care whether I lived or died. And then you almost magically appeared and literally got me back up on my feet again. I don't know what would have happened if you hadn't come."

"If I helped in any way, I'm glad." Jeb looked down at the sidewalk and then at Ginny. "You've always been special, Ginny, to me…and to many people around here."

"What do you plan to do now that you're out of the Army, Jeb?"

"I want to go to college. I wasn't financially able to go after high school, but my uncle left me some money. I've also saved a lot of my Army pay, and now there's the GI Bill coming along."

"That's wonderful. I'm happy for you. You deserve it. I think you'll find college a wonderful experience. I sure enjoyed nursing school. Which college do you want to attend?"

"I'm still trying to decide. I think I'd like to stay in Virginia. What are your plans?"

"Well, I have to report to the Army hospital at Camp Lee in a few weeks. I think the Army may send me off to the Pacific, in preparation for the invasion of Japan."

"Maybe they'll keep you stateside."

"Maybe. Perhaps while I'm at Camp Lee you could visit me. I understand there are lots of things to see and do around there."

"Ginny, before I start college this fall, I have to go back to England for a visit."

Ginny slowed, almost to a stop. "Back to England? Why?"

"There's a girl there that I dated while I was stationed at Waterbridge. After my company left for Normandy, we more or less lost contact. I have to go look for her." Jeb did not tell Ginny that he had written to Katherine but that she had not responded.

Ginny started walking again, and Jeb followed beside her. She looked down at the sidewalk. "She must be a very special young lady, Jeb."

"She is. I need to look for her. I couldn't live with myself if I didn't."

Ginny and Jeb walked back to the Jackson home in silence, and both were subdued as they sat at the dining room table and ate dinner with Ginny's parents.

Chapter 78

August 1945, Great Britain

Jeb was able to find passage to England and arrived in mid-August at the southern British port of Southampton. He presumed that Katherine would now be back in Waterbridge and intended to look for her there.

Arriving in Southampton late in the afternoon, he found a small hotel and then went to a pub for supper. No one spoke to him except an older waitress who took his order. While waiting for his meal, he looked around the pub, which was filled mostly with older English men. He played with his silverware and read the labels on the condiment bottles. *It's strange being back in England after more than a year away.* He felt both foreign and lonely.

The next morning he caught a train north and then one west to Waterbridge. Midway on the trip, a flurry of anxiety washed over him. He asked himself one more time the questions that kept coming into his head. *Where was Katherine? Why had Katherine not tried to contact him after he had visited her cousin in London? Why had she not responded to his letters? Had she found some other man? Did she have the baby, or had she given it up?*

He arrived in Waterbridge shortly before noon. He got a room in a small hotel and decided to stop for a bite to eat at the pub that he and the men of Company N had frequented.

His memory of the pub was of the evenings, when he and other soldiers traveled in the dark from the nearby camp. When they had opened the door of the pub, they had found a warmly-lit space filled with the rich smells of ale and food and the noise of boisterous men bantering back and forth. Now, at noontime, standing in bright sunlight, he opened the door of the pub and found the inside so dark that he could hardly see. Once his eyes adjusted, he saw that the only people in the pub were two older men sitting at a table and the proprietor, who stood behind the bar washing glasses.

Jeb recognized the proprietor and approached the bar. "Hello, Michael," he said.

"Hello, there," said Michael.

"Do you remember me?"

"Well, you look a bit familiar."

"I'm one of the Americans who were stationed at the camp outside town until just over a year ago. We used to come in here a lot."

"Oh, sure. I should have recognized the Yank accent. Those were lively times then."

Jeb sat down at the bar. "We used to fill this place at night."

"Indeed, you did. It's a lot quieter now. Can I get you something? I'd put it on the house, if I could, for old times' sake, but times have been really tough this last year."

"Could I have a small ale and maybe a sausage?"

"Coming right up," replied Michael, as he poured a glass of ale from a keg and set it on the bar in front of Jeb. He got a sausage and began heating it. "So, did you go to Normandy from here?"

"Yes, and then further into France. I also made it into Belgium and Germany."

Michael served Jeb the sausage. "What brings you back to Waterbridge?"

"I'm looking for someone."

"A girl? There have been a couple of other GIs come back here looking for girls they knew."

"Yes, a girl. Maybe you happen to know her—Katherine Tefford?"

"No, I'm afraid I don't. There are several Tefford families in town."

Jeb finished his ale and sausage and paid his bill. He had some walking to do.

Chapter 79

Jeb exited the dark pub and was momentarily blinded by the bright sunlight. As soon as his eyes adjusted, he headed toward the old dance hall where he had met Katherine. When he got to the hall, he found a notice on the door—"Closed until further notice."

He thought for a moment about how to get from the dance hall to Katherine's home. He had made the trip many times. He walked down the main street of the town, recognized a building on a corner, and turned onto a side street. In the block ahead he saw what he was sure was Katherine's house, on the same side of the street where he was walking. He crossed to the other side so he could see more of the front of the Tefford home. No one was outside any of the homes on the block.

Jeb crossed back over the street and approached the house. He took a close look. This was it. He remembered the front door. His mouth was dry, and he felt queasy. Rather than go up to the door, he walked on by house. After about fifty feet, he reversed course. When he got back to the Tefford house, he paused, faced the house, and stepped to the front door. He rapped on the door.

No one answered. He waited a minute and rapped again. He heard something inside. Then the door opened. Standing at the door was a woman who appeared to be in her sixties. She wore a simple housedress. She could have once been attractive, but now she looked run down. She wore no makeup and had deep circles under her eyes. "Yes?" she said.

From within the house came the cry of a baby.

Jeb smiled inwardly. *Is that my child?*

The woman turned toward the noise. "Hush, you sweet little rascal," she said in a gentle voice. She turned back to Jeb. "He's going to be the death of me yet."

She said 'he'—do I have a son?

"What do you want, young man? I'm rather busy right now, as you can hear."

"Mrs. Tefford?"

"Yes."

"I'm Jebediah Fletcher."

Mrs. Tefford took a step backward and gasped slightly. "Fletcher? You mean…Fletcher, the American?"

"Yes."

"Oh, the trouble you've caused."

More baby cries came from within the house. Mrs. Tefford turned again toward the noise. "Hush, I said."

"Is Katherine home, Mrs. Tefford?"

"Katherine?"

"Yes, Katherine."

"You don't know?"

"Know what?"

"Why, my Katherine is dead."

Jeb felt dizzy, as though all the blood was flowing from his head, from his body. "Dead?" he muttered. He reached out and took hold of the door jamb to steady himself.

"Are you all right? You're as white as a ghost. You'd better come inside and sit down."

Jeb stepped inside.

Mrs. Tefford motioned to a chair in the living room. "Sit down."

Jeb sat and put his head in his hands. After a few moments, he looked up. "I'm very sorry," he said, shaking his head.

"I thought you knew."

"I didn't."

"I guess maybe there was no way you would have heard."

"I had no idea. I'm so sorry."

"Katherine was my only child. I miss her dearly."

"I'm terribly sorry." Scooting forward in his chair, he asked in a subdued voice, "May I ask what happened?"

"Well, did you know that Katherine was pregnant— pregnant with your child?"

"Yes, she wrote me that she was pregnant. I've kept the letter and have it with me. I was wounded around that time, and they sent me back to a hospital here in England. When I got better I left the hospital for a day and went to the home in London of Katherine's cousin—her address had been on the letter Katherine sent me. The cousin said that Katherine had gone back home for a visit. I was then sent back to France. I wrote her several times from France but never received a reply."

"I see. Well, Katherine's father warned her to stay away from you soldiers. He knew what could happen. She didn't heed his warning and sneaked around behind our backs with you—oh, I shouldn't say anything bad about my daughter."

"I'm sorry," said Jeb, looking down at the floor and then looking back up at Mrs. Tefford. "It was all my fault. I never wanted to hurt Katherine or your family."

"When she told us she was pregnant, her father flew into a rage. He said he wanted to protect the family's reputation. He insisted that she go away until she had the baby. He insisted that she move to London to live with a cousin and that she give the baby up for adoption after it was born."

"I'm so sorry."

"Katherine came home once when she was pregnant. Her father insisted that she stay in the house and then he sent her back to London after a few days. The baby was born in London. Then one day one of those German V-2 rockets hit the house. It killed Katherine and her cousin. The baby miraculously survived. The government said it was one of the last rockets the Germans fired across the Channel."

"I'm very sorry," said Jeb, again looking down and shaking his head. "I'm truly sorry Katherine is dead, and I regret that my actions contributed to her death. I feel awful."

"Katherine told me a little about you. She thought you were a wonderful person. She said that even after she learned she was pregnant. I think she was in love with you."

"We were in love. We told each other so. She was special. I wanted to come look for her."

"She was special."

"I'm sorry for the grief that her death must have caused you and Mr. Tefford."

"It was very hard for both of us, especially for my husband. After her death, he forgave Katherine, but then he couldn't forgive himself for sending her away—sending her to her death. He was heartbroken. He died in his sleep a month after she was killed."

"I'm so sorry."

The baby let out a loud bawl from a back room, wanting attention.

"Is that the baby?" asked Jeb. "You indicated it's a boy. Is that my son?"

"Yes, indeed, Katherine's and your son. Would you like to see him?"

"Yes, please," replied Jeb, standing up, as a rush of excitement and anticipation overcame the sorrow he felt.

Mrs. Tefford walked down the back hall. The baby cried out again, and Jeb could hear Mrs. Tefford soothing him. She returned in a couple of minutes, carrying the baby, who continued to cry but softly.

Jeb approached for a close look at the baby, who was wrapped in a blue blanket. "He's beautiful. He looks like Katherine."

"I think so, too," said Mrs. Tefford, as tears ran down her cheeks. "Maybe now I see some of you in him, too. Would you like to hold him?"

"May I?"

"Why don't you sit down first? I wouldn't want you to drop him."

"That's a good idea. I don't think I've ever held a baby." Jeb sat, and Mrs. Tefford handed him the baby, who continued to cry, but softly.

Jeb cradled the baby in his arms. He felt awkward. He looked at the baby and smiled. The baby stopped crying.

Mrs. Tefford smiled. "Well, listen to that. He hushed right up for you."

Jeb lowered his face toward the baby and inhaled. "He smells so sweet."

"Doesn't he, though?"

Feeling the baby's warmth, Jeb smiled at the baby. "What's his name?"

"Katherine named him 'Franklin.'"

"'Franklin?'"

"Yes, after your president. She thought the world of Mr. Roosevelt. We all did."

"Hello, Franklin," Jeb said, lowering his face toward the baby's.

"His middle name is 'Winston.'"

"After Mr. Churchill?"

"Indeed. Katherine also thought the world of Mr. Churchill, as we all do. She thought the world of you, too, and she wanted to honor you, so 'Franklin' came before 'Winston.'"

"She couldn't have chosen two better names."

Mrs. Tefford looked quietly at Jeb and the baby for several seconds.

Jeb looked up from the baby and met her gaze.

"His last name," she said, pausing, "is 'Fletcher.'"

Jeb was speechless. Before today, he had not even known if there was a baby, and he had not even thought about names. He was pleased with little Franklin's first and middle names. This last name was something he had not expected. He could manage only one word. "'Fletcher?'"

"Yes. Katherine insisted."

Jeb slid his hands under the baby's arms and lifted him up in front of him, father and son looking each other directly in the face. Jeb smiled at the baby. "Hello, Franklin Winston Fletcher."

"As I said, Katherine thought the world of you. She said she didn't know what would happen to you, or what would happen between the two of you, but she wanted to honor you with the baby's last name."

"I feel very honored, indeed."

"Good. I wasn't sure how you'd feel. Katherine would be pleased."

"Is Katherine buried near here?"

"Yes, she's buried here in the town cemetery."

"Could I visit her grave?"

"Why, surely. It's just a short walk. I'll get the pram for Franklin, and we'll take you there."

Pushing the pram, Mrs. Tefford led the way to the cemetery and to Katherine's grave. "Here we are," she said. "That's my husband's grave next to Katherine's. I'm going to take Franklin for a short stroll. We'll be back in a few minutes."

When he was alone, Jeb said a prayer for Katherine and for her father. He asked for forgiveness from them and from God. Then he wept.

When Mrs. Tefford returned, Jeb said, "May I take Franklin for a stroll and give you a few minutes here, Mrs. Tefford?"

"Thank you, Jeb—may I call you 'Jeb'? That's what Katherine called you."

"Please do. We'll be back in a few minutes." He pushed the pram away.

Ten minutes later, Jeb returned to the gravesite with the pram.

Mrs. Tefford had been kneeling between her husband's and Katherine's graves. She stood and dabbed at her eyes with a handkerchief. "Thank you, Jeb. I guess we should head back home now. Would you mind pushing the pram?"

"I'd be pleased to push Franklin." Jeb grabbed the handle of the pram, and off they went.

Once they reached the house, Mrs. Tefford said, "Would you like to stay for supper? It won't be fancy, but it'll be nourishing."

"I'd like that very much."

They moved to the kitchen. Jeb sat at the kitchen table holding Franklin in his arms, while Mrs. Tefford fixed supper.

"Would you like to try feeding Franklin?"

"Uh, O.K. This will be a new experience."

Mrs. Tefford fixed a bowl of baby food and placed it and a small spoon on the table in front of Jeb. She put a bib on Franklin and placed a cloth on the table. "You'll need the cloth. Just feed him half a spoonful at a time. He's a good eater, but messy."

Jeb began feeding Franklin, watching with amazement as the baby ate. When Franklin managed to get his hands in his food, Jeb promptly cleaned him up with the cloth.

"What are your plans for the future, Jeb?"

"I'm going to go to college. I couldn't afford it before, but my uncle left me some money, and I saved some money when I was in the Army. Also, the government has created a new program to help veterans with college."

"Going to college—that's splendid. If you don't mind my asking, how old are you?"

"I'm twenty-three."

"Katherine would be twenty-two."

Mrs. Tefford put Franklin down for a nap. Then she set two places at the table and served the meal. While they were eating, she asked, "Can we speak frankly for a minute?"

"Of course."

"I'm worried about Franklin's future. I'm getting older, and my health is not good. I love this little boy, but even now I'm having difficulty taking care of him physically, and it won't get any easier when he starts crawling and then walking."

"I can see he's going to be active."

"And financially, I have just enough income for me to live on. I've had to use some of my savings to help with expenses for Franklin, and I know the expenses will increase as he gets older. I have no family. If something happens to me, I'm afraid Franklin will be placed in an orphanage. I'd hate to see that happen to this dear little boy."

Jeb sat quietly, slowing taking bites of food and thinking. He took a drink of water and wiped his lips with the napkin. "Could I take him back to America to live with me?"

Mrs. Tefford put her napkin down and looked directly into Jeb's eyes. "You'd do that?"

"He's my son."

"But what about going to college?"

"I could work out some arrangement. My mother might be able to help, and with some of the money my uncle left me, I might be able to hire some help."

"Are you really sure you want to do this? It's a big responsibility. I'd hate to see you find that it's too big of a responsibility and then have Franklin suffer."

"Mrs. Tefford, Franklin is my son. He's a Fletcher. I pledge to you, and to the memory of Katherine, that I will be a good father to him and raise him well."

"Well, if you're sure, that would be a wonderful thing. I've been very worried about what would happen to the boy."

"Could I take Franklin to America now?"

"We'll probably have to establish that you are his father. I can probably vouch for that."

"And I have Katherine's letter saying she was pregnant with my child."

"Once we're able to establish you as the father, there could be a problem allowing Franklin to leave this country with you and then enter the United States."

"Yes, that could be a problem."

Mrs. Tefford thought for a moment. "When I said I have no family, I misspoke. I have a second cousin who's fairly high up in the Home Office in London. When Katherine died, he told me to let him know if there was anything he could do for me. He might be able to pull some strings with our government and your embassy. I'll phone him tomorrow."

Chapter 80

August 1945, Waterbridge, Atlantic, Halesford

Jeb made arrangements to stay at the hotel in Waterbridge for a week. He spent most of each day at Mrs. Tefford's, getting to know her and Franklin better and telling Mrs. Tefford about his mother and Halesford. To give Mrs. Tefford a little rest and have some time to herself, he took Franklin on long walks in the pram, stopping each time at Katherine's grave. He became proficient in caring for the baby, feeding him, changing his diapers, and playing with him. Jeb could tell that Mrs. Tefford was more relaxed and more rested than when he met her days before.

At the end of the week, Mrs. Tefford's cousin in London telephoned with news that Jeb had been authorized to take Franklin with him to America. Papers had been put in the post to Mrs. Tefford and should arrive within a day or two.

Jeb made arrangements for passage for Franklin and him to New York and bought a small suitcase for Franklin's clothes.

When the day arrived for them to leave, Mrs. Tefford grew teary. She fixed some food for Jeb to take for Franklin. Then she held and rocked the baby until it was time for them to leave. She insisted on walking with them to the Waterbridge rail station where Jeb and Franklin would catch a train toward Southampton. She pushed Franklin in the pram, while Jeb carried his bag and the suitcase for Franklin. As they walked, Jeb promised to write Mrs. Tefford frequently about Franklin, and he gave her an open invitation to visit him and his mother in Virginia.

When they reached the station, Mrs. Tefford picked up Franklin and held him on her lap as she and Jeb sat chatting while awaiting the train. She gave the baby several kisses. When the train arrived, she gave Franklin one last kiss and handed him to Jeb. With tears in her eyes, she leaned up and kissed Jeb on the cheek. "Take care of Franklin and yourself, and please write me often."

"I will. It's a promise. Jeb kissed her on the cheek. "Take care of yourself, too, and thank you for all the love and care you've given Franklin."

Holding the baby in one arm, Jeb picked up Franklin's suitcase with his free hand and handed it to a porter. Then he grabbed his own bag, climbed into the railcar, and took a seat on the side where he could see Mrs. Tefford. She was standing with the empty pram, tears streaming down her face. Jeb held Franklin up to the window and moved the baby's arm in a wave as the train pulled away.

* * * * * * * *

Traveling with a baby was a challenge. Jeb had to navigate from one train to another and then, in Southampton, onto a ship, carrying the baby, his bag, and a suitcase. He had to find food for Franklin, feed him, change and wash his diapers, and share a bed with him.

Aboard the ship to America, Jeb and Franklin piqued the curiosity of many travelers who asked if Jeb was traveling alone with the baby and where the mother was. Jeb limited his responses to saying that Franklin was his son and that Franklin's mother had died.

When the ship arrived in New York early one morning, Jeb purchased a ticket for a train to Bedford. He sent his mother a telegram: "Arrive Bedford 8 pm tonight stop Please meet us stop Jeb."

Helen read the telegram several times. *'Us'? Who is 'us'? Is he bringing his girlfriend Katherine back to Virginia?*

As the train pulled up to the Bedford station, Jeb saw his mother waiting on the platform. He picked up Franklin in one arm and the bag in the other. A fellow passenger offered to carry the suitcase to the door.

Helen saw Jeb step off the train, some forty feet away. *What's that he's carrying? It's a baby! But no one else is getting off the train.* She was confused. She rushed forward, calling, "Jeb, welcome home." She gave her son a hug and a kiss on the cheek.

Jeb returned the kiss. "Hi, Mother." He held up Franklin. "Mother, meet Franklin, your grandson."

She arched her back. "What? My grandson?" Her forehead knotted in puzzlement. "Where's Katherine?"

"Here, Mother, take Franklin," he said, as he handed the baby to Helen. "Let me grab the bags."

Helen took Franklin and cradled him in her arms. Franklin smiled at her. "Well, aren't you just the cutest thing?" she said with a smile.

"We should head home, Mother. I've got a lot to tell you on the way."

"I guess you do, son. You surely do."

Jeb loaded the bags into the back of the truck and opened the passenger door for his mother. Helen handed Franklin to Jeb and climbed in. Jeb then handed Franklin back to her, and she cradled him in her arms. Jeb got in on the driver's, started the truck, and headed toward home.

"We have a thirty minute ride," said Helen, looking at Jeb and then at Franklin. "We also have all of the rest of the night. I want to hear every bit of detail, Jeb, every last bit."

By the end of the thirty-minute drive home, Helen had fallen in love with Franklin and had begun to delight in her new role of grandmother. It took the rest of the evening, until midnight, for Jeb to answer all the questions his mother had about Katherine, Franklin, Katherine's parents, and Jeb's trip to England and back.

Chapter 81

September 1945, Halesford

Word about Jeb and his new son spread quickly throughout the Halesford community. Many fully embraced Jeb and Franklin, but some gossiped, mostly about loose morality.

Jeb had applied to and been accepted at Roanoke College, which was a little more than an hour's commute from Halesford. Helen applied for retirement so that she could help watch Franklin. Jeb would be home with Franklin except when he had classes.

Jeb learned that, after Japan announced that it was surrendering, Ginny had applied for a discharge from the Army and was returning home to Halesford from Camp Lee.

On a bright Saturday morning, Jeb was pushing Franklin in a stroller on a walk downtown when he saw Ginny come out of a store across the street. "Hey, Ginny," he called, a big smile showing his excitement at seeing her. He waved to get her attention.

"Hi, Jeb," Ginny called back, in a voice that was courteous but lacked emotion.

"Can you come over here, please? I want you to meet someone."

She hesitated, then called back, "Oh, I'm sorry, but I have to run. I have an appointment."

Jeb watched as she walked away. He turned and continued down the sidewalk in the opposite direction.

From a distance he heard a loud, deep voice from down the street behind him call, "Ginny!" He paused and turned to see who was calling. Even from a distance, he was able to identify Dick Drumheller.

He saw Ginny stop and Drumheller cross the street and eagerly give Ginny a big hug.

Jeb watched for a moment and then looked down at Franklin and adjusted the small, light blue cap on the baby's head. He glanced back at Ginny and Drumheller, who stood talking. Then he continued pushing the carriage toward home.

The next day was the Halesford Labor Day Picnic, an event held each year in the town park.

With Helen cuddling Franklin in the seat next to him, Jeb drove to the park about 3 p.m. They found an empty picnic table, and Helen spread out a cloth and placed their picnic basket atop it. Many people came over to say hello and to see the baby. Several women picked up Franklin, who was dressed in a powder-blue playsuit. They played with his tiny hands and tickled his cheeks. Jeb noticed that some people, however, seemed to shun them. Neither he nor his mother said anything about this.

An hour later, Jeb saw Ginny and her parents arrive and select a table. He handed Franklin to his mother. "I'll be back in a few minutes."

He walked over to the Jackson's table as they were unpacking their picnic basket. "Hello, Ginny. Hello, Mr. and Mrs. Jackson."

The Jacksons looked up. "Well, hello, Jeb," said Ruth, with a smile.

"Hi, Jeb," Ginny said quietly.

"Hello, young man," said Randolph, pulling at one ear. "I understand you're a father now."

"Yes, sir. I have a son. His name is Franklin. He's seven months old."

"Well," said Randolph, "that's…well, that's really something. I'm sorry, but we just arrived, and our food is hot."

"Oh, excuse me," said Jeb, his face reddening. "I'll see you all later."

"Certainly," said Ruth, her face turning crimson.

Jeb turned and walked back to his mother and Franklin. He took Franklin from his mother and sat cradling him in one arm. Several more people came to see the baby, and Jeb stood up each time so they could have a better view of the little boy.

Ginny had also blushed at her father's rudeness. "Mother, I see some friends. I'll be back in a few minutes."

She had seen two of her old classmates from the Class of 1940, Charlotte Biggs and Frances Murdock. She walked over to greet them. "Hey, Charlotte and Frances, how are you?"

"Hey, Ginny. Wow, it's been a long time since we've seen you," said Charlotte.

"Hi, Ginny," said Frances. "It seems like ages."

"It's been quite some time," said Ginny.

"You went to nursing school, didn't you?" asked Charlotte. "How was that?"

"I really enjoyed it."

Charlotte raised her eyebrows. "Really?"

"And then you joined the Army, right?" asked Frances.

"Yes, I just spent two years as an Army nurse. I got back from Europe recently and was discharged earlier this week."

"Did you get to see gay Par-ee?" Charlotte said with a smile.

"I spent a couple of days in Paris."

"That must have been fun being in the Army with all those young men. I'll bet you had a date every night," said Frances, smiling and giving Charlotte a quick wink.

"Although," said Charlotte with a laugh, "I don't see how you could ever attract a man with those ugly uniforms they made you wear. We saw pictures of them in *Life Magazine*."

"It would probably be hard for you to imagine Army life," Ginny said, no longer smiling. "We actually thought the uniforms were pretty special. We were proud to wear them."

"Oh, well, anyway," said Frances, "we're glad you're home now. Maybe you can join us for a game of bridge sometime. We've gotten pretty good. There sure wasn't much else to do in the evenings these past years, with all the men gone. Just give us a call if you want to play."

"Well, I'd better get back to my folks," said Ginny.

From behind the three young women a deep voice called, "Hello, ladies." The women turned to see who it was.

"Hello, Dick," said Ginny, greeting Dick Drumheller.

"Hey, Dick," said Charlotte, with a broad smile. "How are you feeling today?"

"That was some party last night, wasn't it?" said Frances.

"I'll say," said Dick. "I'm glad I could sleep in this morning. I'll bet Halesford hasn't seen anything like that for years." Dick looked across to the other side of the picnic area. "Speaking of unusual sights, isn't that Jeb Fletcher over there?"

"Yes, that's Jeb. We were talking about him before Ginny came over to see us," said Charlotte.

"We think he's got a lot of nerve coming here," said Frances, "coming here to show off his son."

"Indeed," said Charlotte, "his illegitimate son."

"You mean his little British bastard?" said Dick.

"Oh, 'British bastard,' that's good," said Frances, as she, Charlotte, and Dick broke out laughing.

Ginny looked over and saw Jeb looking at them. She felt her face flush, as a wave of shame swept over her. She abruptly walked away and returned to her family's table, where her father sat eating chicken. "Mother, would you go with me to say hello to Jeb and his mother?"

"Why…" her mother hesitated, glancing at her husband. "Why…certainly, Ginny. We'll be back in a few minutes, Randolph."

Randolph stared up at his wife and daughter for a moment, started to say something, and then went back to eating his chicken.

Jeb saw Ginny and her mother walking toward him and his family.

"Hi, Helen," said Ruth, as she and Ginny neared the Fletchers' table.

Helen and Jeb rose to greet them. "Hello, Ruth," said Helen.

"Hello, Mrs. Fletcher," said Ginny.

Helen took Ginny's hand. "Oh, Ginny. It's great to have you back home. I've been looking forward to seeing you. I've heard of some of the wonderful things you and the other nurses did for our boys over there, including one young man who's very special to me. Thank you." She gave Ginny a big hug.

"Thank you, Mrs. Fletcher. You have no idea how much that means to me right now," Ginny said as tears welled in her eyes. She looked at Jeb and smiled. "Jeb, we've come to see your son."

"Yes," said Ruth. "May I hold him?"

"Yes, of course," said Jeb, handing the baby to Ruth. "His name is Franklin. He's named after President Roosevelt. And his middle name is 'Winston,' after Mr. Churchill."

"Oh, he's adorable," Ruth said as she cuddled the baby. "Ginny, would you like to hold Franklin?"

"Uh, well…not right now. Maybe later."

The three women and Jeb chatted for a few minutes.

"Ginny," said Jeb, "would you take a walk with me?"

Ginny hesitated. She looked over and saw Charlotte, Frances, and Dick, who continued to look in the direction of the Fletcher table and laugh. "I'd like that very much."

"Mrs. Jackson, would you mind if I take Franklin back?" Jeb said, holding out his arms.

"Why, of course not." Ruth handed the baby back to Jeb. "Thanks for letting me hold him. He's a sweet baby."

As Ruth and Helen chatted, Jeb, carrying Franklin, motioned Ginny toward a path that led away from the picnic area. As they strolled along, Jeb said, "Ginny, the day that we had lunch at your house, I told you I was going to go back to England to look for a girl I had dated when we were training there."

"Jeb, I don't think I want to hear about this."

"Please, let me finish. What I didn't tell you was that we had fallen in love. A few weeks before D-Day, I talked her into spending a weekend together in London. She later wrote to me in France that she was pregnant."

Ginny stopped. "Jeb, I really don't want to hear this."

"Please, let's walk a little further, and let me finish." Jeb continued down the path, and Ginny walked with him. "I went back a few weeks ago and went to her home. Her mother was there. She told me that Katherine—Katherine Tefford was her name—had been killed by a German rocket in London, where her father had sent her when he learned she was pregnant. A cousin had also been killed, but Franklin survived. Katherine's father died shortly thereafter of a broken heart."

"I'm sorry."

"I felt awful. I was responsible in many ways for what happened to Katherine and her father."

"A lot of awful things happened in the war," said Ginny.

"Yes, they did. I could tell Mrs. Tefford didn't think highly of me. Then I heard a baby cry from a back room, and Mrs. Tefford brought him out and introduced me to Franklin. She had been caring for him, and it wasn't easy. She's an older woman, whose health isn't good. She had lost her husband and Katherine, her only child. She barely had enough money to live on. I could see for myself that it was true what she was saying about her circumstances. She was very concerned about what would happen to the baby in the future, especially if her health worsened. She had no other real family. When she told me that Katherine had named the baby Franklin Winston Fletcher, there was absolutely no room for doubt. I knew immediately what the right thing to do was—to bring my son home with me to Virginia."

Ginny raised her head and looked at Jeb as they continued down the path.

"Fortunately, Mrs. Tefford had a cousin in the Home Office, and he was able to expedite things so I could bring Franklin to America. In the short time I was there, Mrs. Tefford and I grew to be friends, and I believe she thought Franklin was in good hands when we left. So here we are."

"Thanks for telling me all of that, Jeb. I owe you an apology."

"No, you don't."

"Yes, I do, for judging you, or maybe prejudging you."

"Nonsense."

Ginny stopped and looked directly into Jeb's eyes. "You'll make me feel much better if you accept my apology."

"Well, O.K. If you put it that way, apology accepted."

Ginny smiled. "Thanks. I feel a lot better already."

They walked further along the path that led through beds of flowers, shrubs, and small trees.

"So what are you plans, Jeb?"

"Well, I've enrolled at Roanoke College. I'll live at home and commute to school. My mother has retired, and together we'll take care of Franklin. My uncle left me some money, and with what I saved from the Army plus the GI Bill, I think I can make ends meet. I developed an interest in the law and would like to go to law school after I get my bachelor's degree."

"That's great."

"And what about you, Ginny?"

"Well, I want to continue with nursing. I find it very rewarding. But the Army's not for me, not any more. I enjoyed getting to travel and seeing places I would never have seen, but I want to find a nursing job around here somewhere and settle down."

They came to a wooded section of the park where there was a bench and a shelter not far away. "Let's rest a minute," said Jeb, sitting down on the bench. Ginny sat down next to him.

"Ginny, I need to run over to that shelter and use the restroom. Will you hold Franklin? I won't be long."

Ginny hesitated. "Well, O.K."

Jeb handed Franklin to her and headed to the shelter. He took his time using the facilities. He washed his hands three times. When he came out of the men's room, he peeked around the corner of the shelter and looked at Ginny and his son. Ginny was holding Franklin close, talking to him, and playing with his hands. Jeb took his time returning to the bench.

He sat down next to Ginny. He leaned over, turned her face toward him, and kissed her on the lips gently.

Ginny did not pull back. She returned the kiss.

Their next kiss was deeper and even more satisfying.

"We'd better be getting back," said Ginny.

"I guess so. People might talk."

Ginny smiled. "Oh, some people are probably already talking. But what do they know? What do they know about anything?"

They strolled back to the picnic area, with Ginny carrying Franklin.

Chapter 82

July 2009, Halesford

Earlier in the day, Jeb, Ginny, Bill, and Billy had sat around the kitchen table and later on the front porch as Jeb and Ginny told their stories of growing up in Halesford and graduating from Halesford High. Ginny spoke of going to nursing school in Richmond, and Jeb talked about finding a job and joining the National Guard. They both went into detail about their wartime experiences and touched on their returning to Halesford at the end of the war.

When in the late afternoon Jeb fell asleep in his chair on the porch, Ginny had to wake him to come to supper. After the meal, they took their dessert and coffee to the living room. Jeb reclined in his favorite chair, with his feet up on a hassock. Ginny sat in the easy chair where most evenings she read and sewed. Bill and Billy sat on the sofa.

A light rain fell outside, and a gentle breeze blew moist, sweet-smelling air through the open windows. Two floor lamps near Jeb's and Ginny's chairs provided the only light in the room.

Jeb resumed the storytelling. He told of courting Ginny after the Labor Day picnic, of their falling deeply in love, and of their autumn wedding. He told of using the inheritance from his Uncle Jonah and the GI Bill to enroll at Roanoke College and moving the family to Charlottesville so he could attend law school at the University of Virginia. He spoke briefly of settling back in Halesford, setting up a law practice, and buying the old farm where he had grown up. He spoke of his mother's death, and Ginny spoke of her parents deaths.

When Jeb finished his story, he took the last bite of his apple pie and washed it down with coffee. He looked at Bill and Billy. "You know, of all the things I've told you about the war, what really stands out in my mind is not all the hardships—the training, the combat, and all the suffering. Oh, I remember some of the horror, men getting wounded and dying. Both your Grandma and I used to have nightmares. One of us would wake up calling out in the middle of the night. At least we knew what the other was suffering. We'd hug each other and usually fall back asleep, at peace. Fortunately, those nightmares subsided with time. No, it's not the horror and suffering that stands out. It's the people that I got to know and serve with. I didn't get to know them well, but we developed a special bond because of the rough things we went through together. They were a great group of guys. We used to have reunions, and I always looked forward to those. Unfortunately, almost all of the men have now passed away."

"We're all getting older," said Ginny. "We used to have reunions of our high school class, but now all our classmates have died."

"Yep," said Jeb, "we're the last two members of the Class of 1940."

Ginny picked up her cup of coffee from the small table beside her chair, took a sip, and held the cup in both hands in front of her chin, reflecting. "My experience in the war was different. As I've told you boys, I didn't serve in any single unit for very long, so I didn't form a lot of close bonds. I met a lot of nice people, but I didn't get to know many of them well. Your grandpa jokes that that's because I volunteered too much. He volunteered only twice—for the National Guard and to become an officer. I volunteered four times— to become an Army nurse, to serve overseas, to serve in an evacuation hospital, and then to serve in a field hospital. I guess I just kept moving on. I did finally bond with someone—my best friend—your grandpa. That is if you call 63 years of marriage 'bonding.'"

Bill and Billy laughed.

Ginny continued. "Of course, I had a close bond with Liz for four years, going through nursing school and serving in the Army together. When I came home in 1945, I felt I should go to Big Stone Gap to see her parents. I dreaded that trip. I was so nervous. But the Hawkinses were so nice to me and so understanding. They and that visit did so much to put me at ease, at ease with Liz's death and with the whole war. The trip to Big Stone Gap is something I'll never forget."

"Well," said Jeb, "we've told you our war stories and a little about our returning to Halesford."

"Thanks to both of you for sharing that with us," said Bill. "It means a lot to both Billy and me to hear your stories, especially to hear them directly from you. I'm going to write some of it down so we can pass it along to Billy's family, when he grows up and has one of his own."

"Yes, thanks, Grandpa and Grandma," said Billy. "I now have lots of things to share with my friends. I've got some other stories from the book Grandpa bought me on D-Day. When I get home, I'm going to the library and look for some more books on World War II."

"Well, good," said Jeb. "I feel much better for having finally told you everything. Ginny, why don't you tell them a little more about what you did after the war. They also want to hear everything we can remember about raising Franklin. If you'll excuse me, I'll just sit here quietly and listen, perhaps with my eyes shut." He reached up and shut off the floor lamp beside his chair.

Ginny told some stories of Jeb's courting her and then their getting married. She spoke of staying at home taking care of Franklin for the first couple of years after they were married and then resuming her nursing career, part-time for several years, and then full-time when Franklin reached the eighth grade. She said she worked for fifteen years in the maternity ward of the local hospital, something she had always wanted to do.

Mostly, she spoke about Franklin. She told how Jeb and she had wanted to have children of their own but were not successful, and how blessed she felt to be able to raise Franklin. She talked about him as a baby and a toddler and of his school days and going off to college and getting married.

She recalled how happy and proud Franklin had been when Bill was born. Then her eyes glistened with tears. "I could not have loved Franklin any more if he had been my own flesh and blood. I feel the same way about both of you boys."

Bill and Billy, who had been listening intently, asking questions, and laughing over many of the things Franklin did as a child, grew quiet. "Thanks, Grandma," said Bill, as he stood and leaned over her chair to hug her.

"Yes, thanks, Grandma," said Billy. I'll always remember this visit."

The grandfather clock struck ten. "Boys," said Ginny, "I think that's enough for the day. Don't you think we'd better get ready for bed?"

"Yes, I think so," said Bill. "It looks like Grandpa is sound asleep already."

Ginny stood up and walked over to Jeb's chair. She took his wrist and shook his arm gently. "Jeb, it's time for bed." He didn't move. She took hold of his shoulder and shook a little harder. "Jeb." Then she lifted his chin and put her hand on his neck, feeling for his carotid artery. "Jeb, Jeb honey." She began to cry, softly.

Jeb had passed—passed on his story, passed on his legacy, and then, unburdened and among those he loved, passed on to a more peaceful place.

About the Author

James W. Morrison spent a career in the Department of Defense, including three years as a U.S. Army officer and nearly 27 years as a civilian executive in the Office of the Secretary of Defense. A graduate of Indiana and Columbia Universities and the National War College, he also served as a visiting fellow at the National Defense University, where he wrote and had published scholarly work.

After moving to southwest Virginia, he conducted research and interviews with veterans and their families on Bedford County's experience in World War II, a war in which the county lost 20 men on D-Day and more than 140 men throughout the fighting. His historical drama, *Bedford Goes to War*, won a contest sponsored by the Sedalia Center in Bedford County and was performed eight times over three summers. His history, *Bedford Goes to War: the Heroic Story of a Small Virginia Community in World War II*, was selected from 60 non-fiction books nominated for the 2005 Library of Virginia Literary Awards as one of five finalists for a People's Choice Award. The book is in its third edition.

Class of 1940, in which the author draws on his research for *Bedford Goes to War*, is his first novel.

In addition to history and other scholarly work and drama, Morrison has written essays, short stories, plays, and poetry. He has been active in the Virginia Writers Club, its Valley Writers Chapter, and the Lake Writers, and has led each group for varying periods.

He lives with his wife, Edie, at Smith Mountain Lake. They have two grown children and two grandchildren.

Visit the author's website at http://morrisonjamesw.com

You May Also Enjoy Reading the History

BEDFORD GOES TO WAR

THE HEROIC STORY
OF A SMALL VIRGINIA COMMUNITY
IN WORLD WAR II

James W. Morrison

Third Edition

Bedford Goes to War is available at Amazon.com and other
retail outlets and is also available on Kindle and other devices.

Suggested Additional Reading

Bedford Goes to War

The Heroic Story of a Small Virginia Community in World War II

"…truly fascinating…the stories were riveting…outstanding…"
David Burton, retired managing editor
Richmond Times Dispatch

"…a wonderful book…immensely valuable…"
George Garrett, former professor
University of Virginia

"…a wonderful tapestry of patriotism, sacrifice, love, loss…"
Michael Ramsey, president
Roanoke Public Library Foundation

This compelling World War II story of Bedford County, Virginia, is one of heroism, sacrifice, and remembrance. From a population of 30,000, some 4,000 men and women served in the military.

➤ Over 50 fought in the Normandy Invasion, and 20 were killed in action on D-Day—19 in the 116th Infantry's Company A, which had been a National Guard unit in Bedford. The county is believed to have lost more men per capita on D-Day than any other community in America.

➤ As tragic as D-Day was for Bedford, its sacrifice throughout the war was far greater. Its men fought and died on the ground, in the air, and at sea in all major theaters. Over 140 were killed or died, many more were wounded, and over twenty were POWs.

➤ On the home front, citizens produced war material and food, prepared for civil defense, bought war bonds, contributed to the Red Cross and USO, restricted consumption, salvaged scarce materials, grew Victory Gardens, prepared surgical dressings for the military, and wrote to loved ones in the service. Bedford has honored and memorialized those who fought and died. It also proudly hosts the National D-Day Memorial.

Bedford Goes to War is available at Amazon.com and other retail outlets and is also available on Kindle and other devices.

Visit the author's website http://morrisonjamesw.com

Made in the USA
Charleston, SC
12 April 2014